NOTHING PERSONAL

a Hit Lady for Hire novel

LAURYN CHRISTOPHER

Camden Park Press

Nothing Personal

I assumed he was moving drugs, weapons, maybe bringing in imports from sanctioned countries. Not activities I necessarily condoned, but considering the ethical glass house I lived in, there was a pretty long list of sins I wasn't in a position to be judgmental about…

— Meg Harrison
Hit Lady for Hire

Chapter 1

I smelled him before I saw him, the unmistakable scents of whiskey, cigars, and breath-mints too strong in the close confines of the hallway to have lingered from his recent passage. I knew he was close, even though I couldn't see him, half-blinded as I was after coming into the dim space from the bright sunshine. I could barely make out the notices pinned to the wall or the worn carpet on the gently sloping ramp beneath my feet.

But there was no time to do more than acknowledge both his presence and my own disadvantage before the burly man dropped on me with all the force of the forklift he normally drove.

We hit the floor hard, rolling a few feet until we crashed into the door that had closed behind me only a moment before. We were a tangle of limbs; the bulk of his body behind me. I rammed my elbow into what I hoped was his gut, and was rewarded with a satisfying grunt. He'd tried to throw an arm around my throat and catch me in a choke-hold, but my backpack had shifted as we'd rolled, messing up his aim.

When his forearm landed across my mouth, I bit it.

"Yeowch!" he yelped. "No fair biting, Meg!"

"No fair dropping on me in the dark like a big, hairy spider," I replied, grabbing a handful of his long, greasy hair, and tugging him away from my back. "It's *Tuesday*, Joey," I said, smacking the back of his head against the door. "You know better. What if it had been a newcomer? You'd have scared the spit out of her."

"You always get here early," he said, shoving my hand away and repositioning, his thick arms coming around my midsection and catching one of my arms, smashing it to my side. "I'd never challenge anyone here for the self-defense class. 'Specially not a newcomer."

But I was done talking. My eyes were already adjusting to the lighting, and even as we tussled, I was getting my bearings and deciding how best to use the environment to my advantage.

Door: At my right shoulder. Glass warm from the summer afternoon, black privacy paint getting a few more scratches in it where thin lines of light seeped through.

Ramp: Beyond my left foot. Fifteen feet, about a four-degree slope, and covered with some sort of industrial-grade non-skid carpeting that probably looked better in the dim lighting.

Walls: Ahead of me and to the right, exterior brick. Painted over enough times that it barely looked like brick, and felt more like the layers of dark gray latex paint that covered it. Up close and personal like I was, I could even see some of the old, dried drips.

Behind me and to the left, interior drywall-over-plywood painted in the same dark gray. Not built to be pretty, and only seven feet tall, it was just designed to separate the entry and ramp from the workout area on the other side. Our fellow gym rats were peering down at us from over the top of the wall, watching us from the shadows, hooting and hollering encouragement at each grapple and feint. Probably had money on which of us they thought most likely to win.

And Ian would be somewhere nearby. Watching. Ready to step in if the challenge went too far.

I wanted to take it too far.

Had to remind myself that it was Tuesday. It was only a friendly challenge. This was Joey, not someone I'd been paid to kill.

Oblivious to my internal turmoil, or the potential danger he'd thrown himself into, Joey gave up trying to squeeze the stuffing out of me, and heaved most of his considerable weight across my body in an attempt to keep me pinned down.

Rather than hit him, or try to shove him off – neither of which would have done any good at all – I raised my arms up over my head and planted my hands flat to the floor.

Then I mirrored the action with my feet, pulling my knees up and pressing the bottoms of my feet on the rough carpeting, hoping it would give me the traction I needed for the stunt I planned to pull. I'd lost my left shoe – in all honesty, I wished I'd lost them both, because the low heel on my right shoe was going to make what I was about to try a little more difficult.

Using all my strength, I pressed down with my hands and feet, struggling to raise my body like a table, while the gym rats hollered above us. I was no more than three inches off the ground when Joey began to shift, his feet scrabbling against the brick wall as he fought to keep his balance.

I didn't give him the chance.

I twisted, throwing myself to the left and rolling out from under him as he slid off me. He hit the floor with a *whuf*, and I scrambled up and onto his back, pinning his thick neck between my knees.

The gym rats cheered.

I leaned down and pinched his ear. "Give up?"

"Shure," he said, his mouth pressed against the dirty carpet muffling his voice.

I looked up. Now that I could actually take the time, I could see six... seven... no, eight gym rats leaning head and shoulders along the top of the wall.

"Show's over," I said.

They drifted off with the usual jokes and cat-calls, teasing Joey over losing to a girl – again – the winners collecting on their bets from the losers. Moments later the usual gym sounds of fists on punching bags and footsteps running along the overhead track had resumed.

I grabbed my pack from the corner where it had ended up and looked for my missing shoe. Joey was sitting on the floor, leaning against the brick wall, and nursing a rug-burned forearm.

"You see a shoe anywhere?" I ask.

He looked up at me blankly for a second. Then he reached behind him and produced a somewhat squished ladies' shoe.

I inspected it. It was a bit mashed, but the heel still seemed solid and the sole was unbroken, so I put it on, then held out a hand to Joey.

"Come on," I said.

He took my hand and I pulled, giving the big man the leverage he needed to get up off the floor. He stood there, dusting himself off, while I peered up into the gloom at the exposed piping hanging just below the gridwork of the upstairs running track.

"How the hell did you get up there, anyway?"

"Wasn't easy," Joey said with a grin. "Got my fingers mashed a couple of times when someone ran by."

"Serves you right," I said.

He looked down at me, just as I swung. My fist connected with his jaw, and he rocked back, bouncing off the brick wall.

"Never on Tuesday, Joey," I said. Then I settled my pack on my shoulder and walked up the ramp and into the gym, Joey's laughter echoing behind me in the narrow passage.

♦

Ian was waiting for us at the top of the ramp, muscular arms folded across his broad chest. As the owner of the small street gym, he officially disapproved of the gym rats' random attacks on each other – for liability reasons – and he glowered appropriately at us as we walked toward him. But the penalty for an infraction was seldom anything more onerous than having to help clean up after everyone else went home for the night, while Ian provided a blow-by-blow critique of the fight.

"It's Tuesday, Joey," Ian said when we were about three feet away. His deep voice was low and icy calm – a sure sign that he was a lot angrier than he was letting show.

"Yeah," Jody replied, rubbing his jaw. "Meg told me."

"Nice of you to volunteer to help with tonight's class," Ian said.

"Huh?" Joey asked.

Ian didn't answer. He just gave him the Special Forces-turned-Zen master look that nobody at the gym was stupid enough to argue with – even Joey.

With a heavy sigh, Joey nodded, then moved forward making sure to step around Ian rather than attempt to plow through him, which he probably would have done if it had been anyone else. He might have been big and often clueless, but he wasn't stupid.

"And Joey," Ian said as the larger man passed him, his voice so low that as close as I was, I barely heard it. "Never again. If you can't follow the rules, you're not welcome here."

Joey barely paused, but I saw the slight dip of his head, heard the faint, "Sorry," before he hulked off, grumbling mostly to himself.

I bit the inside of my mouth to keep from reacting. Joey had started the fight, but that didn't mean that I was going to get off scot-free.

Sure enough, as I started to move forward, following Joey, Ian stepped into my path.

"Where do you think you're going?" he asked, his deep voice butter-smooth, the iciness from a moment before melting away.

"I have a class to teach," I said, keeping my tone casual. "Need to get changed, stretch out first. Why do you ask?"

"You know I don't like fighting in my gym."

I was already looking up at him – at six-foot-three, Ian is several inches taller than me – so I just tilted my head a little to one side. "So… what? I was just supposed to lay there like a doormat after Joey jumped me? I don't think so."

"You hesitated."

"What?"

"When you came in. You knew he was there, and you froze. If you'd kept moving while you assessed the situation, even as little as two steps, he'd have hit the floor. No fight. Instead, you gave him three seconds – time to get the drop on you."

"Literally," I said, nodding. "I was blind – he had the advantage—"

"Doesn't matter. If it had been a real attack…"

He left the sentence hanging. We both knew the rest: If it had been a real attack – the kind my off-the-books line of work sometimes throws my way, the kind Ian had trained me not only to survive, but to win – I'd have been dead. Or seriously injured, which was almost worse.

I accepted the criticism for the combination of professional assessment and personal concern that it was. Ian and I have a long and complicated history, and were currently four months into the non-exclusive dating relationship that we found ourselves in every few years. Ours is an odd blend – friends, lovers, teacher and student – but with an underlying respect and mutual admiration that keeps us from ever drifting too far from each other.

"I'm off my game," I admitted.

"The ribs?" he asked, referring to the cracked ribs I'd suffered the previous autumn.

"That was months ago," I said, stepping around him to head deeper into the gym. Even Ian didn't know the whole story behind that injury – which I'd sustained in a fight with a target – and believed the lame explanation I'd given everyone about having hurt myself in a fall.

I have trust issues. Even with the people I trust the most.

"What then?" Ian asked. He'd turned to walk with me, shortening his stride to match my pace, his voice a low rumble of concern that only the two of us could hear.

"Don't know," I said. "Think I need to get away for a few days; couple of weeks, maybe. Sort some stuff out. Get my head together."

We walked in silence toward the locker rooms. About two steps from the ladies' room door, Ian touched me on the arm. He gestured to one side, and I followed him into his small office, perching on the corner of his desk, facing the door. The blinds on the door's window were tilted at a slight angle, allowing a filtered view out into the gym, but none of the gym rats appeared to be paying any attention to us.

Ian closed the door, then stood there, hand on the knob for a fraction of a second too long – almost an eternity in Ian-time – before he reached up and closed the blinds.

I was immediately on alert. Ian is as human as any of us, but he rarely lets anyone see him with his guard down. So when he turned to me, his expression the same Zen-calm he usually wore, I didn't believe it for a moment.

He stared at me for a long moment, then ran his fingers through his close-cropped hair, which was barely longer than the semi-permanent five-day growth of beard he habitually wore.

"Is it us?" he asked finally.

Of all the things he might have said, that was the one I least expected. I didn't even have to think about my answer.

"No," I said. "Not even a little bit." I stood, letting my pack slide off my shoulder to the floor, and crossed the small office to him.

"We said 'no strings,'" he continued, "but if it's still too much—"

It *had* been too much, once, years ago when I was so focused on building my career that I couldn't handle the complexities of a relationship at the same time.

Resting one hand on his chest, I raised my other to his face, pressing two fingers to his lips to silence him. "Of all the things going on in my life, Ian Mitchell, you're one of the few that's *right*."

The tension beneath my hand eased. He slid an arm around my waist, and I reciprocated, leaning my head against his chest.

On the other side of the door, the gym rats hit punching bags, groaned and shouted as they sparred, ran the upstairs track in foot-slapping laps. Soon the members of the self-defense class would begin to trickle in.

But for a few moments, all that mattered was the steady beat of Ian's heart.

Chapter 2

By the time I got home, I was too wound up to sleep.

Volunteering as one of the instructors at the gym's weekly self-defense class was usually a good thing for me. I understood the fear so many of the participants were living through.

Teaching the class usually grounded me. Every time we told the members of the class that they could take control of whatever situation they found themselves in – or at least how they responded to it – I was reminding myself that I didn't need to be a victim again, either.

From the first time I'd walked in off the street years before, Ian had helped me find my balance.

But if I likened my own emotional stability to a three-legged stool, one of the legs – the one I use to beat back my anger issues, metaphorically speaking – had been pretty wobbly over the last few months. And Joey's unexpected attack on the one night of the week that was supposed to be safe, when challenges were never, ever, supposed to happen, had knocked that wobbly leg right out from under me. I'd kept reminding him it was Tuesday not so much to pound it into his head, as to remind myself *not* to pound his head in.

And now as steady as I thought the remaining legs of my emotional stool were – the personal leg and the relationships one – I also knew that two wasn't enough. I was teetering, and afraid of what might happen to me and anyone who happened to be around if I fell.

I tossed my pack on the couch, then crossed the miles of faux-Persian carpeting to get to the bar tucked into the wall dividing the living and dining rooms and poured myself a scotch. I carried the drink with me as I paced from the living room across the entry hall to the library and then back, sipping the drink slowly to prolong the burn. The tension began to ease as the warmth spread across my chest and down into my stomach, and I made myself take a slow, deep breath.

I looked around the large living room. Two couches faced each other in front of a large, only slightly ornate fireplace. A pair of Queen Anne chairs flanked a small table near the window overlooking the side-yard. A loveseat and pair of easy chairs formed a third grouping around a low coffee table near the large window looking out at the front yard.

All those places to sit, and even steadied by the scotch, I stood there, incapable of making a choice.

Why the hell had I bought such a big house? Even after four months, it still only occasionally felt like home. What was I ever going to do with six bedrooms, anyway?

A scrabble of claws on tile answered part of the question. I looked over as Glau, a six and a half foot long adult male iguana, headed toward me from the plant-filled, two-story conservatory that occupied the center third of the house. I loved the room, and from the first time I saw it, I'd known it was destined to be Glau's home.

I knelt to him and rubbed the top of his knobby head, just behind his large eyes.

"Yes, I bought the house for you," I told him. "Come on, let's go find you a treat."

He followed me to the kitchen, climbing up onto the perch I'd had installed for him along the far wall, similar to the one I'd set up for him in the rowhouse we'd lived in until late the previous year. Though the house – and this kitchen – was nearly three times as large as my old rowhouse, I still didn't want a large lizard underfoot when I was cooking.

"What am I going to do, Glau?" I asked the lizard, recounting a much abbreviated version of Joey's sneak-attack as I pulled a variety of fresh fruit and veggies from the fridge and made a small pile on the kitchen island. "Joey's mostly harmless," I finished. "But for half a second, I really wanted to smash his head against the brick wall."

I reached for a cutting board, a knife, and a large, shallow bowl and began chopping broccoli, cantaloupe, and bell pepper into large chunks.

Unlike my back-door neighbor's little yapper dog, iguanas don't make a lot of noise. But I've had Glau long enough now that I have a pretty good idea what he's saying when he gives me that long, baleful stare like he was doing now – and it wasn't just his way of telling me to hurry up with his snack.

I looked away. It's hard to lie, even to yourself, under that kind of stare.

In my opinion, a person doesn't become a paid assassin unless they're carrying around a lot of very nasty baggage. It's risky, dangerous work, and contrary to what the movies would have you believe, there are better ways to make an extremely good living, on both sides of the law. The house I was living in was proof enough of that – as I'd bought it using only the legitimately-earned funds from my "day job" as a corporate consultant.

But for years, private side-gigs in corporate espionage and insider trading had served as a "relief valve" when the memories of childhood abuses turned into nightmares I couldn't run away from. When combined with the complexities of my day job, the intrigue of the illicit work kept my waking mind so busy that even in sleep I was often too exhausted for the nightmares to find me.

It worked… until it didn't anymore. Until becoming an assassin had become the way I exorcised my darkest demons, all the while earning more money than I could ever spend.

I glanced over. Glau was still staring at me. It was possible that his attention was mostly on the fruit and vegetables, but we both knew better.

"Okay, okay," I said, chopping the cantaloupe with probably more force than the sweet, juicy flesh deserved. "I've been having nightmares again. And I haven't taken on an outside job since…"

Since my last job put two of my good friends in danger.

I tossed the chopped fruit and veggies into the bowl with a handful of cilantro leaves, then waggled the bowl at Glau.

"Want this?" I asked him.

He mirrored the gesture, waggling his head back at me. Clearly, we weren't finished talking.

"All right," I sighed. "I'll take a job. Something quick, simple, anonymous. Out of town. Nothing personal this time. Just getting back on the horse."

Glau stared at me for another two seconds, then he then turned and scuttled down off the perch and followed me to the conservatory. I put the veggie bowl on the mat, replacing an empty one, refilled his water and checked the heat lamp above his primary perch. Then I closed the four sets of French doors leading from the conservatory to other parts of the main floor, wiped down the kitchen counter, shut off all the downstairs lights, and headed up to my room.

Glau was right.

It was time to go back to the dark web.

♦

One of the advantages of having an enormous house is that no one notices when you partition off a sliver here or there. A thickened wall near the downstairs library held a hidden bookshelf filled with titles I found useful, but which my friends might have considered questionable.

A panel under Glau's primary perch in the conservatory concealed a gun safe that usually held at least two unlicensed firearms and their ammunition.

And what was originally a second walk-in closet in the master bedroom was now a compact office, accessed by way of a panel at the back of a freestanding wardrobe I'd bolted to the wall.

It was this hidden office that I went to now.

I slipped past the clothes hanging in the wardrobe, slid open the back panel, then opened the closet door and stepped through.

It was a generous space, as closets go – seven feet wide by nine feet deep, with the door centered on the long wall, about twice the size of most of the cubicles I'd worked in during college. I'd removed the hanger rods and most of the shelving, keeping only the upper shelves that ran around the entire room just above the door.

To say the décor was Spartan was almost an understatement. Sure, I'd set up a workstation with large, dual monitors and a filing cabinet next to the desk, stocked the necessary office supplies, and hung a whiteboard on the wall. But the whiteboard was clean, the shredder empty, the pad of sticky notes unused, the collection of burner phones in the locked desk drawer still awaiting activation.

Even the mini-fridge humming quietly in the corner by the door was empty.

I must have stood there for two or three minutes, just looking at the room before I realized what I was doing – rather, what I *wasn't* doing, namely, going over to my desk, powering up the laptop, and navigating to the dark web listings site where I picked up my illicit contracts.

So, before I could find another way to procrastinate, I did just that. A few minutes later, I was staring at the familiar green text on black screen of the covert listings queue.

As the letters scrolled quietly up the screen, I felt the tension that had been winding me up like a spring begin to ease – just a little. Not enough to make any real difference, but enough to confirm that this was exactly what I needed.

Like a shark smelling blood in the water, I began to scan the listings.

◆

Listings on the dark web don't use words like 'steal' or 'infiltrate,' 'murder' or 'kill.' As secure as the site is, there's no sense in taking that kind of risk.

Instead, the requests are presented like poorly-written classified ads, using terms like 'research' and 'relocation,' and you learn to read between the lines.

So when I saw a listing that read:

> HR *department will pay top dollar for immediate replacement of a skilled research assistant with excellent references*

I didn't even have to think about it to understand exactly what it meant.

A corporate executive needed to eliminate an employee who had learned too much about a sensitive – probably criminal – operation. They needed the job done quickly and quietly, before the employee passed the information on to the authorities. And they were willing to pay well for it.

I was intrigued.

The site is set up in such a way that listings appear at the bottom of the feed and scroll up one line at a time, old-school style, until they work their way off the page. As I understood it, everything that transpires on the site is live, posted and responded to in real time, rather than saved or held in memory. So if a listing wasn't picked up by an operative during the few minutes it was on the screen, the client would have to try again.

I'd seen listings scroll through several times in succession, appearing at the bottom of the page even as they were disappearing at the top, as clients re-posted jobs over and over in the desperate hope that the right operative would pick it up – "right" being defined as an operative who was both interested in and qualified to do the job.

Sometimes the technique worked, but as far as I was concerned, the more desperate the client seemed, the less likely I was to take the job.

This one, though, looked interesting. And since no one had claimed it by the time it was about two-thirds up the screen, I clicked on it myself. The listing continued to scroll upward, but the text changed from green to yellow, a signal to any other operatives online that it was under consideration, and a private chat box opened on the right-hand side of my screen.

I don't waste a lot of time in chat. So my questions were short and to the point:

Location? Timeframe? Payment?

The reply was quick and concise:

> *Charleston, S.C.*
> *Within the next 72 hours.*
> *$250K by wire transfer; double if completed w/in 36 hours.*

While there was never any guarantee about just how stable a client might be, I preferred to work with the ones who were straightforward and to the point. The more they rambled, tried to justify the reason for the contract, the more trouble they usually proved to be. This one knew exactly what they wanted and didn't waste their time or mine with long-winded explanations. With any luck, it would be the simple, straightforward job I'd been looking for.

Target ID?

Mindy Collier

The client also provided the target's address, SSN, and phone number, and I copied the information to a separate file. I had no idea who Mindy Collier was, or what information she'd stumbled onto. I didn't know if she was a college student working as an intern or a grandmother who saw something she shouldn't have in the Client's briefcase during Sunday brunch. It didn't matter.

It wasn't personal, at least not as far as I was concerned.

The fact that someone was serious enough about it to find their way to the listings site and issue a contract for her death, meant that Mindy Collier's days were numbered, regardless of who pulled the trigger.

It might as well be me.

Accepted.
The clock begins when payment is received.

I entered the account details for one of the many bank accounts I use for wire transfers. His reply appeared almost instantly.

Sent.

In another browser window, I logged into the account, and waited, passing the time by pulling an unused burner phone from the supply I keep in my desk and activating it. Three minutes later, the payment appeared in the account. As soon as it did, I replied to the client:

Received.

The funds wouldn't actually be available to me for several hours – with as late as it was, it could be Thursday morning before the transfer fully processed. I wouldn't eliminate the target until the payment had cleared.

But there were several things I could do while I waited. I would monitor the account, and as soon as the new balance was registered as fully available, I would transfer the funds to an account at a different bank. I often moved large sums of money around – sometimes receiving client payments, sometimes using my own money from other accounts. I would pool funds into a single account, then split the balance, transferring portions into other accounts that offered better interest rates or allowed me to make a large payment from a single account. Because my money movement was routine behavior, it didn't raise the kind of red flags it otherwise might.

In the meantime, I had one more message for my new client:

Secure a burner phone. All future communication to be sent/received at this number, text only. To continue, provide contact number within twelve hours.

I provided the client with the number to the burner phone. When the client acknowledged the message, I logged out of the listings site, and cleared my computer cache.

I checked the time. It was 11:37 p.m. There was a lot to do, and the clock was ticking

The Researcher – my teacher in all things hacking-related – had taught me to generate a random IP address for each new task, as a way to better obscure my activities. I did this again now, then booked a one-way flight to Charleston for the following day using a fake ID and a VISA gift card, also reserving both a car and a room in a local hotel. I printed out the travel confirmations, then repeated the process of clearing the computer cache and generating a new IP address.

Then I logged in through a back-door into a background checking tool I'd invested in some years prior. Using admin codes that would have made the managers of the otherwise perfectly respectable service cringe at the multiple laws I was breaking behind their backs, I set the system to running a deep background check on Mindy Collier.

Chapter 3

First thing Wednesday morning, I called my office to let my assistant, Jessica, know I'd be working from home for the rest of the week. I often sprang random changes to my schedule on her with little notice, so she took it in stride.

"Is everything okay?" Jessica asked.

"Yes, just a bit under the weather," I said. It wasn't entirely a lie. Several nights of broken sleep had left me feeling drained, and though I'd slept well the previous night, it was going to take more than one good night's sleep to reverse the toll stress had taken on me. "Please change this afternoon's meeting with McCann to a conference call."

"You got it," she said.

"I reviewed the preliminary packet for the Samuels merger yesterday. It looks good, thank you. Go ahead and send it over with a note that I'll follow-up with Chaz by middle of next week."

"Okay," Jessica said, her keyboard clattering as she took notes from our call.

"And see if Joe Benson at SCH has any time on his calendar on Friday – late morning or early afternoon. Nothing urgent, just to touch-base."

Southern Coast Holdings was a major client, based out of Raleigh-Durham, North Carolina, and maintaining that working relationship was high on my priority list. If all went as planned in Charleston tomorrow, it would be an easy drive north, through pleasant, early spring greenery to the SCH offices. I'd catch a late afternoon flight home from there.

And if things didn't go as planned, or the weather took a turn for the worse, well, Joe would have been expecting a phone meeting anyway. It would all be business as usual.

With the day job taken care of for the moment, and Jessica none the wiser to my other activities, I turned my attention to the background check on Mindy Collier.

Her driver's license photo showed a tired face, framed by long, dark hair, with bangs that nearly brushed the upper edge of dark-rimmed glasses.

She was in her early forties, divorced, with two teenaged children – a boy and a girl – who split their time between their parents' homes. I paused at that, but only for a moment. I knew what it was to lose parents – my father, when I was seven, and my mother, when I was fifteen – and I generally avoided jobs that would impact young kids. But from what I was reading, Mindy's two teens were in a much better situation than my siblings and I had been when our mother died. They'd be okay.

Besides, if I didn't take Mindy out of the picture, my client would just hire someone else who had no qualms about it.

"Don't let it get to you," I muttered, chastising myself as I set a second, far less invasive search running on Mindy's ex-husband and his wife before returning to my review of Mindy's report.

Mindy worked as an executive secretary for one of the many shipping companies headquartered in Charleston, which explained how she might have become privy to the information that had resulted in the contract on her life.

Data gathered from bank records and credit card spending showed her to be financially conservative, living just within her means, and with a tidy nest egg that had been growing over the years – likely a fund for her kids' college education. There was no record of payments to a home security service, which removed a layer of difficulty getting into her house, should it be necessary.

The results of her browsing history, online purchases, and an assortment of online surveys suggested that she was interested in vegetarian cooking, liked mystery novels, and owned one or more cats. But while the data provided me with a basic sketch of my target, it was her web searches that revealed a potentially useful detail.

Based on the percentage of web searches on the topic, and the consistency of repeat searches, indicating that it wasn't simply a one-time curiosity or the subject of one of the teenagers' homework assignments, it appeared that someone in the household was allergic to peanuts.

I felt the pleasant little 'pop' of dopamine hitting my system. If Mindy was the one with the allergy, and not one of her children, I might have found the key to eliminating her quickly and quietly. I pushed back my sleeves – literally and figuratively – refilled my coffee, and dug deeper into the data.

It felt good to be working again.

HIPAA laws have made it all but impossible to gain access to medical data. And while the Researcher could have dug into the records with less difficulty than I could, there were other ways to find out which of Mindy's family members had the deadly allergy.

Mindy used an online receipt-organizer, and as organized as she appeared to be with her finances, I suspected that she would have scanned the receipts for both doctor visits and prescription purchases. I didn't even attempt to hack that account – while it still required a good deal of effort, it was easier to dig into her cloud backup and find copies of the categorized receipts there.

Just as I'd expected, when I narrowed my search, I found several receipts from her local pharmacy that shared the same date stamp as scanned copies of the accompanying prescriptions. I had to review the images manually, but the effort paid off. Dated seven and a half months earlier, I found what I was looking for: a prescription for an EpiPen, made out to Mindy Collier.

Now I just had to figure out how I was going to get her to ingest the killer peanuts.

♦

The burner phone buzzed with a text message at 11:37 a.m., exactly twelve hours from my last communication with the client on the listings site.

Go ahead.

Some clients waver during the twelve-hour window. Some back out altogether – and no, I don't refund their money, even when they beg for it. I just destroy the burner phone and move on.

But everything about this client had led me to believe they knew exactly what they wanted, and were determined to see it through.

My reply was direct and to the point:

Confirmed.

Twenty-nine minutes later, I was boarding a plane bound for Charleston.

♦

I was standing in my closet, one of the business-focused podcasts I usually listen to during my commute playing through my earbuds while I chose a simple wardrobe that would fit into my carry-on bag, when the podcast was interrupted by Sinatra singing *Fly Me to the Moon*.

I smiled. It was Kyle Herriman.

If Ian knew my dark side better than most, Kyle was well acquainted with my professional side. I'd met him the previous fall while negotiating the sale of his company, and we'd started dating just after New Year's, shortly after the deal was finalized.

Ironically, I'd started seeing Kyle the same week I'd begun dating Ian again.

The challenge of juggling my corporate and clandestine jobs was nothing compared to the challenge of dating two compelling, intelligent men, both of whom I found utterly fascinating for entirely different reasons – and both of whom seemed willing to be patient, for a while at least, while I spent time with the other.

All that flashed through my mind in the first notes of the song I'd set as Kyle's ringtone.

I tossed a blouse and a lightweight turtleneck sweater onto my bed, then tapped the headset to accept the call.

"Hi," I said. "What's up?"

"I was going to stop by your office, drag you away from your desk for lunch, but it's been one thing after another, and the day is getting away from me," Kyle said, his smooth, warm baritone hinting at a touch of frustration.

"Just as well," I said, choosing a wrinkle-resistant charcoal blazer and matching slacks and tossing the combination onto my bed. "I'm working at home today. But we're still on for dinner Friday, yes?" Kyle and I always planned for late dinners, to allow for both our sometimes demanding work schedules and Philadelphia's inevitable traffic delays. I was confident that whether I flew back from Charleston or Raleigh-Durham, I'd easily make it back in time for our eight p.m. dinner date.

"That's that thing," he said. "I just found out that I need to be in Charlotte for the next couple of days – flying over this afternoon. I'd hoped I could take the meetings remotely, but the customer is old-school—"

"Like your grandfather?" I asked. Kyle had taken over management of Herriman Industries when his grandfather retired. I'd met the man once, and he was definitely the product of a different age.

I added a tan raincoat to the growing pile on the bed. I'd have to carry it separately, but I'd long ago learned to never trust spring weather.

"Like my grandfather, yes," Kyle said. "And he's insisting on the whole face-to-face thing. Including dinner."

"Good thing he didn't insist you bring your wife," I teased.

"Actually…," Kyle said, "How would you like to come to Charlotte with me? Join me for dinner?"

"Nice try," I said with a laugh as I laid a long, black, paper-wrapped wig – it was as close as I had to Mindy's shade – in the small suitcase, then began folding clothes and tucking them around it. "But I'm literally packing for my own trip as we speak. Not that I'd have gone in any case."

"Of course not – I was teasing," he said. "Where are you headed?"

"Charleston."

"That's right next door," Kyle said. "You could—"

"No, I couldn't," I said, cutting him off. "It's close enough to be a tease, but too far to make it over in time for a business dinner."

"True…," he said, stretching out the word as though toying with an idea. "But I could hop over the following morning, if you're still going to be in town. We could make a weekend of it."

Between his work and mine, Kyle and I had rarely spent more than a few hours together. Dinner here, a lunch there, with only the occasional Saturday morning or Sunday afternoon when a phone wasn't ringing or pinging. I'd warned him during the negotiations that brought Herriman Industries under the SCH umbrella that his workload as the company's new CEO was going to increase, but neither of us had expected it to be quite so non-stop as the past four months had been.

I liked Kyle. I liked him a lot. And the Charleston contract had already lightened my mood enough that I thought I just might enjoy a couple of actual vacation days.

"Deal," I said. "But you have to turn your phone off. Or let the battery die or something. No calls, or we go straight home."

"You drive a hard bargain."

"You know it."

"Send me your hotel details," he said.

"Let me know when your flight is getting in," I said at the same time.

We both laughed, then spent the next couple of minutes sorting out details. When the call was over, I added a pair of capris, a casual blouse, a sweater, and a pair of flat sandals to my suitcase. It was a tight fit, but I was smiling as I shifted things around to make it all work.

I had a job-in-progress that was already relieving my stress levels.

I had a weekend getaway planned with an intelligent, gorgeous man who, for some crazy reason, enjoyed my company.

And in just a few hours, I had a plane to catch. As far as I was concerned, things could only get better from here.

Chapter 4

I ran, screaming, through the shadow-world that lies between wakefulness and dreaming…

…I was a child, running down the long hallway of a building I'd never seen, not knowing how I'd gotten there, only that my father was there, unlocking a door near the end of the hall.

"Papa, wait!"

My father looked over and smiled, waved. And then the door opened, and he went through, leaving it to slam in my face.

I pounded on the door, kicked at it, screamed for him to open it.

Just as the doorknob started to turn, a movement caught my eye. When I looked, the hall had grown longer and my father was about halfway to the end, standing in front of another door.

Then the door in front of me opened, and Eddie was there. Horrible Eddie, who my mother had married after my father went away. Nasty Eddie, who smiled at me and licked his lips, his bathrobe falling open as he reached toward me with his mean, groping hands.

I stepped away from Eddie, knowing that if I could just catch up with my father, bring him back, then Eddie would go away, and our family would be right again.

I turned and ran down the hall, chasing after my father.

Over and over again, each time I got close, my father would go through, the door would slam shut behind him, and when it opened it would be Eddie…

A door slammed across the hall – reality intruding into the dream – and I woke in a cold sweat, disoriented, my heart racing, my face wet with tears. In the near total darkness, lit only by the greenish glow of a digital alarm clock, it took several seconds before I remembered where I was – in my hotel suite in Charleston – and not still in the madhouse of the dream.

I pulled the puffy duvet up around my shoulders and rocked back and forth in the middle of the big bed, clutching a pillow to my chest.

"Eddie's dead," I said, repeating the words over and over. Maybe I was reminding myself. Maybe I was trying to console the child he'd forced himself on time after time, the one who still hid from him in the deepest, darkest recesses of my mind. I didn't know.

But it was the child's voice that answered.

"Kill him again. Kill him for me."

"I will," I whispered. "As many times as it takes."

♦

I woke early, as I usually did, less rested than I wanted to be, but about as much as I'd grown accustomed to over the past few weeks, which was rather annoying. I knew from long experience that trying to go back to sleep was a lost cause. Whether I liked it or not, my day had begun. I was in no mood to be social, but I didn't feel like pacing around my room, either. So rather than take advantage of the hotel's reputedly excellent, in-room breakfast service, I dressed, grabbed my raincoat – I didn't trust the overcast sky to stay that way – and headed downstairs in search of a cup of coffee and a place to drink it.

In exchange for a recommendation for a local coffee shop, I gave the concierge a generous tip. She directed me to a nearby café that she said was about four blocks from the hotel. I decided to tempt fate and walk, confident in the knowledge that because I was prepared for inclement weather, the promised rain would fail to materialize.

Charleston is a lovely city, and after my conversation with Kyle, I'd cancelled my reservation at the chain hotel near the airport and taken a suite in a hotel along the city's scenic waterfront. I was glad, now, that I had. I felt surprisingly less like a tourist than I'd expected, even though I openly admired the signature colonial décor of the buildings as I passed. Oddly, other than the humidity and prevalence of thick sabal palms, I felt almost at home.

I'd made the mistake of turning right instead of left when I left the hotel, and then wandering even further off course just out of curiosity. When I left the main tourist area, with its signature colonial décor, I found myself walking along streets which, though the buildings were different in style, were packed together and up against the curb in a manner that reminded me a little bit of the way rowhouses lined Philadelphia streets.

I was fascinated by the long narrow, brick and cobblestone-paved alleys I seemed to encounter almost at random. Being in the historic district, I suspected they were remnants of the city's past – and as clean and quaint as the two I wandered down were, with glimpses over vine-covered walls into private courtyards or old-fashioned sconces and signage announcing back-door entrances into businesses, I was almost certain of it. I found them charming, and wished more alleys in other cities boasted a similar ambience.

By the time I found my way to the café, and from there along a more direct route back to the hotel, I'd gotten in a good morning's walk. The activity had gone a long way toward clearing away the vestiges of the previous night's bad dream. The caffeine from my first cup of coffee was hitting my system in a good way, and I was energized and ready to get to work.

Taking a sheet from the complimentary notepad and the to-go cup of coffee I'd gotten from the café – it usually took well over an hour for me to drink my second cup, and I hadn't wanted to stay that long - I went out onto my small balcony, sat down at the little table, and made a list of the things I needed to do that day.

One: Locate a hardware or auto parts store for tools I would need, but that would have caused problems if I'd tried to pack them in my carry-on luggage.

Two: Pick up a nutritional supplement I needed at a local health food store.

Three: Find Mindy Collier's house, the best routes into/out of the neighborhood, and locate a fast food restaurant, preferably near Mindy's home.

Four: Find Mindy's workplace, identify the three most likely routes she was likely to take to/from work, and decide on the best place along each route where I could intercept her on her end-of-day commute. A quiet kill eliminated either her workplace or her home. Besides, I had no desire to harm her children, or kill her in front of them.

When I finished making my list, I sat there, sipping at my coffee, and observing the comings and goings both on the street below and out on the water. The hotel was literally a stone's throw from the harbor, and the air carried the salty tang of the ocean. The wind had picked up since I'd returned to my room, kicking up white, choppy wavelets, and the breeze blowing in off the ocean sent a chill through me. I had no idea what that meant for the day's weather, only that it was time to head inside before the wind did more than just ruffle my hair.

I transferred a few things I was going to need from my overstuffed suitcase to my computer bag – it often did double-duty as a shoulder bag – and with a last look around, headed out, not bothering to hang the "do not disturb" sign. I'd left nothing of particular value in the room, and was taking anything that might be potentially incriminating with me. Might as well go ahead and have the room made up while I was out and let the housekeeping staff earn the twenty dollar tip I'd left, along with a note, on the table.

Downtown Charleston sits at the end of a peninsula, one of a group of four peninsulas formed where three rivers – the Ashley, Cooper, and Wando – converge to flow into the Atlantic Ocean. Suburbs spread out across these peninsulas and neighboring coastal islands, amid marshlands and waterways too numerous to count. The airport is actually located in North Charleston, about a half-hour drive inland from the downtown area.

The port area where Mindy Collier worked was in Mt. Pleasant, the suburb occupying the majority of the northernmost of the four peninsulas, along the Wando river. Mindy lived in the suburb of West Ashley, which was on the southernmost of the peninsulas.

According to my GPS, the most direct route from her house to the port would have her take the expressway across the Ashley River, past the airport in North Charleston, over the Cooper River, across Daniel Island, and then across the Wando River. It seemed like a long way at first glance, but the app clocked it as between twenty and thirty minutes, depending on the time of day, which wasn't as bad as it might otherwise have been. A more easterly route, which passed through Charleston proper, would nearly double that commute.

In cities not divided by rivers, there are often numerous routes from one point to another. Here, regardless of her street-level choices, one way or another Mindy was going to have to cross one of the three bridges spanning the Ashley River.

It seemed unlikely that she would take the route through the city center unless she had specific business downtown. If Charleston locals were like their Philadelphia counterparts, they tended to avoid the touristy areas, which, at almost any time of day, was going to extend their commute.

Ninety to ninety-five percent odds said Mindy would hop on the expressway, circling back toward North Charleston. Once there, it was a fifty-fifty shot whether she would continue across the Westmoreland Bridge, or head east to the Cosgrove

Bridge, again depending on traffic load and whether or not she had business in that part of town.

Regardless of which bridge she crossed, once she reached West Ashley, her options multiplied exponentially. As a result, once I completed the other errands on my list and picked up the tools and other supplies I needed, I spent the rest of the morning familiarizing myself with the community of West Ashley. Not only would it assist me in deciding the best place to intercept Mindy, but having a general idea of how a town is laid out has proven to be helpful on more than one occasion when I needed to make a quick getaway.

I spotted grocery stores and fast food restaurants, shopping plazas, the movie theater, and the local high school. And I found Mindy's house – a split-level sitting on a corner lot in an established, working-class, residential neighborhood. Homes and yards were well-maintained, and the streets were in good repair, but the trees were old and multiple vehicles – including the odd clunker up on blocks, boats on trailers, and RVs parked on the lawn – were common. The houses weren't all crowded together like those in the city – four rowhouses could have easily fit in the space between Mindy's house and her nearest neighbor. I was still new at suburban living, but from the way the houses were spaced, it seemed like the residents would have to work at it to pay attention to what their neighbors were doing.

There were five routes in and out of the neighborhood, some leading more directly to the house than others. I followed them all, noting dead ends, hidden driveways, and the orange cones in the road where a work crew was repairing a broken pipe. Mindy might follow any of these routes on her way home, and I wanted to be prepared.

I was approaching her house from the northernmost route into the neighborhood, which was the most out-of-the-way, but had the benefit of having the fewest twists and turns, when an approaching school bus stopped at the corner ahead of me, in front of Mindy's house. I pulled over to the shoulder of the road, to wait and watch.

Three teenagers got off the bus. One crossed the street in front of the bus and disappeared down the intersecting street. The other two – a tall, sandy-haired boy and a girl, shorter, but also fair-haired – headed up the sidewalk to the front door of Mindy's house, stopped to unlock the door, and went in.

Her children.

I checked the time. It was just two forty-five. Okay.

I was about to ease back onto the road when a blue minivan pulled into Mindy's driveway. The driver honked the horn twice, but when no one responded, the driver's side door opened and a tall, skinny woman with short, fiery red hair got out. She was heading toward the house when the teenagers burst through the door, backpacks in hand. I couldn't hear their conversation, but watching their body language it didn't look like anyone was angry, just running late.

The teens tossed their packs in the van, the boy and the woman climbing in while the girl paused to talk to someone who was already in the vehicle's rear seat. A moment later, she climbed in as well, and the van sped away.

I followed it. I had a guess as to who I thought the woman was. I just needed to get close enough to see the license plate, confirm my suspicion.

She didn't make it easy.

If I'd thought the redhead zipped like a racecar driver through the winding neighborhood roads, she completely let out the throttle when she got to a longish, unpopulated stretch. If I hadn't been chasing her, I'd have been impressed. I hadn't known minivans handled that well.

As it was, I only caught up with her when her route took her into another neighborhood, and she had to wait for a school bus.

I grabbed my phone and snapped a photo of the minivan's license plate, then turned aside at the next intersection. A few minutes later I pulled into a shopping plaza, parked, and used a free online license plate search tool to look up the van's information.

It was registered to Trevor Collier, Mindy's ex-husband. That would make the redhead Sarah Collier, his new wife and the teenagers' step-mother. As I recalled, Trevor and Sarah had a child of their own, a girl who was five or six years old, and a James Island address that put their home about twenty minutes to the east. The court had awarded Trevor shared custody of his two older children, and there was a visitation schedule in place, but the details eluded me.

With any luck, Sarah and the teenagers were headed to some sort of family activity that would keep them occupied for the next few hours. I hoped the teens had a decent relationship with Sarah and Trevor, because they were all going to be spending a lot more time together very soon.

◆

An hour later, I sat outside the office building where Mindy Collier worked – one of the many warehouses with attached offices that littered the port area along the Wando River shoreline – and watched as it emptied and refilled at the end of day-shift workday and the evening crew arrived. When Mindy appeared, I recognized her from the driver's license and social media photos I'd found during the background check.

Mindy was two inches shorter than me, and probably ten or fifteen pounds heavier, with long, dark hair pulled back in a ponytail. She crossed the lot, first swapping a pair of dark-framed glasses for sunglasses as she walked, then fishing keys out of her oversized, patchwork shoulder bag. She paused, looking back toward the building after she reached her car – an older, but well-maintained Chevy Malibu – then got into the car and drove away.

I eased into traffic behind her. It's easy to follow someone in a city. There are enough cars that nobody notices one more on the road a few cars back.

I'd expected Mindy to head home along one of the routes I'd identified earlier, but wasn't too surprised when she turned off the main road and pulled into the parking lot of a small, nondescript bar whose name I recognized from Mindy's receipts.

She parked, hopped out of the car, and practically ran inside.

I pulled into the lot and parked a few spaces farther down the row. Before I got out of my car, I pulled a small tracking device from my bag and made sure it was powered up. As I walked past Mindy's car, I bent down to dump a pebble from my low-heeled dress shoe, reaching under the rear bumper to attach the tracker. If she made any other side-trips on the way home, I wanted to know about them.

That done, I went into the bar and took a seat at the far end of the counter, opposite from where Mindy was sitting.

The bartender came over, flipping a short towel over his shoulder. "What can I get you?"

"Gin and tonic," I said. "Tanqueray."

"Lime?"

"A splash."

"On it."

At the opposite end of the bar, Mindy raised an empty tumbler and asked for a refill.

"Is everything okay, Mindy?" the bartender asked her, glancing over as he finished making my drink.

Mindy jerked her head up and gave him a sharp look. "Sure. Why would you ask that?"

I'd seen enough receipts for this bar to know that Mindy was a regular, but didn't know if the bartender was a personal friend or just being friendly to a customer. He set my glass in front of me without comment and went back to talk to Mindy.

I busied myself studying my phone screen, watching Mindy over the top of it, pretending not to listen. I didn't want either of them to worry about whether a stranger overheard their conversation.

I needn't have bothered. Mindy staring into her empty glass, utterly oblivious to everyone. A trio of new arrivals came to the bar, asked for and received their own drink, and wandered off in search of a table, and she didn't even look up. From their sturdy boots, worn jeans, canvas jackets, and rough hands, I guessed them to be dock workers.

After a couple of minutes, Mindy shook her head, as though trying to pull herself together, "Sorry, Nick," she said, pushing the glass toward him. "I'm just a little stressed out. Haven't been sleeping well."

I could relate.

Nick took Mindy's glass and refilled it – whiskey, neat.

"This should help take the edge off," he said, adding as she grabbed it and gulped it down, "Hey, slow down!"

She stuck the glass out toward him. "Another."

He took the tumbler, but this time slowly, methodically rinsed then dried the glass. "What's going on?"

Mindy shrugged. "Work stuff. Makes me jumpy."

Absently, she reached out toward the snack dish, then jumped when Nick abruptly scooted it away from her.

"What?" she said, glaring at him.

"Peanuts," he said, tilting the bowl so she could see its contents.

Mindy recoiled like the nuts were about to attack her. Then she shrugged. "Not that it matters. Pretty sure my boss is planning to kill me anyway."

"It can't be that bad," Nick said.

"You don't know. He's just been… I don't know. I'll look up and he'll be watching me, all intense-like. So, I smile and get right back to work because the last thing I want is for him to be upset with me."

"Sounds like his problem, not yours."

Mindy shook her head.

"I know stuff," she said, her voice barely audible. "Stuff I shouldn't. He might not have realized it yet – he hasn't said anything, but the way he keeps looking at me... I just know, when he figures it out, he's gonna be pretty pissed. I don't know what to do."

Nick tried to coax more out of her, but Mindy had apparently decided she'd said enough – or too much. And when Nick set the drink down in front of her, she just sat there, staring off into space, her hands surrounding the glass, her expression glum.

She looked over at the peanuts. "Maybe I should just choke down a handful of those, get it over with." She held out her hand. "Gimme that bowl."

Nick shoved the bowl farther down the bar.

"Do I need to cut you off?" he asked, eyeing the as-yet untouched drink in front of her.

"No." Mindy said. "It's all good. This is a safe place." She looked around the dim, half-empty room. "I know everyone here."

I didn't follow her gaze; I'd scoped out the place when I entered. It wasn't large, and though it lacked the hominess of the one immortalized on television, the nods and greetings exchanged I'd observed as customers arrived were all indicators of a local's bar. The mood was relaxed, the bartender knew his customer's names and preferred drinks, and the customers, stopping for a drink on their way home from work, knew – or at least recognized – each other.

In my charcoal slacks, pale blue blouse, and charcoal blazer, I was clearly part of the after-work crowd, if slightly over-dressed for this particular establishment.

I raised my head, watching openly as Mindy's gaze tracked around the room. And then her scan came full circuit, and she was looking at me at the opposite end of the bar, and she froze.

Our eyes locked.

I can be a nice person. I really can. But when I'm on a job, I don't even try. What would be the point? So I raised my glass, tilting it slightly toward Mindy in a pseudo-toast, then took a sip, never taking my eyes off her.

Mindy just about fell off her barstool.

"I've gotta go," she said, tossing back her drink. She rummaged through her bag for her wallet, and shoved some bills across the bar toward Nick, then stood and walked with deliberate, forced calm toward the door.

I pretended not to notice as she passed, wobbling a little as she gave me a wide berth. I almost managed not to smile.

I took my time finishing my drink, tipped the bartender, then left the bar about three minutes behind Mindy.

Chapter 5

The tracker pinged at ten-second intervals across the map displayed on the burner phone's screen, showing Mindy's car heading toward the expressway. I followed, not even bothering to try to catch up. She continued along the route I'd mapped out earlier, passing the airport, and staying on the expressway until after she crossed the bridge over the Ashley River.

"You're making this too easy," I said when the blips left the expressway, then pulled into the parking lot of a grocery store a few blocks from her home. The tracker stopped sending data after she parked, and was still quiet five minutes later when I cruised past the store. I went a half-block farther, then pulled into the drive-through lane of a fast-food restaurant. While I waited for my turn in line, I pulled on the dark wig I'd brought with me, checking in the mirror to make sure none of my short blonde hair was visible around the edges. The car in front of me moved forward as I pulled on a pair of lightweight, beige driving gloves.

"Can I get a combo number seven, with fries," I asked when I got to the speaker. Listed on the menu between combo six – a bacon cheeseburger – and combo eight – a grilled chicken sandwich - combo number seven was the restaurant's vegetarian burger. Asking for the wrong number when intending to choose one of its neighbors was the simplest mistake a person could make. And it would appear to have been a lethal one for Mindy.

According to my research, some meat substitutes – including the brand of veggie burger served by this chain – were made with concentrated pea-protein isolate, which had been known to trigger severe allergic reactions in some people with peanut allergies. I planned to capitalize on that bit of notoriety.

"What drink do you want with that?" the attendant asked, after repeating the order back to me.

"Cola." I had no idea what Mindy drank, but the ubiquitous brand seemed like a safe-enough choice.

"Sure thing," came the chipper reply. She told me the total and which window to pull up to.

Mindy's tracker was still silent. I pulled forward, paid in cash, and accepted the folded-over bag, cup, and the bundle of napkins folded around a straw from the smiling teenager working the window – all fingerprint-free, thanks to my gloves.

In the unlikely event anyone ever questioned the girl, she would remember a woman with long dark hair who had ordered a vegetarian burger and paid in cash. It was still light enough that my sunglasses obscured most of my features, and my rental car wasn't particularly flashy or memorable.

The scent of the fresh, hot fries set my stomach growling. I spread a couple of napkins out on the seat next to me, dumped a few fries onto it, and put the pouch back in the bag. Then I pulled off my glove so I could nibble on the fries.

From the grocery store, there were three routes Mindy might take to get to her house. The first backtracked a couple of blocks to a main thoroughfare, which she would need to follow until getting to a cross street that would take her almost directly home. It was the least complicated and most direct, but also the most out-of-the way. It also offered only a single opportunity for heading her off – a long stretch of road between the main street and the first house in the neighborhood. I would have to pull directly across her path somewhere along that stretch and hope she didn't hit me – and hope no one else happened by in the time it would take me to kill her and make it look like an accident.

The second route would take her almost all the way around the neighborhood, stair-stepping from one block to the next. There were no houses along the half-block section at the end of each street, and few visible lines of sight. With the addition of the dark wig and swapping the charcoal blazer for the light sweater, I could take my pick of places to pretend to be a distressed driver, flag her down, and overpower her before she recognized me as the person from the bar.

Unfortunately, I had a hunch that Mindy would take the third route, which wove through the neighborhood. Both my mother and my Aunt Ruthie, who had taken my brothers and me in after our mother died, were masters at navigating the surface streets and back roads. There were times they had races getting from one house to the other where the only rule was to not go over the speed limit or put anyone in jeopardy.

Mindy didn't strike me as having the daredevil personality of her husband's second wife, or the competitive streak of my aunt, but I suspected she'd acquired the suburbanite's arcane knowledge of navigation. The odds on her taking what I'd dubbed "the overland route," which had were too high to dismiss.

I was going to have to confront her in her own driveway.

The thing about a quiet kill is that it needs to be done in such a way that the victim's death doesn't call attention to itself.

For example, drown someone in their bathtub, fully dressed, and the police feel the need to investigate a suspicious death – and rightly so. But if the victim has been drinking, and you added bath salts to the water while the tub was filling – you have to do that part, or the water filling their lungs won't match the water they're soaking in; coroners notice that sort of thing – and then drown them, you can then stage the room at your leisure with a partial glass of wine, a few lit candles, and a romance novel, conveniently dropped in the water, and the death would be blamed on the wine.

Using the veggie burger as the primary murder weapon would be chalked up to a simple – if tragically fatal – accident.

To ensure her demise, I had stopped at a local health food store earlier in the day and picked up a small container of the pea-protein isolate powder. I had dissolved a triple dose of it in a small amount of water, which would ensure that the mild allergic reaction I expected the veggie burger to trigger would appear to have been severe enough to kill her fairly quickly.

I hoped to make her drink it. If she refused, I had a filled syringe in my pocket and could inject her with a lethal dose – but I wanted to avoid that option, as a decent medical examiner would notice an injection site, and we'd be right back to the "suspicious death" situation my client wanted to avoid.

And if Mindy had no reaction to the protein, there were many other ways I could kill her if I had to, each less "quiet" than the last.

I slowed as I drew near her house, studying it as I rolled by. There were no lights on, no sign of anyone nearby. I hoped that meant Mindy's teenagers were still with their step-mother.

I don't generally give much thought to my victims' personal lives, outside whatever I need to know to do my job. But in this case, I conceded that having the empty house to work in made everything so much easier. For all concerned.

The tracker began to ping again just as I was passing the house, as Mindy's car moved slowly through the grocery store parking lot.

"Showtime," I murmured when she turned into the neighborhood, then congratulated myself on correctly guessing the "overland" route she'd chosen.

I pulled around the corner and parked along the curb, wiped the last of the fry grease from my hand and put my glove back on. I double-checked my wig to make sure it was still settled, then got out of the car, draping a sweater over my arm to conceal both the fast-food bag and the long, thin strip of metal I'd retrieved from the backseat floor. Hoping anyone who saw me would think I was Mindy, I walked quickly to the gate at the side of the house and slipped into her back yard.

The house was a split-level, with four windows at this end of the house – two just above ground level and two higher up. A small deck sat at about the center of the house, raised to what I assumed corresponded to the house's main level. There was a deadbolt lock above the handset, and while I could pick the handset without thinking, deadbolts always took longer than I liked to admit.

I moved back to the lower-level window closest to the gate, set down the food and sweater, and put the Slim Jim skills I'd acquired during my misspent teenage years to good work. In two pings of Mindy's tracker, I had the screen off. I dropped it rather than setting it carefully aside, wanting it to look like it had fallen of its own accord. A moment later, and I'd found a tiny space between the window frame and the casing, and managed to wiggle the thin metal into it.

It was looser than I expected – not at all a bad thing in my opinion – and the window moved slightly. I nodded in satisfaction. It wasn't even locked.

Holding the window steady, I fished the multi-tool from my pocket and slid the blade into the space I'd opened with the Slim Jim, working my way in until I'd managed to get the window open a good inch. But that's where it stopped.

"Dowel," I said, almost growling when I glanced at the phone screen to see where Mindy was. Two blocks away. Great.

I turned to the other side of the glass panel, and pushed the Slim Jim in along the window casing, easing it forward until I found the dowel. Wiggling the thin metal around a bit, I finally caught the dowel with the hook at the end of the tool, and flipped the dowel out of the track. The glass slid free.

I pocketed the burner phone and multi-tool, grabbed the food, my sweater, and the Slim Jim, and was climbing through the window and over the back of a small sofa when the garage door mechanism engaged.

"Nothing like cutting it close," I muttered.

There was enough light coming in from the windows that it was easy to see I was in a family room, this level just a few steps down from the kitchen-dining room that opened out onto the deck. I slid the window closed and replaced the dowel, much to the annoyance of the large yellow cat that had jumped up onto the couch to investigate.

"Let's wait for Mindy, shall we?" I said, picking up the bag of food and moving it out of reach.

I dusted off the couch, then took a seat in an easy chair positioned just to the left of the couch, both oriented toward the large flat screen television mounted on the wall opposite the windows. A long, low coffee table sat in front of the couch, with enough scuff-marks on it to suggest that it was frequently put in service as a footrest. At the moment, however, the table was empty save for a chunky universal remote.

My chair was just far enough into the corner to be slightly in shadow, but also give me a decent view of the kitchen. I pulled off the dark wig I'd worn to fool the neighbors and folded my sweater around it, and had turned to set the bundle on the floor next to me when the cat jumped up on my lap.

"Well, hello," I said.

After a moment's turning this way and that, the cat lay down, apparently quite content to let me stroke his back.

The cat and I had no sooner gotten settled than the connecting door from the garage opened and Mindy came in, her arms loaded with what appeared to be reusable grocery bags. She deposited them on the small dining room table, switched on the kitchen light, then went back for another load.

I was in no hurry. I waited in the shadows, stroking the cat.

It took two trips to the garage to bring everything in. Mindy then bustled around the kitchen, emptying the bags, and putting the food away. The cat on my lap watched attentively, and after a couple of minutes a second cat – this one a small calico – wandered into view. It paused at the top of the steps leading down to the room where I sat, and stared at me, then apparently decided what was going on in the kitchen was more interesting, and leapt up onto the table for a better view.

"Shoo, Sunny!" Mindy said when she turned and saw the cat. She swished a towel in its general direction, and Sunny jumped off the table and ran down to the family room level, ducking out of sight behind the couch. "You know better..."

Mindy's voice faded as her gaze followed Sunny and then came to rest on me.

"You... you were at the bar," she said, her voice barely loud enough for me to hear from across the room. She grabbed the back of a chair like she was steadying herself.

"Good evening, Mindy," I said, feeling like a Bond villain as I sat there, my hand resting casually on the cat's back. "We have some things to discuss. Why don't you join me?"

◆

"You're here to kill me, aren't you?" She had come downstairs slowly, cautiously, and was now perched on the edge of the couch beneath the window. "Please. I won't say anything. You don't have to do this."

"That's not how this works," I said. "If I don't do it, someone else will."

I glanced meaningfully at the photos on the wall of Mindy with two teenagers, a boy who looked to be in high school and a girl of about thirteen or fourteen. "The next person might not be so nice about it."

Mindy followed my gaze and gasped. "Stay away from my children!" she said, half-rising from the couch.

"That's up to you," I told her. "Keep them out of my way, and no harm will come to them."

"They're not here. They're at their father's – it's his weeknight to have them…," she paused, sitting back down before continuing. "I can ask him to keep them longer."

"That would be best." I said. "Why don't you call him.?"

She pulled her phone out of her pocket, and sat there for a minute, holding the device in trembling hands.

"Make the call," I said. "But say anything wrong, try to give him a clue that anything at all is out of the ordinary, and it won't be pretty… for you, or your family."

She set the phone on the coffee table in front of her and placed the call. She had put the phone on speaker, and the ringing seemed to echo in the dimly-lit room, filling the silence between us.

The call was picked up after four rings.

"The kids are here. Did you forget?" a man's voice asked. In the background, intense music and the sound of crashes – or possibly explosions – suggested we'd interrupted a movie.

"I didn't forget," Mindy said. "I was hoping you and Sarah could keep the kids for the rest of the week… maybe through the weekend?"

Maybe for the rest of their lives, her eyes said as she looked at me. I met her gaze, my expression carefully neutral.

"What's going on, Min?" Trevor asked.

"Big project, that's all," she said, breaking eye contact with me. "I'm going to be at work almost round-the-clock for the next few days."

I had to hand it to her, she kept her cool, never letting her voice waver.

"You need to stop letting them take advantage of you so much." From the sound of it, Mindy working overtime was a common complaint. Trevor sighed before continuing. "I don't think there's enough food in the house to last us a week with two teenagers."

"That's what grocery stores are for, Trevor," Mindy said, her tone unexpectedly sharp.

"Hey, chill out," Trevor said. The background noise grew muffled, as though he'd stepped into another room or closed a door. "I just said it was *inconvenient*. Didn't say I wouldn't do it. What's wrong with you?"

"Nothing's wrong with me. I'm just tired. I don't feel well, and as soon as I grab a bite to eat, I have go back to the office," Mindy said, with a quick glance in my direction. She'd dialed her tone back and managed to sound almost sincere. The strain in her voice could easily be attributed to exhaustion. "It would be really good – a huge favor – if you kept the kids. Please?"

"Yeah, sure. Do you want to talk to them?"

"No, they'll just worry. Tell them I have to work, but that I'll pick them up on Sunday afternoon. We'll go to the beach or a movie or something."

"Okay. They'll probably want to stop by the house after school tomorrow to get some clean clothes. I'm not sure what they've got here, but they only brought enough for overnight."

"Yeah, no problem. Thanks."

"Sure. Are you sure you're okay?" Trevor seemed genuinely concerned.

It was time to get him off the phone before Mindy broke and said something compromising.

Holding the cat with one hand to keep from jostling it too much, I reached down with my free hand and picked up the fast-food bag sitting on the floor next to my chair. I set it on the coffee table near the phone, letting the paper rustle a little, then gestured for Mindy to wrap up the call.

"Yeah. It's just been a long day," she said, nodding. "There's nothing you can do to fix it. Just look after the kids – that will be help enough."

But Trevor wasn't quite finished. "You've been at that place for a long time, Min," he said. "Maybe it's time to look for something better."

"You're probably right," she said, an almost palpable touch of regret in her voice. "But for right now, I just need to get this project done."

"Promise you'll look?"

"I will," she said. She continued, winding up the call like everything was perfectly normal. "Next week, I promise. Look my dinner's getting cold. I've got to go. Tell Sarah I said thanks, and give the kids my love, okay?"

"Yeah, Okay."

Mindy ended the call before he had a chance to say anything more.

I gave her a minute to regroup; but she broke the silence in about forty-five seconds.

"Last meal?" she asked.

"You could say that. It's gotten cold – I'm sorry about that."

She nodded. "Couldn't be helped. What is it?"

"What would you have gotten?"

"Burger and fries. They make a good bacon cheeseburger. A cola, or maybe root beer."

I reached down for the cola, napkins, and straw and passed them to her. She took it all, and set the drink down by the bag, using one of the napkins as a coaster.

"Go ahead," I said, nodding at the bag. She opened it, picked out a few of the fries, and popped one in her mouth.

"You're awfully calm about all this," I said.

She swallowed. "Jazzy likes you."

"Jazzy?"

"The cat," she said, waving the second fry toward the big yellow cat on my lap. "Mostly we call him Jaz. He likes you." She popped the fry into her mouth.

"And that means what, exactly?" I asked, trying – and failing – to follow her logic. I wouldn't have trusted someone just because Glau liked having them pet him.

"I don't know. But you're treating him well, so it must mean something. Besides, you're holding a gun on me," Mindy said, pointing with the last of the fries she'd been holding. "I could attack you – or try to run away – and either way, I'm still dead." She ate the fry and reached back into the bag for the paper-wrapped burger.

It was beginning to get dark outside, and the light filtering down into the family room from the kitchen wasn't doing much to effectively light our conversation. In the dim light, Mindy had misinterpreted my holding the cat as a way of concealing a weapon beneath or behind him. It was an understandable mistake.

I didn't bother to correct her.

"And like you said," she continued, peeling open the paper, "I'd rather not have the rest of my family caught up in this. None of which is to say that I've given up, I just haven't figured a way out of it yet."

"That's one way of looking at it," I said, watching closely as she took a bite of the burger.

She started to chew, then stopped, her eyes going wide as she looked down at the burger in her hand and then over to me, the realization dawning. With one hand, she grabbed a napkin and raised it to her mouth.

"Swallow it," I said, stroking the cat.

She sat there, frozen, napkin halfway to her mouth, a slight whimper escaping her lips.

"Swallow it," I repeated, emphasizing each word as I patted the cat meaningfully. "And then take another bite."

Mindy complied, her earlier composure shattered. Her hands were shaking now, and she not only dropped the napkin she'd been holding, but she nearly dropped the burger as well.

"I am curious," I said as she chewed the second bite. "What did you learn about your boss that was so damning?"

Mindy reached for the cola, popping off the plastic lid and gulping the liquid down, not bothering with the straw. "Trafficking," she whispered after she set the cup down. "Names. Dates. Bank accounts."

"Digging where you shouldn't have," I said, shaking my head in sympathy for her situation. "Too bad."

I pulled the vial of pea-protein isolate from my pocket and held it out to her. "Drink this, please."

"What is it?"

"Something that will make this go much easier for you, and will be masked by the food in your system," I told her.

Mindy's shaking fingertips touched mine as she took the vial. "I didn't go digging," she said. "Not at first. Mr. Bouchard prefers to dictate memos and other notes. He gave me the wrong files to transcribe. After what I heard… that's when I went looking for more."

That was cold. She had to die because of his carelessness. I actually felt bad for her.

"Drink that," I said, attempting to sound friendly. "Your death will look like an accident. If I were to shoot you—" I saw no reason to tell her I didn't have a gun, "—or you were to die under other suspicious circumstances, there would be an investigation. It would be messy and painful for your family. This way, yes, they'll grieve, but they'll suffer less, be able to move on. Do you have life insurance?"

"Yes," she whispered. The calico cat, Sunny, jumped up on the couch next to her, and nudged at her for attention. "Not now, baby," Mindy told it, gently pushing the cat aside. Her breathing was already starting to sound raspy, and she was starting to itch the backs of her hands.

"Good. An accidental death won't nullify it. Your children will be taken care of."

Mindy nodded. "Why?" she asked. "Why do you care?"

"I lost my mother when I was about their age," I said, shrugging. "We didn't have it as good as your kids will." I gestured at the vial. "Go ahead and drink that now."

She started to twist the lid, then abruptly stopped, set the vial on the table, and reached into her pocket. I braced, ready to throw Jaz at her if she tried something desperate, but my concern was unnecessary. When she pulled her hand out of her pocket, she was holding a slim, black flash drive.

She held it out.

"What's this?" I asked, not taking it.

Mindy had to clear her throat a couple of times before she could speak clearly, and it took several seconds for her to get it all out. "It's all the data I have on Bouchard's operation…. The only copy… Take it…." She thrust it toward me. "Destroy him… for me. For my children."

I took the drive, turning it over in my gloved fingers. "Passcode?"

"None. I was going to turn him in, but I didn't know who to send it to."

I considered. I'd never had a target try to hire me to go after the original client before. I wasn't morally opposed to it – I wasn't morally opposed to much – but I wasn't fully on board with the idea either.

"I don't work for free," I said, knowing I was taking the easy way out.

"I have jewelry, money in the bank—"

"And if I took any of either, it would look like you'd been robbed," I said. "No deal."

Mindy squeezed her eyes shut, folding her arms over her stomach like it hurt.

"Are you going to be sick?" I asked.

She shook her head. "Stomach hurts," she whispered.

She was progressing through the stages of anaphylaxis that I'd read about right on cue. Part of me – the part that killed dispassionately and without remorse – watched with cold, clinical detachment. But there was another part of me that felt sorry for her, for the bad situation she'd had the misfortune of stumbling into and the grief it was going to bring to her family.

I nodded at the television. "Do you have a favorite show?" I asked. "Or a playlist you'd like to listen to?"

"Playlist," Mindy said, frowning as though trying to follow the direction the conversation had taken.

"Set it up," I said.

"Okay," she said. She leaned forward, bracing herself against the table with one hand while she reached for the remote. She stared at it for a moment, like she was trying to remember what the buttons did, then pointed it at the television.

It took a few attempts, while Mindy's breathing became more labored and her actions grew increasingly disoriented, but then the room filled with the sound of orchestral music, and a woman's voice began to sing.

"*Les Miserables*," I said.

"Movie soundtracks," Mindy whispered, falling back against the couch cushions, her expression softening. "I've loved musicals since I was a kid."

I nudged Jaz from my lap, put the flash drive in my pocket, then scooted forward and picked up the vial. "I'm sorry," I said. "But you really need to drink this now."

Mindy looked up at me, her expression almost unreadable in the shadows. I opened the vial, gently gripped her by the chin, and poured the contents into her mouth. When it was empty, I followed up with cola, forcing her to drink until she began to choke.

"Where is your EpiPen?" I asked.

"Purse," she croaked. She swung her arm, pointing in the general direction of the kitchen.

"I'll spill the bag. Make it look like you couldn't find the pen in time. Everyone will think this was an accident."

Mindy stared at me for a moment while she processed what I'd said, then nodded.

"In my closet... on the top shelf... back corner," she said, the effort to force the words out coherently clearly costing her. "Shoebox... money... was hidden in Bouchard's desk... Took it, thought it might stop the deal... No one knows."

Her eyes began to glaze as her breathing faltered. "You seem... like a decent person...," she said as I stood and capped the vial. "Please, save those girls..."

The music swelled. Mindy's eyes rolled back, her body slumped, and her breathing stopped.

I toyed with the flash drive in my pocket. I'd been prepared to walk away, call the client, tell him the job was done. But her last words had me wondering.

I'd just killed her, and she thought *I* was a decent person? What was on that drive that she thought was worse?

And what was I going to do about it?

Chapter 6

I took the money.

Mindy had been halfway out of her mind when she'd told me where to find it, but her instructions were spot on, and I found the shoebox exactly where she'd said it would be.

It was full of bundled stacks of bills. I didn't take the time to count them; just set the box on her bed and arranged the items on the closet shelf so no one would notice anything was missing.

I'd already scattered the contents of her purse, leaving the EpiPen just poking out from under the couch, where it might have looked as though Mindy wouldn't have been able to see it in a panicked state. Before I left, I made sure all the drapes were pulled shut, put away the last of the perishable groceries, and turned on the family room light.

Then I tossed the receipt for the meal in the fast food bag, set out some food for the cats, and retrieved the tracker from under her car's bumper.

I let myself out through the back door, locking the handset behind me. I'd found a roll of clear packing tape in the kitchen junk drawer, and had used a folded length of the sturdy tape to lock the deadbolt. Once the lock slid into place, I tugged more firmly on the strip of tape I'd attached to its handle. The tape pulled free of the handle and slid through the thin gap between the door and the doorframe. I wadded it up and stuck it in my pocket to throw away later.

I'd left nothing out of place, nothing to suggest that anyone else had been there. Nothing to indicate that Mindy's death had been anything other than a tragic accident.

The wind had picked up and a light rain was falling, the wind-driven droplets hitting like needles. I ran back across the yard and through the gate, glancing around to see if anyone was paying any attention as I hurried to my car, but other than a pickup truck driving through the intersection, water spraying from his tires and wipers running, I saw no one.

Shivering, I drove away, heading out of the neighborhood. A few blocks later, I spotted a store parking lot, pulled over, and dug the burner phone out of my bag. It was time to update my client.

Completed.

44.25 hours from contract start; no additional payment required.

The reply came swiftly.

How?

I didn't want to go into detail. Besides, he'd hear about it from the family the next day. So I responded with a single word:

Accident.

Bouchard would assume an automobile accident. I didn't care. He'd wanted something quick and quiet, and a toxic allergic reaction was about as non-suspicious as I could pull off.

I was about to power off the phone when it pinged with another message.

Did she say anything?

I knew what he was asking. Knew also that I had to be vague with my answer. Without even a second's hesitation, I responded.

Never saw me.

When a full minute passed with no reply, I powered off the phone and pulled the battery. This phone had no SIM card or extra memory. I tossed the pieces in my bag to dispose of later. I never used the same phone for multiple jobs. It was too risky.

I drove back to my hotel, the flash drive Mindy had given me burning a figurative hole in my pocket. She'd talked about trafficking, and asked me to "save those girls." Had Bouchard had her killed because she'd found out he was involved in *human* trafficking?

I'd assumed he was moving drugs, weapons, maybe bringing in imports from sanctioned countries. Not activities I necessarily condoned, but considering the ethical glass house I lived in, there was a pretty long list of sins I wasn't in a position to be judgmental about.

But if he was smuggling "those girls," to sell them as sex workers…

The abused child in the back of my mind began to whimper, and my heart began race, the pulse pounding in my ears. I clutched the steering wheel, forcing myself to stay focused, breathe calmly. Not jump to conclusions until after I'd reviewed the information on Mindy's flash drive.

After all, I'd taken her money. It was sitting there in a shoebox on the seat beside me. It didn't matter that she was dead, or even that I was the one who'd killed her. I had a new client.

I was working for Mindy now.

♦

There were three files on the drive – an audio recording, a simple text file, and a spreadsheet. I skimmed the text file while I listened to the audio.

The first few minutes sounded like routine business – Bouchard dictating a memo dealing with a forklift that needed servicing. I didn't follow the technical details.

But just as he was beginning the next memo, his train of thought was interrupted by a ringing phone. After some shuffling and rattling noises that I at first thought were him looking for the ringing phone and later decided were him attempting – and failing – to turn off the recorder, he took the call. The recording only had his side of the conversation, but it was damning enough.

"This is a bad time. I'm at work… You'll care if anyone suspects…. No, no problem with the shipment. As far as I know, everything is running smoothly… No, I haven't seen them. When would I have? They're not here yet. Won't be until Friday. We'll make sure they all survived the trip, then lift the container directly from the boat to the truck. They'll get to you Sunday morning, early… No, the driver doesn't know who you are. He'll just get an address for where to deliver the container… How would I know? I sent you the photos I got from the supplier. I didn't see any blondes in this batch… It's not like we take custom orders. If your buyer wants a blonde that badly, you'll have to bleach one of the girls' hair, or tell him to wait until next month…"

There was more, but it was all along the same lines. Bouchard was importing girls picked up off the streets in various Central and South American cities, using his connections to smuggle them into the U.S., and selling them. It made me want to vomit.

It made me want to go hunting.

♦

Mindy's write-up of Bouchard's operation was a good starting point – especially considering the fact that she'd gathered this information in only a couple of days. She had tracked back through the company records and found that missing or mis-counted containers had been marked down as clerical errors on a not-quite monthly basis for most of the previous year – ever since Bouchard had risen to his current role of General Manager. I suspected a review of Bouchard's financials would show a corresponding uptick in his net worth.

The spreadsheet she'd included was a goldmine of information. In addition to the details of each of the missing containers, including their origination point, the customs official who cleared them for entry into the country, and their final destination, Mindy had listed the contact name for each shipment, and the bank account numbers and fees corresponding to each transaction. But while she'd listed the number of girls in each shipment – an average of seven girls each, with the occasional group of nine – there had been no personal data about any of them, or records of where the individual girls had ended up.

The line for the current shipment was missing critical details.

According to the spreadsheet, there were six girls, in a shipment arriving on Friday – but it was one of three freighters coming into port that day that Raeburn Shipping had contracts with, and she didn't know which ship the container would be on or its point of origin.

The fields listing the buyer and bank account had been filled in, but the arrival time was blank, as well as the container number. And she knew that someone named "Richard / Richards / Richardson" was supposed to handle the customs inspection for the container, but was uncertain enough about the name to have listed all three, followed by a double question mark.

She'd been playing a dangerous game, collecting this data.

If Bouchard had known she'd gathered this much on his operation in so short a time, he probably would have killed her himself, rather than waste time ordering the hit.

It's what I would have done, in his position.

Questions of morality aside, from a strictly business standpoint Mindy had been a liability – and Bouchard had been a fool. He'd kept records that incriminated him up to his eyeballs in the trafficking ring – probably as some sort of underworld insurance policy – and not made sure they were properly secured.

And while she almost certainly would have refused, he hadn't even tried to buy her off – or better, bring her into the scheme. Instead, he'd allowed himself to feel threatened and gone straight to eliminating her. If he'd presented it properly, there was a small chance – a *very* small chance – he might have convinced Mindy to join him in the business, help him streamline his operation. Maybe even expand it.

Having a skilled bookkeeper on his side would have been useful. I knew that much from my own one-person operation. Paperwork could be such a chore.

I glanced over the spreadsheet one last time before closing the file. Mindy had tagged all but one of the containers as "reefers." The term meant nothing to me, but a quick internet search provided details. Reefers – in the shipping container context – were the refrigerated containers, used to transport cargo that needed a climate-controlled environment, with settings ranging from sub-zero to the mid-eighties.

I supposed the smugglers thought they were being considerate, ensuring the girls would have air to breathe and not be subjected to the extreme temperatures of the non-regulated containers.

I couldn't imagine the hell of being shoved into a refrigerator and shipped halfway around the world, only to be sold as a sex slave.

I pushed back from my laptop, fighting back my emotions.

This was supposed to have been a routine job. Nothing that would push my emotional buttons. Nothing personal.

But Bouchard, that conniving scumbag, had made it personal.

And as soon as I beat the information I needed out of him so I could save those girls, I was going to kill him.

And I was going to enjoy it.

♦

I changed from the blouse I'd been wearing into the darker, more functional turtleneck, and hung up my blazer. I wouldn't need it to go skulking around the port offices. It was bad enough that I was probably going to ruin an otherwise perfectly good pair of slacks. And while sneakers would have been better, my low-heeled loafers were an excellent choice for the well-dressed sneak-thief. They were also the only shoes I had, other than the sandals, which would have been a poor choice for the kind of sneaking I needed to do.

Whatever. I'd manage – and I'd look good doing it.

The rain had let up, and was no longer pelting the windows, but there was still a good stiff breeze coming off the ocean. I wasn't crazy about being out in a coastal storm, I needed to get to Bouchard's office tonight, while there was less of a chance of getting caught snooping. I grabbed my raincoat and headed out.

The travel brochures said the best time to see the Ravenal Bridge was at night, when the diamond-shaped towers shone like twin blades of light against the darkness, but as I crossed the bridge to Mt. Pleasant, I wasn't thinking about the scenery.

My reconnaissance of Raeburn Shipping's main office had been minimal, to say the least. I knew its location, where employees parked, and where the front doors were. I had no idea how the interior of the building was laid out, how many people might be onsite at night, or what security I might encounter.

Nothing like rushing in without a plan.

Ian would have advised caution, but the lack of detailed information wouldn't have stopped him.

And it wasn't going to stop me, though it might slow me down some. I wasn't too worried. It was barely after ten o'clock; I had all night.

I'd seen Mindy's keycard when I'd spilled the contents of her purse, and now I was kicking myself for not taking it, so getting into the building was the first hurdle I had to overcome.

A fictional thief would have miraculously consulted the internet and discovered the floorplan, complete with security schematic and a back-door for disabling those safety measures. They'd be carrying a cell phone-sized tool that granted them magical access to any keycard locked door. And to take advantage of the special effects budget, they'd have also been equipped with heat-sensor goggles, allowing them to track the movements of employees, guard dogs, and even the stray rat or bat.

Lacking any of that, I catalogued my resources.

I had a wig and a pair of dark-rimmed reading glasses, which might make someone who'd never actually met her or seen her up close think I was Mindy.

I had a multi-tool, a Slim Jim, and a set of lock picks.

That was it. I'd travelled light. Breaking into an office hadn't been part of my original plan.

I had a decent amount of skill with switching circuits around in a few models of security panels, and the multi-tool had everything I needed to do the job, but I hadn't put those skills to the test in nearly a year. The building would have to use exactly the right system and model for me to be willing to risk hacking it.

I set the problem to simmering in my back-brain. One way or another, I would get inside the building. The next order of business was to have my goals clearly in mind so that once I got in, I could do what I needed to do and get out.

One: find Bouchard's office.

Two: find the answers to the questions Mindy had been unable to answer - the identity of the customs official, the container number, who and where "the 4:30 truck" was delivering the girls.

What I would do once I had those answers, I had no idea – I was flying by the seat of my pants here, figuring it all out as I went along. But this much I did know: without those answers, the girls Mindy had tasked me with saving were still in jeopardy.

Chapter 7

The containers stacked on the dock rose like a blocky city skyline backlit by the glow of the lights on the massive cranes as I approached Raeburn Shipping's office-warehouse.

Fortunately, the Raeburn office was set well back from both the river's edge and the hustle and bustle of the dockworkers loading and unloading the massive freighter currently at anchor. I was grateful for that, as the idea of ducking through the container stacks didn't appeal to me.

There were about three dozen vehicles in the poorly-lit lot – probably belonging to the dockworkers currently on shift at Raeburn and the neighboring warehouse closer to the lot. I pulled in among them, then once again pulled on the dark wig. I didn't anticipate fooling anyone I came face-to-face with – but the disguise would obscure my appearance on any security cameras.

I hadn't thought to check the strength of the lenses when I'd picked them up – I'd just grabbed the first pair of reading glasses I saw that looked like the ones Mindy had worn. As a result, the distortion in my vision when I put them on made my head swim as I walked across the parking lot and to first warehouse. As soon as I reached the shadows near the building, I tugged the glasses off and just kept my head down as I walked the length of the building. I didn't want to wear them if I didn't need to.

I stopped when I got to the end of the first warehouse and studied the Raeburn building.

The Raeburn warehouse sat at a right-angle to the first warehouse, the two buildings forming a slightly off-centered "T." I was just to the right of the office portion of the building, a single-level box with a window at the front next to a glass door with a dim light over the door. There were three windows along the side of the box, all were dark, except for the one closest to the point where the office adjoined the warehouse.

To the left of that window, a door provided the only entry into the warehouse from this side. That door, the "Employees Only" sign on it, and the black box of a keycard reader mounted beside it, were illuminated by a bright overhead light.

The only windows on the warehouse were up high, running the length of the building in a faintly glowing dotted line tucked just under the slight eaves.

Movement at the far end of the building caught my eye, and I watched as a forklift backed out of an open container, carrying a loaded pallet toward the back of the warehouse.

While I watched, a tractor-sized forklift emerged from the shadow of the building, carrying a container on its blades. I watched in fascination as it altered its course, taking a long, slow, lumbering curve to position the container alongside the first, then slowly lowered the heavy box to the ground. It wasn't until the driver hopped out of the forklift's cab that I realized how large the tractor-sized vehicle actually was.

This was not the corporate world I was accustomed to.

Nevertheless, I'd gained some important information: there were people in the building, and at least one open door at the back – probably one of the large, garage-door style.

I could work with that.

Believe it or not, people are often easier to manipulate than locks. And if I couldn't slip in unobserved, I'd go to Plan B: a little social manipulation. I headed for the far end of the building, staying in the shadows whenever possible.

One way or another, I was getting into that warehouse.

◆

I stood at the end of the Raeburn warehouse, my body pressed close to the wall as I peered around the corner. I had been wrong in almost all of my assumptions. The warehouse might not have been at a full crew, nevertheless, it was a hive of activity. In addition to the ground-level forklifts and containers I'd seen as I approached, a half-dozen semi-trucks sat at a series of raised loading docks. A fleet of smaller forklifts – these driven by standing operators – buzzed around, driving directly into the containers, then emerging a few moments later, carrying pallets loaded with shrink-wrapped stacks of boxes which they whisked away into the interior of the building.

Periodically, a truck would leave, hauling its empty container away only to be replaced by another as soon as it had cleared the dock. After a momentary consultation between the driver and the foreman who guided them into the loading dock – presumably to verify the container's contents – the unloading process would begin anew.

The nearest door was only a few feet from me, a heavy-duty steel door, a few steps up from the open bay, putting it at the same level as the loading docks, and lit by a weak, yellow bulb. I dismissed it almost immediately. I would be too exposed there, in easy view of the forklift drivers.

However, just beyond the door a ground-level garage door stood open, seated forklifts using that bay to unload a container that sat on the ground, its canvas side open to the building.

I ducked back around the corner as one of the seated forklifts trundled forward. The ground-level by doors appeared to be my best bet.

I would have to time it just right.

There were three forklifts emptying the container, moving in and out of the warehouse on a well-timed rotation. They were smaller than the tractor-sized one that had brought the container over from the yard, but larger than the standing forklifts buzzing around the loading dock. These also had a small, covered area for the driver to sit in, which I thought might be to my advantage, in that it would be a tiny bit harder for one of the drivers to jump out of his rig and chase after me than for the standing drivers.

Of course, they could also move pretty quickly, so I was still going to have to stay out of sight.

I put on the reading glasses, ignoring the almost instant wave of nausea that washed over me. Blinking and squinting, I concentrated on bringing the rain-soaked, funhouse vision of the activity at this side of the warehouse into focus, grateful that I only needed the glasses for a short time.

The forklifts moved in dizzying blurs, but I could see well enough to gauge their timing, and slipped into the warehouse behind one of the inbound forklifts just after its outbound partner passed my hiding place. I moved quickly, the sound of my footsteps on the cement floor lost under the machine noise as I half-ran up the slight ramp into the building. I had about twenty feet to cross before I could duck into the stacks of boxes and only seconds to do it – but I couldn't run, or I'd pass the machine I was following. The forklift currently loading up would be right behind me in only a moment, and the third coming soon to take its place.

We reached the end of the ramp just as the third forklift came around the corner toward us. I stayed behind my machine as it turned, stepping off to the side into the opening between the shelving, and then running for the shadows at the far end of the row, hoping that the driver of the second machine – the one behind me – hadn't seen me.

Luck was with me. I heard no shout, no blasting of an airhorn, no footsteps following me.

The row ran the length of the warehouse, with a series of shorter rows heading off to my right at regular intervals. All were wide enough for the forklifts to drive down and gave them enough room to maneuver the pallets onto metal shelving grates that must have risen fifteen or twenty feet into the air. The air was heavy with humidity, the not-quite briny scent off the river, and the smell of cardboard and sawdust.

I pulled off the glasses, and kept moving, listening for the telltale whine of the small forklifts echoing though the vertical canyons as I approached each intersection. Twice I had to backtrack, ducking back around the end of the previous row when the lawn-mower-ish sound of one of the larger forklifts headed toward my long corridor. I was grateful for the relative shadow that helped to conceal my presence – the overhead lights above this row were off, but toward the center of the warehouse the lights blazed like a sunny afternoon.

With all the back and forth, and staying out of sight of the forklift drivers, it took nearly ten minutes to walk the length of the warehouse. I peered around the end of the final row and breathed a sigh of relief as I watched one of the standing forklifts heading down the row in the opposite direction, one of its wheels clacking against the concrete like it had a rock stuck in its treads.

A set of double glass doors to the office section were centered along this wall, about forty feet down the row, which ran the entire width of the building. On this side of the doors was the windowless Employees Only door I'd seen from the outside, a timeclock and rack of old-fashioned punch cards mounted to the wall next to it. About fifteen feet beyond the glass doors was a second set of double-doors, these solid and painted a dark gray with bright yellow trim around the framing. The doors were labeled in white lettering, but I couldn't read it from this distance and angle.

All of the doors were outlined with bright yellow trim around the framing and hashed lines in both red and yellow extended in a large rectangle on the floor. I assumed this was a safety measure, an indication to the forklifts that they shouldn't drive in the foot-traffic zones.

The row was wide and well lit, with nowhere to hide.

I would be completely exposed.

I put my "Mindy" glasses back on, straightened my raincoat, and walked down the row, focusing on the pale, blurry rectangle where I knew the glass doors to the office were.

There was another forklift ahead of me, but on a different row, possibly the one next to me, I wasn't sure. The constant squeal of wood sliding on metal as the pallets scraped against the shelves was almost deafening, making it difficult to tell where the various forklifts were when I couldn't see them. I only knew if they were close when the cement floor vibrated under my feet.

I kept walking.

The row ended in an open area about ten feet away from the office door. I was three steps across when one of the approaching forklift drivers waved at me. I waved back, but kept on walking, averting my head slightly.

"Bouchard's not here," he shouted, slowing his forklift as he rolled past, no more than ten feet away. He didn't seem surprised to see "Mindy," but I doubted he knew her well – my excuse for a disguise wasn't that good. I stayed back and kept my face turned a little away from him, just to be on the safe side.

He pointed toward the loading dock. "Took some bigwig out to see the freighters."

"Thanks," I shouted, nodding and waving, because I wasn't sure if he could hear me through his heavy-duty, noise-cancelling headphones. As he revved up his forklift, I raised my hand to cover my ear – and further block his view of my face – then pointed toward the office with my other hand. "No earplugs."

He laughed, gave a thumbs up, and sped away, disappearing down a nearby row.

I walked quickly to glass double-doors, which, thankfully were unlocked. If Bouchard was on site, I needed to work fast. He might return from the freighter any moment.

♦

The office followed a simple layout – from the double doors there was a short hallway, with the mens' and womens' room doors on my right, flanking a drinking fountain, and a wall filled with OSHA posters and other posted notices to my left. A few feet ahead, the room opened up into a small cubicle farm which would seat no more than a half-dozen workers.

The mechanical smells and sounds of the warehouse faded almost immediately as I walked down the hallway – helped along, no doubt, by the air freshener hanging on the bulletin board. It was less humid here, too. By the time I got to the end of the hall, and into the office portion of the building, it was easy to almost forget about the warehouse behind me.

Mindy's space, which I identified by the photographs on her desk of her with her children and cats, was along the outer wall. A small vase with vanilla scented sticks sat next to her monitor. Right next to her cubicle was a closed office. A large window reinforced with wire mesh between the panes and narrow slat blinds open just enough to allow a view of the lighted office beyond, occupied the bulk of the wall between them. As if I needed confirmation, the door next to the window bore a nameplate reading "General Manager."

The door was locked, but that's what lock picks are for.

Bouchard 's office was large by comparison to the cubicles. A narrow, rectangular table with a pair of folding chairs sat just below the window overlooking Mindy's desk, and a long, low, uncomfortable-looking, cracked vinyl futon couch with wide armrests and a sloping back ran along the adjacent wall, with an exterior window just above it.

The opposite wall was dominated by a large wall-mounted screen displaying an automated, color-coded diagram of the warehouse. I stared at it for a few seconds, fascinated, watching the LED display update with codes and numbers as the forklift drivers delivered new pallets and registered their location with handheld scanners.

A row of tall, slightly dented, putty-colored filing cabinets ran the length of the far wall, the old-style locking mechanisms pushed in on all of them. I could pop the locks if I needed to, but hoped I'd find what I was looking for in Bouchard's desk.

The desk sat in front of the filing cabinets. It was an oversized, wooden monstrosity that looked like it had seen better days. A large, high-backed, executive-style desk chair that probably cost as much or more than all the other furniture combined took pride of place at the desk. A third folding chair holding a torn-open flat of water bottles sat beneath the diagram, next to the desk.

The blinds were closed on the exterior window, but the interior window blinds were open. I closed the door behind me, twisted the blinds closed, and moved into the room. There was no time to go through the filing cabinets. That would only have been an option if I'd known exactly what I was looking for or had all weekend to comb through the records. Instead I went straight to the desk, and began going through the drawers.

I found three flash drives in the top left-hand drawer. I had no idea what was on them, but pocketed them anyway, tucking them in my raincoat pocket with the glasses, which I'd abandoned as soon as I'd entered Bouchard's office. There was also keyring full of small keys, presumably for the filing cabinets behind me, which I hoped I wouldn't have to dig through.

The top center drawer protested when I opened it, squealing slightly as one of the metal glides scraped along the track. But the Glock 19 Bouchard kept in the drawer made the shiver-inducing squeal worthwhile. I popped a loaded magazine out of the gun and cleared the chamber, then pocketed it and a spare magazine that had shifted to the back of the drawer in my raincoat pocket. Once empty, I left the gun on the top of the desk – I'd tuck it into the back of my jeans when I was ready to go. There was no sense leaving it behind. Bouchard wasn't going to need it much longer.

The lower right-hand drawer was locked. I once again pulled out my lock picks, but when I opened the drawer, I was surprised to find it empty. I patted the interior, and the underside of the drawer above to see if there was perhaps a secret panel or compartment, but found nothing.

I was pushing away from the desk when my toe bumped against something squishy. I looked down, and saw a soft-sided leather briefcase tucked just under the edge of the left-hand drawers. I pulled the case out and unzipped it. Bouchard 's laptop – a state-of-the-art, ultra-light PC model – was inside.

Bingo.

I set the laptop on the desk, and was starting to rifle through the several file folders full of miscellaneous paperwork in the briefcase, when I heard voices in the hallway on the other side of the thin wall next to where I sat.

There was no way to know if it was Bouchard coming back from the docks, or one of the workers heading to the restroom. It didn't matter. I couldn't afford to take the chance.

I stuffed the briefcase back under the desk, grabbed the gun and laptop, and looked for someplace to hide.

Including the wide, bulky armrests at each end, the couch was a little over seven feet long, and sat a few inches away from the wall, probably to allow space for adapting the futon cushion into a sleeper. Its angled back slanted away from the wall, creating a small tunnel.

It wasn't much, but it would do – I hoped.

I practically dove behind it, shoving the gun and laptop deep under the three-inch space under the futon and wriggling my way into the tight space against the wall. I was still on my side, scooting forward – and hoping my feet weren't hanging out in the open – when a key rattled in the office door.

Chapter 8

"We can talk privately in here," a man's voice was saying as the door swung open. "It's better than trying to shout over all the noise out in the yard or in the warehouse."

I froze, laying on my side, my left arm awkwardly supporting my head, the gun's magazines pressing into my hip, and my back to the wall. Based on where I was relative to the couch's short legs, I thought I was well-hidden. The next few minutes would either confirm or deny it.

Peering under the couch, I saw a pair of well-worn steel-toed, leather work boots, the hem of a pair of blue jeans caught on one of the knotted laces enter the office. Work Boots stepped aside for a pair of fancy cowboy boots – alligator skin, I thought – the textured, amber-colored hide contrasting with the crisp sleekness of neatly-pressed black dress slacks. Beyond those two, I barely glimpsed more than six inches of off-the-rack navy slacks over cheap wingtips taking up a guard stance in the hall before the door closed.

Alligator Boots moved to the center of the room, then stopped directly in front of the middle of the couch – and my waist – but facing the opposite wall. I guessed that the LED display had caught his attention, as it had mine.

But instead of the good-ol' boy voice I'd assumed would come with the boots, it was a woman's voice that responded.

"This is quite the operation you have here," she said. Her voice was low and smooth, her tone professional, not gushing.

"It works for us," Bouchard said, the steel-toed boots walking past the woman's alligator boots. There was a rustle of plastic. "Water?"

"Thank you."

I hadn't been thirsty until he offered her the water, damn him.

Now I listened to the crack of the plastic lids being opened, acutely aware of both how dry my mouth was and the dust I'd raised while squeezing into my hiding place. I was wrinkling my nose, trying to prevent a sneeze, when the woman took a step back, then sat down, crossing one leg over the other as she settled onto the cushion. I caught a glimpse of dark, auburn hair as the couch shifted. It was no more than half an inch, but now the frame pressed me against the wall.

To be fair, it could have been worse. If she'd been the large man I'd expected, and dropped onto the low futon as a tall man would almost invariably do, I'd not only have been even more thoroughly pinned than I already was, but it was a good bet I'd have given myself away with an "uhf" as the air was crushed out of me.

It's the little things.

Strands of my wig's long, dark hair had twisted loosely around my neck while I'd edged my way into the space, and I couldn't get to it without hitting the back of the futon. As long as I didn't move, I was okay. Focusing on the conversation going on above me was the only way to keep from reaching for it. I exhaled slowly, still twitching my nose and gently blowing the dust away from my face.

"…How many don't survive the trip, on average?" the woman was asking. "We're not paying to ship corpses."

"We've only lost one girl since Haskell suggested we use the reefers," Bouchard said. "We were using regular containers, before, but the losses…" He left the sentence unfinished. From the angle of his boots, it looked like he was sitting on the front edge of his desk. Both of his feet were flat on the floor, not raised or angled, not stretched out in front of him. Between that and his boot size, I guessed him to be a few inches taller than my own five-foot-seven.

"What's the container number?" she asked.

"Nnn-hnnn," Bouchard said, the negation diluted by the water he was drinking. "Never gave it to Haskell, not giving it to you either, Renee. The fewer people who know, the safer for all of us."

"I want my own people present," the woman – Renee – said casually, but with an underlying steel in her tone not dissimilar to the one I used when negotiating corporate deals. "To make sure everything goes smoothly with the inspection, loading the container onto the truck."

"I've got all that covered. This isn't my first rodeo, sweetheart," Bouchard said, his tone dismissive.

I grimaced. The man was an idiot, speaking to his client that way – and a new client, too, unless I missed my guess. My esteem for him – already as low as I thought it could go – dropped several more points into the negative. And though I had no use for her, either, Renee rose a few points in my book when she replied.

"Is that so?" she said. "After the trouble you've already had…"

She never moved, but even tucked behind the couch, I could feel the temperature in the room plummet at the ice in her voice. Bouchard's booted feet twitched, then he abruptly stood and walked around to the other side of his desk.

The wheels on the executive chair crunched across the plastic floor mat, and the chair's pricey springs creaked slightly as he sat down.

"I told you," Bouchard said, once he was safely ensconced in his seat of power. "I took care of it. She won't be a problem."

"So you said," Renee said. "But who's to say she didn't tell someone? Or report you to the authorities, before you took care of things? Can she be trusted? How much did you pay her?"

"She won't be talking to anyone," Bouchard said. He sounded pleased with himself.

"You killed her?"

"Hired it out. Too risky to do it myself." The big chair squeaked and his boots *thumped* onto the desk. He was clearly satisfied with himself.

"Of course. The killer – someone you know?"

"Not personally, no," Bouchard said. "And they don't know me. It was all negotiated remotely. Anonymously."

"I see."

If I hadn't been so close to her, I doubt I would have heard the slight, frustrated sigh that accompanied Renee's words. I understood how she felt. Bouchard's carelessness had exposed the entire operation. And having Mindy killed before he'd learned who she might have told had been a tactical mistake – one he seemed completely unaware of. The strikes against him were adding up.

The tension in the room was almost palpable.

Bouchard must have felt it, too, because he was quick to justify his actions.

"I'm not even sure she realized what we're doing here – Mindy, I mean," he said. "She never said anything, never even looked at me funny. It just seemed safer to be proactive. You know, deal with her before she became a problem. I told the contractor to make it quick and quiet. Something that wouldn't raise suspicions."

"How did she die?"

"An accident."

Renee was silent, and after an uncomfortable pause, Bouchard added, "I don't know. Might have been a car wreck, might have been pushed down the stairs in her house. Doesn't matter. Dead is dead, and as long as it looks accidental, there's nothing to connect her death to us."

"To *you*," Renee corrected. I heard a soft, rhythmic tapping vibrating through the couch, as though she was tapping her fingers on the vinyl cushion.

My fingers twitched involuntarily in response. I winced. I was rapidly losing sensation along my left side, and my hand was going numb from lack of blood flow.

Renee was still talking. "All the more reason why I want my own people involved from this point forward," she said. "The container number, please."

Bouchard was quiet, but I heard the now familiar squeal of metal on metal as he opened the desk's sticky center drawer.

Papers rustled, and Bouchard made a small choking sound as he looked under sticky notes and receipts for the Glock that the scraps of paper couldn't have hidden. Other than the single bullet that had dropped into the drawer when I'd cleared the chamber, there was no sign that the weapon had ever been there.

It was all I could do to suppress a chuckle.

"Is something wrong?" Renee asked.

"Um…" The drawer closed. "No. Not at all."

"The number?"

The chair creaked again – in such a humid environment, he really should have had both it and the desk oiled – and his booted feet hit the plastic floormat.

"What's your hurry, Renee?" he asked, all charming-like. He stood, and moved around the end of the desk. "We've got plenty of time before the freighter arrives…"

I couldn't believe it. He was attempting to seduce her. Not that it seemed at all out of character for him to try it, but if she took him up on it, I didn't know if I'd survive them bouncing on the futon above me. I'm not a religious person, but as Bouchard came around to stand in front of Renee, I was praying to any god that might be listening to please, *please* intervene on my behalf.

Bouchard took a step forward.

Renee had been sitting with one leg crossed over the other throughout the conversation. As Bouchard moved toward her, she shifted.

"*Ulggg*," Bouchard grunted, staggering back. He stopped near the center of the room, his feet spread wide, breathing heavily.

If I were a betting woman, I'd have guessed that she'd planted her alligator boot in his crotch. Not hard enough to bring him down – which I had no doubt she could have – but just firmly enough to get her point across.

"There was no call for that," he said, his voice rough. "I was just tryin' to be friendly."

"I'm not one of your container girls," Renee said, her tone steely. "The number, please."

Bouchard shambled over to the desk. Maybe he was leaning against the desk, maybe he was looking for something on it, I couldn't tell. I only knew that his feet were still facing the desk, meaning his back was to Renee when he spoke.

"I don't know who you think you are," he said, pain still evident in his voice, "coming in here and acting like you're running the show. Haskell and I worked together for quite a while. There's a way we do things."

"A way you *did* things," Renee said. "Haskell is gone. And now there's a new way. *My* way." She stood, then, and walked past him, going around the desk and sitting in the big chair. It barely creaked under her, even when she tilted it back and deliberately *thunked* her boots on the desk.

"Now look, Renee—" Bouchard said.

"I might have to set up a secondary office here in Charleston," she said, ignoring Bouchard. "Build a house with an ocean view…"

"You killed him, didn't you?" Bouchard asked.

"Who? Haskell?" she said, coming back to the conversation. "He was old-school. Didn't want to keep up with the times. Forget about him. Is that the number?"

"Yes." There was the whisper of paper rustling on the desk.

"Excellent. And the cash for the customs official and the drivers?"

"I don't keep that here."

"Of course you do," she said.

I almost felt bad for him. All that bluster and show – and he was utterly weak in the face of someone who actually had a backbone. Not that I would add Renee to my Christmas card list or ever invite her to the house for a barbecue – I recognized some of my own darker shadows in her – but if this conversation was typical of either of them, she definitely had the upper hand.

And possibly a weapon, now that I thought about it. I couldn't decide if she'd threatened him openly or just intimidated him. Not that it mattered either way.

"Bottom drawer," he muttered.

The drawer rattled.

"The locked one?" Renee asked, her voice dripping with insufferable patience.

There was a rattle of keys. "Here," he said.

The alligator boots hit the floor.

As the keys rattled again, followed by a dull *click*, I knew exactly what Renee was going to see when the drawer slid open: nothing. Because the money she was looking for was sitting in a shoebox I'd retrieved from Mindy's closet and stored in the locked safe in my hotel room.

"Very funny," she said, sounding not at all amused. "Where's the money?"

"It's right there, in the shoebox…" Bouchard said. One of his heels left the floor as he leaned forward over the desk. "No, no, that's not right," he said, his voice rising in panic. "Someone took it!"

"Back off, Bouchard," Renee said. She stood, coming around the desk.

Bouchard took one step back, then two, as she advanced. He nearly tripped over the chair full of water bottles, and only stopped when his back hit the wall. I decided then that Renee definitely had a gun. Even the threat of the wingtip-wearing bodyguard outside the door wouldn't have caused him to retreat like that.

"I fronted you five hundred thousand dollars," Renee growled. She stood close to him, only separated by a couple of feet. "Where is my money?"

"I used some of it to take care of Mindy—"

"How much?"

"Two-fifty. And another fifty to hire the truck to take the container to Kansas City," he said. He was talking fast, and probably sweating like a stuck pig. "Richardson – the customs agent I work with – and the driver, they each get fifty. And I always keep ready cash around for emergencies, to pay off any forklift drivers who need to look the other way. That sort of thing."

"So you're telling me that you left *two hundred thousand dollars* in a shoebox in your desk drawer?" Renee said, speaking with exaggerated patience, as though to ensure there was no mistaking her words. "And there are people here who know about it."

"It was locked," he said, as if that should have explained everything. "And I keep my door locked. It's always been safe before—"

"Like that ever stopped anyone who wanted to from getting in," Renee said, cutting him off. "You're running a sloppy operation here, Bouchard. I don't know what Haskell ever saw in you."

"I paid the hitter by wire." Bouchard said. He sounded desperate.

"I'll want the transfer number."

"Yeah, yeah," Bouchard said. "It's on my computer. And I've got their phone number." There was a pause, presumably while he pulled out the burner phone and showed it to her. "They don't know who I am. No names – except for Mindy's, of course – had to give them that much. We did everything by text message."

"Really?" Renee sounded intrigued. "Call them."

"Sure. Okay."

I had a sinking feeling I knew where this was headed. He thought he could pull the funds back from my account to give to Renee. Bouchard wasn't thinking clearly, but Renee had to know that I would go after him if he stole from me.

Bouchard was an idiot.

And I was glad I'd grabbed his computer.

And Renee was as sneaky as the alligator her boots were made from.

They stood there, facing each other in silence for a couple of minutes listening while a phone rang on speaker. I didn't think I'd ever been so grateful to the Researcher as I was at that moment for having drilled into me the habit of immediately disabling the burner phones I used for each job.

I focused on the ringing phone, rather than think about the sweat trickling down my face and neck from beneath the dark wig or the cramp forming in my leg. One of the magazines was jammed right up against a bone and there was no way I could safely shift to relieve the pressure. I was just glad I'd put the reading glasses in my right-hand pocket, or they'd be digging into my leg as well – and might have given me away with a telltale 'crunch' beneath my weight.

"Doesn't look like your hitter wants to talk to you," Renee said.

"I guess not," Bouchard said, ending the call. "But the wire transfer number is on my computer, like I said."

"Then maybe this won't be a total loss," Renee said. "The rest of the plan? Freighter schedule? Driver information?"

"It's all on my computer."

"Which is where?"

"Under the desk," he muttered. He sounded like a petulant child.

Renee turned and took a couple of steps toward the door. Bouchard started to follow, then stopped when she did.

"I'll cover the costs, *this* time; collect this container," she said. "There had better be a blonde."

"I told you I can't promise that," Bouchard said. "We sometimes get one in the South American shipments, but almost never from Colombia."

She stood there for a long moment, facing him.

"We won't be working together in the future," she said. Her tone was back to the cool, level professional, the statement a simple one that expressed all her frustration with him without descending to his level. I had to respect her for that much.

"Now wait a minute," Bouchard said, his bluster returning. "You can't do that."

"Yes, I can," Renee said.

"But we had a deal."

"Deal's off."

She fired. Two quick shots.

I somehow managed not to jump in surprise, give myself away. I knew she was running out of patience with him, had figured she might put him out of her misery once the deal was done, but I hadn't expected her do kill him right then. I wondered about Haskell, the former business partner, and if she'd taken over his business in a similar fashion.

Bouchard hit the floor, his face turning toward me as he landed. I knew, from the hole in the center of his forehead, that he was already gone, but it was still unnerving to see his dead eyes staring at me under the couch.

Renee stepped over the body, went to the desk, and pulled the computer bag out from under it. She must not have checked it – or mistook the weight and shape of the file folders it held as a lightweight laptop – because she turned and walked back across the room to the door without a pause.

Wingtips turned as she opened the door. "Everything all right, boss?" he asked.

"I don't ask for much," Renee said. "A little professionalism…"

She took two steps past Wingtips, then turned back toward the office.

"I'll want you to check on his secretary," she said. "He says he had her killed. Make sure. And track the number on this phone. It's probably another burner, but still worth looking. Find out who it belongs to, if you can. I want my money back."

"You got it," he said. "What about that? Want me to clean up the mess?"

Renee barely paused before answering.

"Torch it."

Chapter 9

Well, shit.

As if laying on my side on a hard, cold, dirty floor, the long hair of a wig twisted around my throat, a pair of ammo magazines digging odd rectangles into my hip, and the arm awkwardly bracing my head having passed the painful pins-and-needles stage of falling asleep five minutes ago wasn't bad enough, now they were going to set the place on fire.

The two hundred thousand dollars Mindy had stolen from Bouchard was barely worth this. On the bright side, at least there weren't any vermin or insects under the couch with me.

I didn't dare move as Wingtips came into the office, closing the door behind him. I caught a glimpse of poorly-pressed navy blue pant legs as he walked over to Bouchard. Without even pausing to think about it, he scooped up the body with no more difficulty than lifting a large pillow, which told me a lot about just how strong he was.

Then he tossed the dead weight onto the couch.

I was prepared for the jolt of the couch against me this time, and had already blown out most of my breath in the half-second before Bouchard landed, but that didn't make the solid wooden bar that ran the length of the futon frame any less painful as it slammed against my body.

I was going to have an odd set of bruises when this was all over.

Rather than think about it, I focused on what was coming next. Wingtips was standing in front of the couch; in just a moment he'd pull out matches or a lighter and apply a flame to the most flammable part of Bouchard's clothing. I didn't know how much hair Bouchard had, but he might light that, too, to help get the blaze going.

If he had a knife… yup, there it was, the ripping sound as a blade tore through the vinyl. The stuffing would make good kindling, and go up quickly, without the need for any sort of accelerant. I wondered how bad it would smell, and how I was going to keep from choking when it started to smoke.

Before he lit the match, though, I was surprised by the sharp scent of whiskey.

Wingtips must have had a personal flask on him – or maybe it had been Bouchard's. From the splatters hitting the wall behind me and dripping over the back of the cushion and down onto my raincoat and hair, Wingtips was giving the exposed stuffing a good soaking.

The temptation to jump up, push the couch over, and take Wingtips on flashed through me – and fizzled out just as quickly as my rational brain took over.

I could almost hear Ian's voice, calm and Zen-like, talking me through an assessment of the situation as though this was nothing more than a classroom exercise.

What do you know? the Ian voice asked.

Wingtips has a knife; I have to assume he also has a gun.

What is your level of readiness?

Bouchard's unloaded gun is under the couch somewhere near my knees; the magazines are in my pocket. I also have a multi-tool with a three-inch blade.

Analysis?

I would be facing an armed adversary who was much larger, much stronger, and – as the numb tingle of my fingertips reminded me – currently much more agile than myself, completely unarmed.

The element of surprise alone would not be enough to get me out of a confrontation alive.

Better, then, to live to fight another day.

So I lay there like a side dish, quietly marinating while the entrée was being prepared, and hoping Wingtips wasn't planning to wait around and watch things cook for too long.

Liberal as he was with the whiskey, he at least had the good sense not to be wasteful with it and moved away from the couch and over to the desk after a couple of minutes.

He wasted little time on that side of the office. Setting the locked filing cabinets on fire would waste time and was an unnecessary risk that would bring little reward. But destroying the old wooden desk was a good idea – once the fire caught, it would burn well. I couldn't tell if he also added liquid fuel to the desk, or decided that the papers there would be enough to set the blaze, but it wasn't long before I heard the flare of a match strike and smelled the first hints of smoke.

He was a pro – I had to give him that.

I willed him to leave.

But he wasn't finished.

He came over to the couch, and for a moment he just stood there. I froze, breathing as quietly as I knew how, worried that I might have made some sort of sound that had caught his attention.

I don't know what he'd been waiting for, but after what felt like an age he began to slowly, deliberately light matches, one after another.

Was he placing them carefully on the body, poking them in the whiskey-soaked stuffing? Was he lighting and tossing them randomly, trusting to fate and whiskey fumes? I had no way of knowing. I only knew it wouldn't be long before the smoke began to fill the room.

There was nothing I could do but lay there, trapped, focusing on the deep, careful breaths I was taking in an effort to breathe quietly and keep my heart from racing at the thought of the fire being lit only inches above me.

Leave.

I could smell the paper burning now, maybe the wood, too, it was difficult to tell the difference. But there was a distinct chemical smell in the room as the vinyl heated and began to melt. I watched as a thin line of dark, greasy smoke curled up over the back of the couch and coiled toward the ceiling.

Lying there in both dark wig and raincoat, I'd already felt like I was roasting. Now, knowing there was fire that close to me, the sensation doubled. I knew it was all in my mind. And I wanted to get out of that room before it became a reality.

Go. Now.

I was going to have to wait for several seconds after Wingtips left the office before I could emerge from my hiding place without risk of being caught. I wasn't sure if it was the fumes or my imagination, but I could feel the cough beginning to form in the back of my throat.

I turned my face forward, staring at Wing Tip's shoes as I breathed in the dusty air from under the couch, then blew it out slowly. I focused on my breathing, taking slow, shallow breaths. To keep from thinking about the fire, I began counting the seconds. I traced the stitching lines and swirling pattern hole-punched onto the shoes, connecting the dots in my mind. I made note of every scuff mark and where the tiny flecks of blood had dripped onto the cracked vinyl from Bouchard's body.

Ten seconds passed, then twenty. At thirty-five seconds, something began to crackle from the heat. At forty-eight seconds, Wingtips cleared his throat. The air close to the floor was still breathable, but with the door closed, it wouldn't last.

Leave, dammit!

Wingtips held out for a full minute, waiting, watching to make sure the fire was established and Bouchard's body – his clothing at least – had caught.

It was one of the longest minutes of my life.

When he finally turned and left the office, locking the door behind him to hinder the efforts of any heroic forklift drivers, I wanted to cheer. I had planned to give him about ten seconds to get well away from the room before I emerged from my hiding place, and began counting as soon as the door clicked shut.

I'd made it to seven when something large and heavy crashed against the window separating Bouchard's office from Mindy's.

That time I did jump.

A second crash followed, and a third, this one sending bits of glass skittering across the floor.

And then it was silent, except for the crackle from the opposite side of the office as the flames began to consume Bouchard's desk.

It was time for me to get out of there.

Like my entire left side, my left arm had fallen fully asleep, and was all but useless to push me along. I tried to force it, the limb flopping ineffectively to the floor. I could barely feel the floor when I pressed my hand to the tile and tried to push myself backward, gritting my teeth against the almost painful rush of blood to my fingers.

I shoved at the futon, pushing at it with my good, right hand, gaining myself a few inches. The back of the futon was already hot from the burning stuffing, and it wouldn't be long before it burned its way through the vinyl. I grabbed the frame, using it as leverage to push myself backward, out of the tunnel.

For the first time, I took the grinding of the magazines against my hip as a good sign – I'd thought my left leg was completely numb, and still couldn't feel the toes on that foot, but at least I had a little sensation left.

It took more than twice as long to back out of my hidey-hole as it took to crawl into it, but I was finally free, sitting with my back against the wall, shaking my still-numb left leg and massaging my left arm, trying to stimulate the blood flow. I wanted to relax, breathe deeply, celebrate finally getting out of the tunnel, but it was too soon to even contemplate that.

I'd merely moved from the frying pan and into the fire.

To my right, the flames were having a party on the desk, dancing merrily along the old wood, and licking their way down the legs.

To my left, the fire had gotten to Bouchard. I'd thought the combined smell of burning vinyl, clothing, and hair was bad; I'd never smelled burning flesh before.

I pulled the collar of my turtleneck up over my mouth and nose, then reached back under the futon for the laptop and Glock. I shoved the empty gun into the pocket of my raincoat, then pushed the laptop ahead of me as I crawled across the floor to the bottles of water on the chair, my left arm and leg threatening to collapse under me the whole time.

I pocketed two bottles, then used the chair to pull myself up to a standing position and soaked the part of my collar I was using as a mask with part of a third. Bracing myself against the wall and clutching the laptop to my chest, I half-walked, half-dragged myself to the door, the flickering LED lights of the warehouse display board encouraging me forward.

Smoke swirled around me as the fire consumed the available oxygen in the room, my wet mask barely filtering the smoke. It occurred to me as I reached for the door, that by locking the door to delay any potential rescuers, the fire would probably burn itself out too quickly, and that breaking the window had been Wingtips' way of providing the additional air the fire would need to keep going.

Points for him.

I opened the door, practically falling into the hallway in a cloud of smoke.

I had to get out of there. Fast. Before anyone else in the building was alerted to the fire.

I couldn't go back the way I'd come, through the warehouse. Instead, I headed forward; pausing to sit on the corner of Mindy's desk and guzzle the rest of the half-bottle of water I was still holding. Mindy's chair lay on its side near the broken window. Smoke seeped through the blinds, through the openings in the glass, random fragments of heavy glass still suspended by the wire mesh.

"Breaking that wasn't as easy as you'd thought it would be, was it, Wingtips?" I murmured, the thought of his frustration at trying to break the reinforced, double-paned glass bringing a slight smile to my face.

My head was clearing. I tossed the empty water bottle in her recycling bin and turned to go.

That was when I noticed that the photo of Mindy and her children was missing from the desk.

Mindy was dead.

Her children were at their father's for the night. Safe.

Still, there was something pinging in the back of my mind

I hadn't gone through Mindy's desk, didn't know if either Renee or Wingtips had taken anything else. But the missing picture bothered me.

I'd figure it out. For now, it was time to go.

On the spur of the moment, I reached down and lifted the handset on Mindy's desk phone. There was still a dial tone, so at least Wingtips hadn't cut the phone lines on his way out. Good.

I pressed "9" to get an outside line, then dialed 911.

I set the handset on the desk before the end of the first ring. I wasn't planning on talking to anyone, but I knew that the emergency services would check out an open call. There was no reason to let the entire warehouse burn down.

There was a fire alarm and extinguisher mounted above the drinking fountain, on the wall between the bathrooms. I crossed to it and pulled the alarm – which, contrary to what they told us in high school, did not spray either paint or ink all over my hand as it began to shriek. Then, still limping slightly, I walked to the front of the building and slipped out the door.

I pulled off my filthy, whiskey-splattered raincoat before I got into my rental car, and tossed the wig on top of it. I put the windows down in spite of the rain, which had gotten heavier while I'd been inside, and drove away as sedately as I could manage, letting my lungs fill with cool, clean air as I passed the emergency vehicles racing in the opposite direction.

Chapter 10

By the time I got back to my hotel, my good mood at escaping the warehouse un-singed had evaporated. I was cold, filthy, and my clothes smelled like smoke. More than that, I was unsettled.

Bouchard was dead. I'd gotten his laptop and potentially the information about the container, which should help me complete the second part of Mindy's assignment – rescuing the trapped girls. So that much was good.

But I was still troubled.

There's a contract of sorts between a client and a contract agent like myself. An unspoken understanding that it is in both of our best interests not to undermine each other.

Agreeing to go after Bouchard had pushed the limits of that understanding – to be honest, I'd probably have left Mindy's money in her closet if she hadn't mentioned the trafficking. By eliminating him herself, Renee had dealt with any trace of an ethical dilemma I might have had, leaving me free to focus on the girls.

And now Renee, herself, was a potential problem.

I wasn't working for her, knew nothing more about her than her first name, hair color, and shoe choice, all of which could have been as artificial as my own often were. I had no way of knowing what kind of skills she had at her disposal, or what kind of opposition she would present if I took the container girls out from under her nose.

I'd already seen how she handled business dealings that didn't go her way.

Annoyed, I paced from one end of the suite to the other, and stopped near the French doors opening onto the small balcony. I stood there, watching the rain beat against the glass, chiding myself for overthinking the situation, letting my imagination drift into dark corridors at the thought of the girls Mindy had asked me to save.

A chill ran down my spine, and I ran my hands up and down my arms, only then noticing just how damp most of the left side of the shirt was. No wonder I was shivering.

I pulled the drapes, switched on the gas fireplace to warm the sitting room, and peeled off my clothes, goosebumps rising on my bare flesh as the air hit my bare skin. After a long, hot shower, I dressed in the yoga pants and tank top I'd brought to sleep in, then wrapped myself in the heavy terrycloth robe provided by the hotel and put my dirty clothes and raincoat out for the valet.

Fortified with a steaming mug of tea, courtesy of the complementary in-room amenities, I retrieved my laptop from the closet safe and carried it to the desk where I'd set Bouchard's laptop.

On the off-chance he was as careless with his computer security as he'd been in his business dealings with Renee, I powered up his laptop. The machine couldn't have been more than a year or two old, and its battery was at about eighty percent, which meant I probably had plenty of time to search the files before I had to worry about running low on power.

I tried the obvious, dumb passwords: first, just leaving the field blank, then entering the word "password." Neither worked, which was somewhat reassuring – it was scary how many personal laptops I'd been able to get into using one of those two non-passwords.

Bouchard had done that part right, at least.

I powered the machine down, then flipped it over. The multi-tool had a small Phillips head screwdriver that, with some care, I was able to use to open the back of the laptop and remove the docking station.

Because I travel so often, both for my legitimate consulting job as well as for my covert operations, I carry a folio in my computer bag that I think of as a "travelling office" of sorts. The folio has pockets and Velcro strips for corralling office supplies, computer tools, pens, sticky notes, computer cables, a compact portable docking station, and a myriad of other items that are so handy to have on the go.

I chose a cable from and the docking station. In a few minutes, I'd connected both my own laptop and Bouchard's hard drive to the dock, powered up my laptop, logged in as an admin, and was scanning the files from his hard drive.

I decided to search the drive by the "last modified" date – since I had no idea exactly what I was looking for, that method at least reduced the number of files I would have to review. It would also give me a logical way of eliminating the ones I'd already scanned.

It took me about thirty minutes to find the details, buried on an innocuous tab on a seemingly ordinary spreadsheet listing the freighter schedule for the current week.

The inbound freighter from Colombia was scheduled to dock in only a few hours. There was only one container in the inventory scheduled to be shipped out by truck later that afternoon – a reefer labeled in the log as containing "flower bulbs."

Knowing as little about the logistics of unloading a freighter as I did, I did a rudimentary internet search on the process, which helped me construct a rough timeline for the following day:

The freighter would arrive just after dawn.

At some point, probably in the early afternoon, the reefer would be taken off the boat and put on one of the many trucks that lined up along the dock to take the containers into the stacks.

The cryptic codes in Bouchard's spreadsheet didn't tell me whether the reefer would be left in the stacks and later picked up by a forklift driver to transfer to the westbound truck, or if transfer and customs inspection would happen right away. But the customs agent – noted in the file as "J. Richardson" – was scheduled to arrive at 4:00.

Just in time to take his cash, stamp the necessary paperwork, and look the other way while the truck drove away with the container full of girls.

All I had to do was stop the transaction.

The thought of simply walking away never even occurred to me.

◆

Once I knew what I was looking for, it was much easier to sort through the data in Bouchard's files. I skimmed back through his records for several months, cross-referencing with the names and dates from Mindy's flash drive. Raeburn Shipping had barely been turning a profit, earning just enough to keep the lights on and avoid too much scrutiny.

But as a smuggling operation – bringing in the occasional load of Cuban cigars and cocaine from Colombia – Raeburn Shipping was raking in the money hand-over-fist. I didn't care about the cigars, and knew the drugs would just find another way into the country. It was the monthly container of girls I was interested in.

It was all there. Everything I needed to severely hobble the import arm of the trafficking ring, if not bring it down altogether.

It wouldn't be easy, but it could be done.

I copied Bouchard's files to my own computer, and entered the specific details about the following day's shipment into a secure, note-taking app on my phone as a backup before shutting down both computers. If I was going to be worth anything tomorrow. I needed to get some sleep.

But it seemed my subconscious wasn't finished with me.

Young teenage girls, dressed in rags, most with skin darker than my own and speaking to me in languages I didn't understand, reached out to me from the dark, tears streaming down their faces. I gave them food, blankets, water – but no matter how many girls I helped, there were always more, an endless stream of them pouring out of a cold, dark shipping container.

"I need a blonde." It was Renee's voice, insistent.

"I've got a blonde for you."

I jerked around when I heard the familiar, leering voice, then watched helplessly as Eddie, my mother's second husband, dragged a young blonde girl – the 13-year-old version of myself, but dressed in the same ragged clothes as the rest of the container girls – out of the crowd and across the asphalt. I tried to follow, but the dark-haired girls surrounded me, burying me under the press of their thin bodies as my younger self's screams faded in the distance.

I clawed my way to consciousness, shoving away the mounds of pillows and heavy comforter I'd gotten tangled in, and lay there gasping for air. The storm had broken during the night, and weak sunlight in shades of pink and peach filtered in through the gap between the curtains.

I glanced at the clock. It was just six-thirty a.m. – and according to Bouchard's schedule, the freighter would be docking now.

I had work to do.

Might as well get at it.

Chapter 11

I enjoyed a lovely breakfast on the hotel's rooftop terrace, and made my third to-do list in as many days while nibbling on delicious pastries and sipping at rather excellent coffee. I checked email on my phone, and confirmed the appointment Jessica had added to my schedule to talk with Joe Benson at two o'clock that afternoon. I was a little bit sorry that I wouldn't be driving up to the SCH offices to meet with him in person, but there were only so many hours in a day, and I wanted to have everything resolved with the container girls before Kyle arrived the next morning.

A trip to Raleigh-Durham would just have to wait for another day.

The fresh fruit on my plate reminded me of one other thing I needed to tend to. I checked the time, decided it wasn't too early, and pulled out my phone.

"You know it's still dark out, right?" a bleary female voice complained through the phone.

"Try opening your eyes, Bonnie," I said, laughing. "You're wasting daylight." Bonnie Kauffman was one of my closest friends, and definitely not a morning person.

"It's not daylight until the sun is directly overhead," Bonnie said, her Jersey accent taking hold as she forced herself to wake up. "Why're you calling me at this ungodly hour, anyway? It's not even eight o'clock. I'm going back to sleep."

"It's almost eight-thirty," I said, nodding to the waiter when he offered a refill on my coffee. "I wanted to catch you before your day got going."

"Yeah, well, you caught me. Not that anything I agree to now I'll be responsible for later."

"I just wondered if you'd stop by the house and look in on Glau. Check his water, make sure he has plenty of food."

Bonnie was instantly alert, the sleepy friend replaced by the professional businesswoman. "Is everything okay?"

"Yes, yes, nothing to worry about," I said. "I'm just out of town, and going to be away longer than I'd planned. Glau will be okay until I get back, but since you have a key…"

"Of course I'll look in on him," Bonnie said. "I've got a couple of showings in No Libs this afternoon – one just down the street from your old place—"

"Next to the park? Tidy three-story with a red door?"

"The one! How'd you know?"

"The couple there was getting too old for all the stairs in a rowhouse. I ran into her in the park with her little dog several times last summer when I'd go over with Glau, and she was talking about looking for a single-level place. Said they hadn't been up to the top floor in months. She was worried someone could be living up there without her knowledge."

"I didn't see any sign of that," Bonnie said, her realtor's ears pricking up at the possibility.

"No, there wasn't. I went over and checked it all out for her, made sure the locks on the windows were good and everything was secure."

"That was good of you."

"It was the least I could do."

"Perhaps, but I'm sure it meant a lot to her. Anyway, Peggy and I will swing by your house this evening. Feed the beast and raid your refrigerator while we're at it."

"You won't find much," I said. "A bottle of white, some cheese. Crackers in the pantry. Just nibbles mostly. I need to go shopping when I get home. Oh, and there's a bag of cut veggies in the bottom drawer of the fridge. Just scatter the pieces around the conservatory."

"Messy," Bonnie said. I could hear wrinkling her nose at the idea. An older woman at a nearby table "tsk'd" at the same time, echoing Bonnie's disapproval.

"A little, but it will take Glau a few hours to find it all, instead of gobbling it down all at once and making himself sick in the process. And I'll mop when I get home. You're not showing *my* house, so nobody will see the mess in the meantime but you."

Bonnie was quiet for a minute while her still-waking brain tried to wrap itself around my logic. "Okay," she said finally. "Wine in the fridge, throw veggies on the floor. Got it. Where are you, anyway?"

"Charleston."

"Pretty town. Had a chance to walk along the beach yet?"

"No, it's been raining, and I've been safe and dry in back-to-back meetings," I lied. "But the weather is supposed to be nice this weekend, and Kyle's joining me—"

"Hold the phone! As in tall-dark-and-gorgeous Kyle?"

"Do we know anyone else by that name? I don't think I do. He's over in Charlotte today, so we thought we'd finish both our trips with a weekend here."

"You take all the time you need with that one," Bonnie said. Her voice grew slightly muffled as she held the phone away from her face and clarified things for Peggy. "Meg's spending the weekend with Kyle. We get to play aunties to the iguana."

She put the call on speaker, and the three of us chatted for a few more minutes before ringing off. I wasn't too worried about Glau, but it was nice to have someone I trusted look in on him when I was away.

One less thing to worry about.

The rooftop terrace provided a nice view of Charleston Harbor, and as I watched a tugboat heading out to meet an approaching freighter, it brought my thoughts back to the container girls.

The trafficking operation – from what I'd seen on Mindy's flash drive and corroborated through my cursory review of Bouchard's files last night – hadn't been limited to selling exclusively to Haskell, and now Renee. He'd shipped girls to a half-dozen buyers from here to Texas – and that was just the ones I knew about.

It was too big for me to bring down alone.

Much as I hated to admit it, I needed to involve law enforcement – probably either Homeland Security or the FBI – without compromising my own position.

I had no contacts in either agency. But I knew someone who just might. I finished my coffee, snagged a couple more pastries for later, and headed downstairs.

That was a call I'd make a little later, when there were no curious ears to overhear.

♦

Say what you will about big box stores, but there's a reassuring level of convenience in knowing that wherever I travel, certain chains will have exactly what I need at a low enough price-point that discarding items I can't pack in my carry-on for the trip home isn't a problem.

Cost of doing business and all that.

My business attire hadn't come back from the laundry yet, and the capris and summery shirt just wasn't right for the kind of work I had to do today. While the look might momentarily distract one of the truck drivers, I preferred to wear more practical clothes when I worked.

First stop, then, ladies' clothing. I blew through the section like a summer squall, grabbing a couple of t-shirts, a package of decent socks, and a good sports bra without giving any of my selections – all known brands and sizes I knew would fit – a second thought. Next into the basket went a pair of jeans, one size larger than I usually wear, because I didn't have time for them to become comfortably flexible.

I'd intended to pick up a jeans jacket, but they didn't have anything in my size in stock. I settled for a wine-red, lightweight anorak-style jacket with a full zipper, high collar, and several functional pockets, both on the inside and the outside. The fabric was a little lighter than denim, and decently flexible, and hung to my hips. It didn't look too bad on me, either – always a bonus.

On the off-chance they'd have what I was looking for and save me another stop, I skimmed the shoe section for a pair of sneakers. I was pleasantly surprised to find a pair of slip-ons I thought might work. They had a deep enough tread to minimize slipping on wet sidewalks, pretended to have a bit of arch support, and were soft enough that I could almost fold them in half.

In the back of my mind, I could hear Ian laughing at me, reminding me that we trained for adaptability, to be ready to fight no matter what we were wearing, what weapons we had at our disposal, and that every minute I spent in the store was a minute wasted.

"I have the opportunity to gear up," I muttered, tugging on a pair of socks I'd pulled free of the packaging. "If a little shopping increases my chances of surviving this, I'm damn-well going to prepare." I pulled on the sneakers, then put the opened sock package and my sandals in the shoebox and set it, wide open, in the front part of the cart – just in case anybody was watching and thinking I was trying to get away with something.

The electronics department provided me with a disposable phone. I found the supplies I needed to clean the Glock over in the sporting goods section, but opted to skip the cheap holster – which looked like it would fall apart under the weight of the gun – and just tuck the Glock into my waistband. I grabbed a set of nice steak knives in housewares, and found a pair of reading glasses with the lowest possible prescription –

one that didn't give me instant vertigo – on a spinner rack near the pharmacy.

Finally, I hit the grocery aisles, where I picked up a box of heavy duty, gallon-sized zip-lock bags, some de-greasing dishwashing liquid, and a small scrub brush, before moving on to the food section. There I stocked up on water, energy drinks, dried fruit and nut packets, and a selection of protein bars. I grabbed more than enough for one day, but I've often found that it was the things I didn't think to pick up that were the ones I usually regretted not having.

I rolled my cart up to the checkout counter, set my obviously-used sandals on the small check-writing counter, unloaded everything else onto the conveyer, and checked the time. The entire expedition had taken only forty-seven minutes.

The clerk eyed the empty shoebox and opened package of socks, and looked up at me with a puzzled frown.

"Airline lost my luggage," I said, forcing a sheepish expression. "All I've got for the weekend are the clothes on my back. And those—" I gestured toward the sandals, "—are giving me blisters."

In reality, the sandals were quite comfortable, but the lie got the clerk on my side. She nodded sympathetically. "Couldn't get out of them fast enough?" she said with a grin.

"You said it," I replied, holding one foot up so she could verify that I was wearing the shoes that matched the box and deactivate the anti-theft device. I waved a hand toward the knife set. "I just hope they find it before my cousin's birthday party tomorrow."

"They'll like the knives. It's a nice set," the clerk said, ringing up items as she talked. "You in town long?"

"Just for the weekend," I said. "Arrived last night, then back to L.A. Sunday night. With my luck, my bags will make it here after I've left." I paid for my purchase, using some of the cash from Mindy's closet.

"Good luck," the clerk said.

I took my purchases out to my rental car.

By focusing her attention on the shoes and knives, and chatting with her while she worked, I'd turned the rest of my purchases into blips of the scanner. She'd remember the encounter until a more interesting customer came along, but the details of a woman buying a phone, a set of knives, and gun cleaning supplies would fade from memory.

It was barely ten o'clock, and the day was already starting to warm up. I started up the car, put the windows down, and turned on the air. While the car aired out, I dug the phone out of the shopping bag and fought with the blister package.

By the time I got the phone free of the packaging and had set it up, the car had cooled enough to be tolerable. I put the windows up and placed the call, dialing the number from memory.

A gruff voice answered, barely audible over the screaming rock music behind it. "Yeah?"

The voice belonged to the Researcher, my mentor in computer hacking and general espionage. He'd never given me his real name, and there were times when I wasn't sure if the smoker's voice I heard was actually his or if he spoke through some sort of filtering device. If there was information to be found, he could find it better, faster, and with fewer traces of his having searched for it than I ever could.

"Do you know where I can find some alphabet soup?" I asked.

"One minute." The rock music faded as he went down the hall or into another room, then was muffled when he closed a door. "It might take some looking," he said. "Always thought you were more of a meat and potatoes type."

Because there was never any way of knowing who was listening, we often spoke in a casual code. "Alphabet soup" referred to any of the three-letter federal agencies – CIA, FBI, DHS, ICE – who we generally tried to stay as far away from as possible. "Meat and potatoes" referred to doing things ourselves, and staying away from the prying eyes of law enforcement.

"Generally, I am," I said. "But you know what they say – starve a cold, feed a fever."

I've stumbled into something big, need to hand it off to official channels.

"You sure? I think the saying goes the other way around."

"Maybe it does," I said. "I'd order take out, but traffic is bad here – you know how out-of-state teenage girls drive."

I'd normally handle it myself, or call on other contractors to assist, but this involves teen sex trafficking across state lines.

The Researcher "hmmm'd" thoughtfully, then was quiet for several seconds. I could hear the heavy bass beat in the background, and the soft tapping of a keyboard not far from the phone. Then there was a rustling as he picked up the phone.

"I might have something for you," he said. "You're in your usual room?"

"No. I'm down the hall, in 843."

You're at home? No, I'm in South Carolina (area code 843).

"Okay," he said. "I'll leave it on a covered tray outside your door."

I'll email it to you in an encrypted file.

"Thank you."

"So you know, this is hot *and* spicy."

Working with the Feds is risky. Be careful.

"I will," I said. "Thanks."

There was a moment's pause.

"Just when I think I know what to expect, you find a way to make my life interesting," he said, his usually brusque voice almost friendly for a change. "Let me know how it tastes."

I was surprised at that. The Researcher had never asked me for any sort of feedback or follow-up on the information he'd given me. If I'd had any doubt about escalating the trafficking ring to the Feds, I didn't now. But he was right – I would have to be extremely careful.

"I'll do that."

There was an awkward silence on both sides of the conversation, and then we both said our good-byes at the same time.

I sat there for a couple of minutes, holding the phone while I watched a woman parked in the row across from me unload a shopping cart with the 'assistance' of a pair of active preschoolers. They made me smile.

I powered off the phone and popped the battery out, then put the parts in separate pockets. I'd need that phone again today, but didn't need to leave it active – and traceable – in the meantime.

◆

Back in my hotel, I got to work.

I checked my email, found and decrypted the message from the Researcher. It felt odd, entering the details for L. Brady into my phone's contact list, but my instincts told me I was going to need assistance, and I'd long ago learned the value of trusting my instincts – or at least giving them due consideration.

Kyle had sent me a copy of his flight itinerary. The flight from Charlotte was barely an hour, but the earliest he'd been able to get a seat on had him arriving in Charleston a few minutes after ten. I replied to his email, teasing him about wanting to sleep in rather than booking an earlier flight, then added the details to my phone's calendar, and set a reminder that would give me plenty of time to reach the airport on time to pick him up.

I scanned the rest of my messages, flagging items that needed attention but could wait until I was back in the office on Monday, and shut down the computer.

Next, I moved to the shopping bags piled on the bed.

I removed the tags from the clothes, making sure to put them all in the empty bag I'd designated for garbage. After I changed out of the blouse and capris and into the jeans and t-shirt combo I thought of as my "work uniform," I put the rest of my clothes – including my clean laundry, which had arrived during my absence – away in the dresser and closet, again, thoroughly disposing of tags and wrappers.

The less I had to do at the last minute to make the room look like this had been nothing more than a normal business trip before Kyle arrived, the better.

With the clothes out of the way, I went into the sitting room and spread a bath towel across the low coffee table, then laid out the rest of my purchases. I also grabbed my travel bag and set it out, open, on the couch, so I could see the items it contained.

Lock picks, multitool, and burner phone went into my left-hand pocket. A stack of folded bills – just a few hundred dollars' worth from Mindy's stash – a substantially funded VISA gift card, a fake driver's license, and the battery for the burner phone went into my right-hand pocket. My personal cell phone was on the desk next to my laptop.

I'd brushed out the dark wig as best I could – it was going to need a salon treatment to fully restore it to its original luster. For the moment, however, I carefully coiled the long locks into a neat bundle and tucked it into a zip-lock bag, along with the lower prescription pair of reading glasses. The high-prescription pair, I tossed into the garbage bag with no remorse. They'd served their purpose, but my stomach flipped at the thought of wearing them again. I pressed the air out of the bag, sealed it, and set it aside.

Next, I took all of the gun-cleaning supplies – the cleaning rod, brushes, and patches – out of their packaging and put them into a bag along with the small containers of solvent and lubricant I'd picked up. I put the bag inside a second bag and set it aside. Gun-cleaning could be messy, and I didn't want any of that mess near any of my other belongings.

Finding Bouchard's Glock had been a possible goldmine, but I wouldn't know for sure until I'd had a chance to inspect, clean, and test the weapon. It would be stupid of me to carry it into a possible fight not having checked it out thoroughly first. That was on my to-do list.

The Glock was in the safe, but I'd picked up an inexpensive, soft-sider gun bag to carry the gun and ammo in, and now removed the tags and wadded paper stuffing from the bag. The state of South Carolina didn't recognize my Pennsylvania-issued concealed carry permit. And while that wouldn't stop me from carrying, until I needed to tuck the gun into my belt, it was safer to keep it in the bag.

I tossed a couple of the empty grocery bags onto the stack of gun-cleaning supplies, then took the dish soap and scrub brush into the bathroom. I'd need them later, to clean up after I'd cleaned the Glock.

Using the blade of my multitool, I carefully cut open the box holding the steak knives and peeled the form-fitting plastic away from the blades. They were nice knives, well-balanced and with full tang blades, the single piece of steel running from tip to the end of the handle left visible, with the contoured plastic handles attached on either side. It takes a lot of practice to throw reliably with kitchen knives – but Ian had seen to it that I'd had plenty.

There were two knives in the box, each protected by its own bubble of plastic and backed with a sheet of light cardboard. I'd chosen this set almost as much for the packaging as for the blades themselves, and after setting the knives and the plastic aside, I began to cut the cardboard into narrow strips, each as long as a knife blade and a little more than double the width.

Next, I folded each in half, length-wise, then I retrieved a small stapler from my computer bag, and used it to staple the rectangles along the bottom and up the long, open edge, creating a simple sheath for each of the knives.

I tucked the sheathed knives into the jacket's interior pockets, one on each side where they'd be easy to get to if I needed them.

I hoped I wouldn't need them.

After I cleaned up the sheath-making mess, I opened the various packages of snacks and divided the individually wrapped packets among a half-dozen zip-lock bags. I added an energy drink to each bag, and a water bottle, pressed as much of the air out of the bags as I could, and sealed them all up.

I stood there, looking at the packets laying on the coffee table. It looked like I was planning to go camping.

I gathered up the discarded wrappers, wondering if the Ian-voice in my had had been right. Maybe I was overthinking all of this. Maybe Kyle and I would be all set with snacks to go wandering the city and coastal beaches.

Maybe you're putting together packets for the container girls, my child voice whispered in the back of my mind.

Maybe I was.

Chapter 12

I carried the zip lock bag of gun cleaning supplies out onto the small patio, spread out one of the empty grocery bags on the glass-topped bistro table, and anchored it in place with the tools. The hotel staff wouldn't be happy to have their room scented with solvent and lubricant.

Since it was a nice morning, I decided to clean the Glock outside and avoid that problem.

I'd put the Glock – unloaded – and the ammo in the room safe when I'd gotten back the night before. Now I retrieved it, checked and cleared it as is my habit whenever I pick up a weapon, and set it on the nightstand while I tucked the magazines into two of the gun bag's three available magazine loops. Then I took the gun out to the patio, closing the door behind me to keep the oil and chemical smells from wafting into the room.

It was a nice day to be working outside. There was a light breeze blowing in off the harbor, and the solid wall surrounding the balcony gave me plenty of privacy from curious eyes. I checked the pistol one more time, racking it a couple of times, before I began the disassembly. Happily, the slide locks didn't stick, and I was able to easily remove the slide, recoil spring, and barrel. I didn't have much good to say about Bouchard, but he appeared to have taken good care of the weapon. It wasn't excessively dirty, and when I checked the parts, I saw no visible damage.

There's something calming in the ritual of wiping down the guide rod, drawing a patch of fabric through the barrel to clean it, then spreading a few drops of oil on the outside of the barrel and spreading it with a clean, soft towel. I took my time, letting the action help me center, before finally setting it aside and picking up the frame. Applying tiny drops of oil at key points of the mechanism with the long, skinny, needle applicator required a bit more attention, but again, the weapon was in good shape, and I had it cleaned, oiled, and reassembled in short order.

All that left was finding a range where I could test it. I hadn't brought one of my own guns, and was reluctant to rely on this one until I'd put a few rounds through a target. But firing the gun would tell me if there were any small quirks I needed to be aware of – if the magazines fed the rounds smoothly, if the firing mechanism worked reliably, if the sight was off center by a hair – all things you can adjust for if you know about them ahead of time, but that can get you killed if you don't.

If I was going to go up against Renee and Wingtips, I wanted to be prepared for anything.

After I cleaned up the mess, packed the cleaning supplies in a zip lock bag, and tucked the bag in the small safe, I went online to find a nearby shooting range. I found a couple of outdoor ranges with good reviews, but ended up calling an indoor range that was also well-rated and was much closer to my hotel.

I called them.

"Hi," I said. "My uncle passed away a couple of months ago, and I'm in town this weekend helping my aunt clear away some of his things."

"I'm sorry for your loss," the clerk said. He was polite, but clearly waiting for me to get to the point. I did.

"Thank you. Among his belongings, he had a Glock 19. My aunt doesn't want to keep it, but she's not sure what to do with it—"

"We don't buy used guns here."

"Oh, no, I didn't think you did," I said. "Anyway, I've cleaned and inspected it – it's not in bad shape – I was just hoping to find a range where I could test it out. I have a Concealed Carry Permit from Pennsylvania, but I know that's not recognized here in South Carolina."

"You don't need a permit to use the range," the clerk said. His attitude had shifted from longsuffering patience with a gun newbie to a more professional tone at the mention of my permit. "And we're happy to let you bring in your own gun. Will you need ammo?"

"Yes. I'll also need safety glasses and ear muffs."

The clerk assured me that they had everything I needed. He also suggested that coming in before noon would be a better idea than waiting until later in the day, as the lanes would begin to fill by midafternoon and stay busy through the weekend.

A half-hour later, I was one of three other shooters at the range, a paper target fluttering slightly as I sent it downrange. The Glock lay on the shelf in front of me, the magazines to one side, along with a standard, 50-round box of 9mm bullets.

When the target was in place, I picked up the gun, verified that it was empty, then racked it, just as I would if it had been loaded. I raised it in a two-handed grip, checking the feel of the weapon in my hands. There was a nick in the grip with a bit of a rough edge that bit at the heel of my left hand when I pressed it tight. I pulled it back and studied it, trying to guess what kind of encounter – or accident – Bouchard must have had to have caused it. It wasn't a large blemish, and wouldn't interfere with the gun's functionality in any way, but there was no way he wouldn't have noticed it.

I raised the gun again. I've done a lot of shooting over the years – Ian had seen to that – and even though I hadn't touched a gun in almost six months, the muscle memory in my arms was as strong as ever. Without even a second thought, I was looking down the barrel of the gun, verifying that the sights were aligned, and then dry-fired a quick double-tap to check the action. So far, all seemed fine.

But I wouldn't be going up against Renee with an empty gun. I popped a magazine in, racked the gun as I raised it, and popped five shots off in quick succession at the target's core. For this exercise, I focused on the target rather than aligning using the Glock's sights. I fired two rounds each into the head, throat, and each of the drawn-on shoulders and then two more into the lower midsection, where the victim's abdomen would be, shooting until the magazine ran dry.

Even from fifteen yards, I could tell my groupings were off. I'd always had a tendency to pull toward the left, and every grouping cluster was slightly left of where I'd intended them to be. To my chagrin, the clusters of holes that should have hit the target's throat and left shoulder were all about an inch outside the line. Ian would have chewed me out if he'd seen them.

If I'd been shooting at a person, those shots would have whizzed right past him.

I dropped the spent magazine, popped in the second one, and repeated the pattern in reverse order, firing off fourteen rounds without a pause.

The fifteenth round gave me a dry *click*.

While the target chugged its way back to me, I took a look at both the gun and the magazine, certain I hadn't miscounted the rounds. Sure enough, when I popped the magazine out, it still held one round.

Frowning, I reloaded both magazines from the box of cartridges I'd purchased from clerk when I'd rented the safety glasses and large, over-the-head ear muffs. I hung another target and repeated the drill, using the faulty magazine, which once again gave me fourteen shots, and failed to load the final bullet.

I set it aside and popped the original magazine. This one fed all fifteen shots smoothly and without issue.

The problem was clearly with the magazine, not the gun. FTF errors – Failure to Feed – happened from time to time for various reasons. Because the problem was consistently with one magazine and not the other, and only occurred with the last round, while the others fed properly, I concluded the fault was probably a too-tight spring in the magazine, and not a problem with the gun itself.

If I'd been planning on keeping the gun and using it on a regular basis, I'd have tried to loosen the spring, or if that failed, simply tossed the magazine and bought a new one. As it was, just knowing I would be one bullet short would have to do.

As Ian often said, if it came down to one bullet, I was already in more trouble than a single shot could cure.

I sent a new target out and repeated the drill, then bought a second box of bullets, refilled both magazines, and ran through drill one more time, letting my body remember the feel of a gun in my hand, the weight of it as I raised it to my chest then extended my arms, pushing it forward, how to move so the gun tracked with where I was looking so my shots would hit the target.

I was on my fourth target sheet before my groupings were finally where they belonged.

The range master brought me another box of bullets, and I ran through one more target sheet before I was satisfied with my performance. I unloaded the gun and stowed it in the gun bag, refilled the magazines and tucked them back in their loops, then dumped the last thirty rounds into a zip lock bag, tucked it away in the gun bag and threw away the box. I cleaned up the spent cartridges, disposing them in the bin marked for the purpose, thanked the range master and salesclerk, and was on my way.

I wanted to stop and pick up some surgical tape to wrap around the grip, and a bandage for my hand, where the nick in the grip threatened a blister. Other than that, and the faulty magazine, I was reasonably happy with the Glock.

Oddly, I found the idea of using Bouchard's gun instead of one of my own both appropriate and somewhat satisfying.

♦

I am a planner.

Not compulsively so, and I'm not at all opposed to spontaneity, but it's been my experience that the more variables I can anticipate and control for, the less likely they are to bite me on the ass.

Now I was going after my third target in as many days, the result of a contract with more variables than I could count and whose timeline was rapidly ticking away.

I had no illusions that rescuing the container girls would be easy. Quite the contrary. I expected it to be so ridiculously difficult that even as I ticked off my mental checklist of preparations, and drove over to Mindy's neighborhood, I found myself questioning my sanity at taking it on.

It was a long-shot, but there was a good chance that Wingtips would show up at Mindy's house at some point, if he hadn't already found it while I'd been running errands that morning. If I could deal with him first, before the container hand-off, it would be easier than trying to take down the entire operation on my own – particularly since I had no idea how big of a "crew" Renee had, or how Bouchard's people would handle the situation with him out of the picture.

It was a little before two o'clock when I parked on the shoulder of the road diagonally across the street from Mindy's house and about two doors down, at what I judged to be the boundary between adjoining lots. There were several trees shielding me from direct view of either house, which served the dual purpose of both shading the car and making it less conspicuous. I put the windows down a finger's width to keep the air moving, and settled in to wait and watch.

From where I sat, could see clearly down the street for several blocks, as well as a couple blocks down the intersecting street which ended in a "T" about fifty feet ahead of me. I had a partial view of the house across the street behind me – also blocked by some large trees – and a clear view of the front and side of Mindy's house, which sat at the corner, though only a partial view of her back yard which was blocked by the tall wooden fence and some mature trees running along the edge of the property.

There was no visible indication that anyone had been in Mindy's house since the previous evening, not that I expected there to be. It was a warm, humid afternoon, and no one was outside that I could see in any direction. Only the occasional barking of a neighbor's dog broke the stillness.

I wanted to check, to see if Wingtips had broken in, found Mindy's body, but returning to the scene of the crime was a bad idea, regardless of the reason. Even parked one hundred yards away in a nondescript rental car with tinted windows that obscured a direct view of the interior of the car, it was dangerous just being here, watching the house.

Instead, I busied myself on my phone, popping in my wireless earbuds, then placing the scheduled call to Joe Benson at SCH. We'd worked together on several projects over the past few years, and spent the first several minutes of the call with the usual pleasantries of long-distance acquaintances who don't know each other well enough to be called friends.

Joe told me about his young son's newfound interest in baseball, and I recounted Glau's antics chasing after a couple of crickets that had invaded the conservatory. At the same time, I dumped a packet of bandages and a roll of surgical tape I'd picked up on my way over out of their bag and onto my lap. I pressed a large bandage over the sensitive place on the side of my hand where the blister was forming.

It seemed secure, but I cut a length of surgical tape using the tiny scissors in my multi-tool, then wrapped it around my hand a couple of times just to be sure it stayed in place. I poked the end of the tape under the strip that ran across the back of my hand to keep it all from coming unwound at an inopportune moment, then flexed my hand a few times to make sure the tape didn't constrict my movement.

Satisfied with the minor first aid, I put the supplies back in the plastic shopping bag and dropped it on the passenger seat, just as the conversation drifted to more mundane business topics.

The call was productive, in a routine-business sort of way. Joe mentioned some new initiatives the corporation was considering as the result of the recent, profitable quarter. I mentioned a few businesses I thought SCH might want to consider pulling under their umbrella and emailed links referencing trends I was seeing that might impact SCH's overall strategy. And while I took notes in a note-taking app on my phone, I kept an eye on Mindy's house.

A big part of my job is waiting and watching, remaining inconspicuous, yet being ready to act when the time came. While Joe and I talked, I had gradually slid a little lower in the seat, stretching my legs out with my feet just beyond the pedals. Leaning my head back against the cushion, I angled my body slightly, the whole goal to make it less obvious to the casual passer-by that there was someone in the car, but not so far as to be uncomfortable.

It was odd, I suppose, watching the house of someone I'd killed to see if another interested party – namely, Renee or Wingtips – showed up, while simultaneously conducting a business call from a car parked across the street. But it was important to maintain a good business relationship with a major client.

The clandestine work paid better, but it was the legitimate work that provided me with a justifiable explanation for my income, frequent travel, and overall lifestyle.

Joe and I talked for about a half-hour, neither making any firm commitments, but each leaving the call with a list of action items to follow-up on and a plan to reconnect in a few days, after we'd had a chance to explore the various options we'd discussed.

We were exchanging the usual farewell pleasantries when a dark gray panel van pulled up to the T-intersection opposite me, then turned the corner and parked directly in front of Mindy's house.

As the van's driver's side door opened, I sank even lower in my seat. Through the upper curve of the steering wheel, I watched as a tall, heavily-built man got out of the van. He was dressed in gray coveralls and wore a dark-colored cap and sunglasses.

I couldn't see his shoes, and since I'd never seen his face, had no way of knowing it was Wingtips or not. All I could do was watch – and continue talking to Joe as though everything was perfectly normal.

The driver glanced up and down the street, then straightened his cap and went around to the opposite side of the van, and out of sight. A moment later he reappeared, holding a medium-sized cardboard box.

So possibly just a deliveryman… in an unmarked rental van.

I wasn't convinced.

I finished my call with Joe while the deliveryman walked to the porch, and powered my phone down and removed the battery while he was standing on Mindy's porch, I was tucking the phone, battery, and earbuds into a zip lock bag when he set the package down, stepped over to the living room window and tried to look inside.

He wouldn't see anything – I knew that, because I'd checked the drapes – but it was odd behavior for an ordinary deliveryman.

When he moved around to the side of the house, glancing around again before slipping through the gate into the backyard, I pulled my gloves from my coat pocket and pulled them on. Then I retrieved the burner phone I'd used with Bouchard, popped the battery in, and powered it up.

Whether it was Wingtips or just a dishonest deliveryman, he wouldn't see anything through any of the windows. But if he had any skills at all, it wouldn't take him long to break in through the back door.

When he hadn't reappeared after ten minutes, I was half-tempted to sneak up to the van and see how my knives did on the tires. He hadn't looked back to the van, or given any indication that there was a second person waiting for him, but that was a chance I didn't want to take. Not there, in front of Mindy's house. There were just too many opportunities for being spotted by a curious neighbor. Much as I wanted to take Wingtips out of the picture, I wasn't willing to risk it here.

I called 911 instead.

"I think someone has broken into my neighbor's house," I said, making my voice sound thin and uncertain. "I saw a strange man go into the backyard, and he hasn't come out. His van is still parked out front. She works all day, so there's no reason for anyone to be there."

I described the van, gave the dispatcher the wrong license plate number, transposing two of the digits, and Mindy's address. When she asked for my name, I made one up. I promised not to go to Mindy's house, and to let the police handle it, then pretended to cry out in alarm and drop the phone, disconnecting the call as I fumbled with the phone.

That would get someone's attention.

I powered down the phone and popped the battery.

Unless there was a cruiser in the immediate vicinity, I estimated it would take anywhere from five to fifteen minutes for the police to arrive. Whether Wingtips ran before they arrived or took off with the police in pursuit, I'd follow him.

No way was I going inside that house.

A movement down the cross street caught my eye and I glanced over, then watched with some concern as the school bus approached. Mindy and her ex had agreed for her teenaged kids to come back to the house for additional clothes today – were they on the bus? Was the skinny, red-haired stepmother going to show up in a few minutes to pick them up, or was she going to bring them over later?

I was still speculating on the possibilities when the bus reached the corner. The red lights flashed, the door opened, and Mindy's teenage son and daughter got off the bus.

Chapter 13

I glanced from the front of the house, where Mindy's kids were crossing the lawn toward the front door, to the fence at the side of the house, hoping the deliveryman would appear. Finding their mother dead was going to be hard enough. Finding a large, probably dangerous stranger in the house with their dead mother...

I shook my head. It couldn't be helped.

I couldn't get involved any more than I already was.

The boy got to the porch and bent down to look at the package, while his sister went around him to the door, looking back at him and talking while she unlocked the door.

They must have been speculating on what was in the package.

I could admit to a certain amount of curiosity myself. But when the boy stood without picking up the box; instead pushing it to one side of the porch with his foot, I had a good guess at what had happened. The deliveryman – who I was now reasonably certain *was* Wingtips – had taken a package from someone else's porch to use as his cover. When Mindy's son saw the mislabeled package, both teens' interest in it evaporated.

The girl pushed the door open, and the pair disappeared inside.

I held my breath, the drumming of my heartbeat a ticking stopwatch as I waited for Wingtips to slip out through the side gate.

The dashboard clocked clicked over.

One minute.

Two.

I ran scenarios in my head, analyzing the possibilities the way Ian had taught me: considering my own behavior in the same situation, then using what I knew about Wingtips to adjust my analysis, make an educated guess as to what was happening inside the house.

Wingtips would have found Mindy's body moments after he first broke into the house. Once he determined she was dead, he would have dismissed her and gone through the scattered contents of her purse as dispassionately as he'd tossed the lit matches onto Bouchard's body.

I tucked the plastic bag containing my cell phone in the cavity under the passenger seat, anchoring it in the springs.

Finding nothing useful, he would have begun a systematic search of the house for any sign of Bouchard's business dealings. But unlike my own through but careful search the night before, Wingtips didn't care if anyone knew he'd been there. So while I'd carefully returned items to their original locations, Wingtips would leave a trail of chaos in his wake. I envisioned him pulling books and movies from the shelves in the family room, dropping them to the floor, plastic movie cases crunching under his feet as he moved through the room.

Staying low in my seat, I twisted a little, reaching behind me to retrieve the gun bag from the shadows of the floor behind the passenger seat and pull it forward and onto my lap.

He would have checked for hiding places in the chair and sofa cushions, probably moving Mindy's body to the floor so he could check the cushions beneath her — a last, best hiding place. He left her body lying in the debris.

I pulled out the defective magazine – identified in the bag with a folded-over strip of paper in the storage loop – then cut a small strip of surgical tape that I stuck to the butt, where it wouldn't interfere with its functionality.

He dumped kitchen drawers onto the counters, poured out containers of flour and sugar and cereal, and swept dishes from their cupboards, glassware and crockery shattering as it crashed to the linoleum, frightening the cats and sending them into hiding.

I put the marked, defective magazine in my jacket pocket. Three minutes.

The living room received the same treatment as the family room – the sofa and chair cushions slashed, the large vase under the main window dumped, the piano ripped open.

I wound the surgical tape around the Glock's grip, covering the rough spot with multiple layers of the heavy fabric tape.

He would have gone through the house quickly, methodically, with no emotional investment in the search. He would find something or he wouldn't, getting worked-up about it would serve no practical purpose. By the time the teenagers arrived, he would have been searching Mindy's room with the same cold efficiency.

Or…

I didn't know Wingtips at all. For all I knew, when the teens went inside, they'd found him standing in the middle of the kitchen, casually polishing off a bag of chips, the cats purring as they wound around his legs.

But I didn't think so.

Unless he'd been as careful in his search as I'd been the previous night, the teenagers would have seen the evidence of a break-in as soon as they went inside. Known someone had been there. Called 911.

Unless he'd stopped them.

Mindy's ghost would haunt me forever if I let her kids get hurt.

The police will be here soon.

Four minutes.

The police weren't going to get here soon enough.

I popped the good magazine into the Glock, pulled back on the slide to force a round into the chamber. Then, against my better judgement, I reached for the car door.

◆

The house's front door flew open and Wingtips burst out before I reached the end of my car.

I dropped down beside the car, peering across the hood.

Wingtips was carrying Mindy's daughter in a football player's hold under his arm, the girl screaming and thrashing ineffectively against him. He paid no attention to her flailing limbs, crossing the porch in two long steps, then pausing at the top of the steps and glancing up and down the street.

I stayed low, scooting backward, keeping out of sight, rising up to look toward the house again only after I reached the rear-view mirror. From this distance, even if he'd been looking directly at the car, he wouldn't be able to distinguish the top of my head from the curve of the mirror.

Wingtips wasn't looking in my direction.

He'd reached the bottom of the porch steps, but he'd made the mistake of leaving the door open, and Jaz, the larger of Mindy's two cats had followed him – aggressively. The yellow tom was clinging to Wingtip's leg and working his way higher as the big man twisted around, swiping at him with one hand, while the girl under his other arm continued to beat at him with her small fists.

I almost wanted to laugh.

Wingtips finally managed to grab hold of Jaz, all but ripping the cat free of his leg – which had to hurt both of them – and threw him back into the house. The big tom collided with Sunny, the little calico, who had just appeared in the open doorway, and the two cats disappeared from view.

But Wingtips wasn't in the clear yet.

He'd barely started down the walk before Mindy's son came barreling out of the house, launching himself off the porch and crashing into the intruder. Wingtip's grip on the girl loosened, and she twisted and turned that much more, slipping out of his hold and tumbling to the ground.

Wingtips tripped over her, but caught himself, turning just in time to take a punch to the face from her brother. I gave the kid credit – the swing looked good.

But Wingtip's swing was better. He returned the punch, with interest, sending the boy toppling back onto his butt on the grass. Then, before the girl had managed to scramble to her feet, he grabbed her by the arm and began dragging her to the van.

This time, when she started to scream, he slapped her. I winced at the sound of the sharp *crack* of his hand across her face, the sound seeming to echo in the otherwise still neighborhood. The girl staggered back, dazed, and Wingtips yanked her forward, propelling her toward the van.

The boy had gotten back to his feet, though, and once again rushed at Wingtips, plowing into him like a linebacker. He had good form, and it was a solid blow that shoved Wingtips sideways off the sidewalk, and onto the grass.

Good form notwithstanding, Wingtips was simply too much larger and stronger for the boy's efforts to have much of an impact. The big man let go of the girl, grabbed the boy, spun around, and threw him at the van. The boy flew through the air, arms windmilling, and collided face-first with the side of the vehicle, bouncing off it and landing flat on his back on the sidewalk, his head only marginally cushioned by the grass just beyond his shoulders.

He lay there, not moving.

Without even pausing, Wingtips turned back, scooped up the girl – who was struggling to her feet – and all but ran the rest of the way to the van, his gait only marginally impacted by the squirming girl he carried.

The squirming *blonde* girl.

"Shit," I muttered, easing back into my car.

The missing photograph from Mindy's desk – the one with her and her children – Wingtips had seen it. He wasn't here to make sure Mindy was dead, not entirely anyway. He was here because Renee needed a blonde for her client.

He'd come for the girl.

I closed my door and shoved the key in the ignition, waiting for the van to move before I started my engine, and was somewhat surprised when Wingtips came back around the van a moment later and climbed in through the driver's side door.

So, he'd been alone after all.

I'd all but decided that he had a partner who had taken the driver's seat, ready to make their getaway, and that Wingtips would stay in the back to make sure the girl didn't try to escape.

But as Wingtips climbed into the van and pulled away from the curb, I revised that assessment. He was alone – which was actually better, as far as the girl was concerned – and had probably cuffed the girl to a support of some sort in the back of the van.

I started my own car, waited for the van to get far enough ahead that Wingtips wouldn't notice me, then eased off the shoulder and onto the road.

As I passed the cross street, I saw a police cruiser approaching, still about a half a block away. Better late than never. They wouldn't see the van in time to give pursuit, but would be able to help the boy, who was just pulling himself to a sitting position on the sidewalk, the big yellow cat, Jaz, creeping toward him.

I drove away sedately, not calling any attention to myself, and keeping a decent distance behind Wingtips. From previous days' scouting, I knew the neighborhood better than he did, and all the ways in and out of it. I wasn't worried about losing him.

And even if I did, I knew where he was headed – back to Raeburn Shipping, to meet the 4:30 truck.

Chapter 14

West Ashley has only a handful of major streets, and at three o'clock on a Friday afternoon, they were busy enough that I had no trouble blending in with the traffic as I followed Wingtips' van through town and onto the expressway.

I was glad he'd taken that route and not only because it let us avoid all the stops, starts, and traffic lights we would have encountered along the routes that wound through the main peninsula. I have a love-hate relationship with traffic lights, which mostly leans toward the hate side of the equation.

Traffic lights aside, I was glad because the long, easy curve of the expressway gave me nearly a half an hour to think.

I'd seen a blue minivan zipping through traffic in the opposite direction just before I got onto the expressway. I hoped it was the kids' stepmother on her way to Mindy's house. The boy couldn't have been in good shape after his fall.

But the chaos I'd left behind was only a small part of my concern. It was the chaos that was likely to follow us that troubled me. Between my own 911 call reporting the break-in and whatever report the boy gave the police about the man who had been in their house, killed his mother – because that would be the initial assumption – and taken off with his sister, it wouldn't be long before the authorities were looking for Wingtips' van.

The sooner we got to the dockyard, the better.

When I'd found the warehouse the previous day, I'd also learned that cars, vans, and other private vehicles took one route to the dockyard, while the semis took another, passing through inspection stations that reviewed their paperwork before letting them pass. Incoming trucks were directed to whatever loading bay or other part of the dockyard their paperwork indicated, while outgoing trucks had to show proof that their load had been inspected and approved by the port authority.

There were two of these inspection stations – one accessed by the main road, and the second a little further to the north, tucked away down a side road. Raeburn Shipping was in one of the smaller warehouses near this northern inspection station.

I wondered if Richardson – the inspector Bouchard had listed on his spreadsheet – had heard about Bouchard's death. If he had, would he show up to rubber-stamp the container for Renee so the truck could pass through the inspection station unchallenged? Would the rest of Bouchard's crew go through with the container transfer – or had she already identified and replaced them with her own crew?

"This isn't what I signed up for," I muttered, hitting my horn as a careless driver drifted into my lane, forcing me to tap on my brakes.

The driver jerked his car back into his own lane and waved apologetically, his cell phone in his upraised hand. I sped up, passing him, and putting some distance between us before I slowed back to my usual just-over-the-limit speed. Last thing I needed was to get in an accident because some idiot decided to text while driving.

Wingtip's van was now only about two cars ahead of me, religiously obeying the speed limit. With a sigh, I dropped my speed, maintaining my distance, watching for the careless driver in the rear-view, and noting the police cruiser who passed us, heading in the opposite direction.

Had the word gone out yet about the kidnapped girl in the gray panel van? Were the police already looking for it? At what point was a cruiser going to pull up behind Wingtips with its lights flashing?

I didn't like it. There were too many unknowns, too many variables on this job.

All I'd wanted was a simple job. Nothing I had to think too much about, no grudges to settle, no vengeance to pursue. Nothing personal. Just a straightforward, easy contract that would engage my mind, settle my traumatized inner child, and let me get some rest.

But by telling me about the container girls, Mindy's last request had found a direct line into my nightmares. My inner child would never stop tormenting me if I walked away without doing everything I could to save the container girls.

And watching Wingtips snatch Mindy's daughter right under my nose, dragging her from her home and her dead mother, with the intention of consigning her to the same fate as the container girls, that was something I couldn't allow.

Variables or not, my "simple job" was now *very* personal.

I accelerated just a little, closing the gap between myself and the car ahead of me before another vehicle moved into the space. I wasn't letting the gray van out of my sight.

Not even for a moment.

◆

After we left the expressway, two other private vehicles joined us on the main road leading into the dockyard. The first, a pickup truck that had come from somewhere to the east, in Mt. Pleasant, continued ahead when the gray van turned down the side road leading to the northern dockyard entrance, following a loaded semi.

That left three of us.

The second, a sedan that was just in front of me, turned off into the parking lot of one of the several warehouse-based businesses along the road. I was right behind the gray van now, a second loaded semi filling my rear-view. I hoped Wingtips hadn't noticed that I'd been following him since he snatched the girl, because there was nowhere for me to go.

We turned the corner, both Bouchard and I staying in the far-right lane while the semis remained in the left lane. We continued past them, turning off to the right as the road widened into the multi-lane inspection station, where several semis waited their turn.

Wingtips turned into the second parking lot entrance. I continued on, taking the third entrance, which was just the next row of the same lot, and the same one I'd parked in the night before. I drove slowly, as though picky about choosing a parking space in the half-empty lot, and watched as the gray van moved through the lot and beyond, heading past the first warehouse and toward the Raeburn building.

I followed, slipping into an empty parking stall near the end of the first warehouse when a utility truck backed out of it. I'd wanted to get closer, but not so close to the Raeburn building that I thought Wingtips would notice. I pulled on the dark wig, put on the new reading glasses, then activated the new burner phone. Grabbing the Glock, I got out of my car, tucked the gun into the waistband of my jeans, and looked over at Raeburn Shipping.

The office portion of the Raeburn building was cordoned off, police tape marking a large yellow "X" across the front doors. Sheets of plywood covered both Bouchard's office window and the next one, burn scars framing them like starbursts, but it didn't look like the fire had spread much. There were no cars in the small lot in front of the building, though there was a lone, dark blue sedan parked along one end of the building.

Unlike the first warehouse, where I'd parked, and around which there was a buzz of activity, the Raeburn warehouse was silent. Between the investigation into the fire and Bouchard's death, and any necessary safety inspections by the Fire Marshall, it would be days – maybe weeks – before Raeburn Shipping was back in business.

And if I turned over Bouchard's second set of books, exposing the smuggling operations, it would close for good. Every box in the warehouse – and every shipment destined for it for the next several months – would be opened and searched for contraband.

It was just too bad that Bouchard wasn't around any longer to take his share of the blame.

I crossed the lot to the warehouse and walked around the far end. People tend not to notice when you dress normally and act like you belong. In jeans, sneakers, and the wine-colored anorak, with the long dark hair spilling down over my shoulders, and the reading glasses, from a distance I looked as much like Mindy as I was ever going to. I walked casually, staying close enough to the building to not draw attention to myself, but not so near that it looked like I was sneaking around. I was just another employee, a familiar presence to anyone happening to glance in this direction.

Only when I got to the end of the building, did I move closer, walking between the blue car – it was a Camry – and the wall, and slowing when I heard the raised voices from up ahead. I stopped at the end of the building, and then, as I'd done the night before, peered around the corner.

The gray van was parked in front of the closed ground-level bay door, its back to me, blocking my view of what was going on beyond it. I pulled out the burner phone and snapped a photo of the van's license, then crept forward, staying low, beneath the level of the rear windows, and looked around the side of the van.

Wingtips had parked only a few feet away from one of the large, tractor-sized forklifts, which had a twenty foot, white, refrigerated container – a reefer – on its forks, the cooling unit letting off a low-pitched hum. He was standing near the lift now, talking with the driver, his voice low and menacing. I couldn't make out what they were talking about over the thrum of the forklift's idling motor, but the driver did not look at all happy.

I raised the phone again, zooming in on the end of the reefer, and took several snapshots of the container number and other registration information. It would be easy to lose a reefer in a yard filled with similar containers, or on a truck headed cross-country. The container number was the only thing that differentiated this one from any other.

There were other voices closer to me, and I ducked back behind the van when Renee, her hair pulled back in a French braid, and a tall, thin balding man with wire-rimmed glasses moved from where they'd been standing at the front of the van, putting themselves between me and Wingtips.

"I told Bouchard he was getting sloppy," the thin man was saying. "Last time the driver got here too soon, asked all sorts of questions about how the load could be certified without anyone opening the container to check it. I had to come up with a quick song-and-dance about having barely finished my inspection before he arrived. I was sure he was going to say something, get us all locked up. I told Bouchard so."

So this was Richardson, the inspector. I checked the time on my phone. It was only minutes after four. The driver would be along soon.

"You're not working with Bouchard any more," Renee said, her voice as smooth as melted caramel. I briefly wondered what she sounded like when she wasn't trying to cajole a man.

A thump from inside the van startled me, and I turned my attention from Renee and Richardson to the van. Was the girl in there? Someone else? I hadn't heard anyone else come up to the van, hadn't heard the door open. I slowly raised my phone to the lower edge of the window, and used the camera like a spyglass to look inside the van.

Except for the girl laying on the floor, curled up on her side just behind the driver's seat, it looked like a standard cargo van. A large cardboard box, a flat or two of water bottles, and what looked like a paint bucket near the back and a pile of blankets near the other wall, similar to one the girl was using as a pillow. Other than that, there were no seats, no built-in fittings. Just an empty shell.

I leaned back against the door and listened. Richardson was still complaining about Bouchard's shoddy leadership, seemingly unaware that Renee was losing interest in the conversation. Wingtips and the forklift driver's argument had intensified.

If I was going to get the girl, this was my chance.

I traded the phone for my lock picks and quickly finessed the van's rear doors open.

The girl gasped when I eased the door open and slipped inside, pulling the door closed behind me.

I raised a gloved finger to my lips and she nodded, her eyes still wide with terror.

"I'm a friend," I said. "Your mother sent me. Let's get you out of here, shall we?"

Chapter 15

I'd been wrong when I saw the interior of the van as just an empty shell. The shadowy view through the tinted windows had been good enough to let me see the girl, but it hadn't been clear enough to show me the heavy mesh separating the driver's section from space behind it.

It also hadn't given me a good view of the multiple sets of handcuffs linked through openings in the interior frame of the cargo compartment.

I scooted forward keeping my movements slow and steady. A trio of dockworkers lingered just beyond the front of the van, near the reefer, visible through the front window. As I moved forward, Renee and Richardson came into view through the front passenger window.

"Did he hurt you?" I whispered to the girl.

She shook her head, then raised her arm, exposing the silver ring of a handcuff, her wrist and the lower part of her hand bright red from her efforts to pull free.

I moved over to her and pulled a handcuff shim from my lockpick kit. But after I popped the lock and freed her wrist, she scooted away from me, backing up until her back pressed against the driver's seat.

"How did you get the key?" she whispered, rubbing her wrist.

I held up the shim. "It's not really a key," I told her. "It's called a 'shim.' It's sort of like a skeleton key for handcuffs – it will open most of them."

I moved toward the back door.

The girl didn't move.

"You got a name?" I asked.

"Kaitlyn."

"I'm Emma," I said, gesturing for her to follow me. The reference to one of my favorite BBC television spies, Emma Peel, would be lost on her, but it made me smile. "C'mon. They won't stand around talking all day. We've got to get out of here."

That seemed to motivate her.

The smooth metal of the cargo compartment floor made it easy for us to slide quietly to the back. Now that I was there, I took another look at the items that had been stacked near the door.

Blankets. Handcuffs. A stack of water bottles and a toilet seat lid on what I'd first thought was a paint bucket.

Were Renee and Wingtips planning to transport the container girls in the van?

There was more to this debacle than met the eye. I wondered about Renee, and Haskell, whom she claimed to have replaced. Was he still an active part of the organization? Had she and Wingtips planned to steal the container girls out from under him? Had she intended to kill Bouchard all along, so he couldn't go over her head, rather than because he'd annoyed her one time too many?

So many questions I would never know the answer to – nor did I care.

However, if they moved the container girls to the van, it would be that much more difficult to find them, and that I *did* care about.

We slipped out of the van. I closed the door carefully, turning the handle to minimize an audible click, then gestured for Kaitlyn to wait on the steps leading up to the gray, steel door. She curled up on the bottom step, pulling her knees to her chest.

I stayed pressed against the back of the van, listening, trying to gauge the situation.

Renee had given up all pretense of patience with Richardson. "I understand," she was saying. "This will be the last time. We won't ask you to do this again." The melted caramel in her voice had cooled, but he didn't seem to have noticed.

This wasn't going to go well for him. He was going to approve the shipment, even if he didn't know it yet. I didn't know what was involved in the process, or how long it would take, but I didn't think it would be very long.

"You don't understand," Richardson said. "I can't certify this, not with Raeburn closed up. They'll flag it at the gates, and it will be my name on the paperwork."

"I'll double your fee."

"I can't spend it if I'm in jail."

"You won't be able to spend it if you're dead, either," Renee said, the too-sweet caramel in her voice turning brittle.

"Hey! Hey! Wait a minute," Richardson said, his voice rising in pitch.

I could only assume Renee had pulled a gun on him. That did seem to be her pattern – cajole, persuade, demand, threaten.

Time was running out. And I still needed to rescue the container girls, if I could.

I slipped around to the side of the van. I reached inside my coat and pulled out one of the kitchen knives. They wouldn't be any good against the tough steel-belts inside the tire treads, but the sidewalls were a different story.

I'd wondered how the kitchen knives would perform, and was not disappointed. The sharp point sank into the rubber like an oversized steak. I drove it deep, then pulled it out slowly, extending the gash. I repeated the movement on the opposite side of the rim, and was rewarded by a barely audible hiss of air escaping the tire.

One flat tire wouldn't seriously or permanently disable the van, but it would slow them down – and keep them from taking the girls away in the van, if that was their plan. I couldn't tell, not with the pressure Renee was putting on Richardson. Either way, whether by choice or by circumstance, they'd have to leave the girls in the easier-to-track container, and that was all I wanted.

I re-sheathed the knife and moved back to Kaitlyn.

"Wait here," I whispered. "I'll unlock the door. You find a place to hide inside the warehouse until the police get here."

"Where are you going?" she said, grabbing at my arm. "You're not going to leave me here."

Most of the time, emotionally-laden situations frustrate me. I'm never sure how to comfort, how to respond. Lying is easier.

But this time I knew exactly what to say. Kaitlyn needed to hear the truth. I put my hand on hers. "You're not the only girl they've kidnapped," I told her. "Your mother…"

"My mother is dead," she hissed. "That man killed her."

"Damn," I said, hoping I looked surprised at the news. "I'm sorry I didn't get here sooner. Mindy found out what was going on – told me she was afraid." I squeezed her hand. "I have to help those other girls, too. You'll be okay."

Kaitlyn nodded, brushing back tears.

Staying low, hoping everyone was focused enough on Renee to not look my way, I worked the lock, every second expecting to hear a shout or – more likely – get a bullet in the back.

In the movies, it seems like they barely have to breathe on the mechanism to open a lock. In real life, it's not like that – especially when you're under pressure. So when I finally felt the tumblers click into place and the handle gave under my hand, I released the breath I'd barely been aware I'd been holding.

I pushed the door open, and turned to wave Kaitlyn forward.

She was bright, I had to give her that. She'd crept to the top of the steps and curled there, her position still hidden by the top of the van, but ready to dart over as soon as I gestured.

The gun went off when Kaitlyn was still two steps from the door. She froze, turning to look, a little cry escaping her lips as she watched Richardson fall.

It was that sound that drew everyone's eyes to us.

I grabbed Kaitlyn and shoved her through the door, diving in behind her and kicking the door as the shots hit it. The steel door vibrated against the impact, but its solid core held. I jumped up and locked it, then turned back to Kaitlyn who was standing only a few feet away, staring at me like a deer in the headlights.

"Run!"

♦

Kaitlyn vanished into the shadows.

I pulled the Glock from my waistband, popped in the magazine, and racked the slide.

And then I ran, too.

With all the bay doors closed, and the overhead lights off, the only light came from the row of small windows that ran along the top of all the walls. If I'd stopped to think about it, it might have seemed as though waiting for someone to come along and tear the roof off along the perforation. But there was no time to think – only to move from shadow to shadow, like a predator looking for a place to lie in wait for its prey.

Unlike my previous visit, when the warehouse echoed with the sound of forklift engines and tires thrummed the cement floor, today the cavernous space was eerily silent, the light taps of our running feet too loud. With no breeze blowing in off the river, the air was heavy, the normal scents of cardboard and sawdust and diesel overshadowed by the residual smells from the fire, which even the wall between the warehouse and office had been unable to completely block.

An engine roared, tires and tires crunched I jumped at the sound, realizing a moment later that it was simply a truck passing by outside, on its way to or from the neighboring warehouse.

There were puddles on the cement floor, as well, which puzzled me at first, until I realized that the sprinklers must have gone off when the fire alarm went off. I took care to avoid the puddles, not wanting to leave even a partial wet footprint to mark my passage.

Forklifts had been abandoned in the middle of rows, many still with pallets on their forks. At one point, I came around the end of a shelving unit to find myself facing one of the seated forklifts, its forks still several feet above me, the pallet it had been unloading not quite fully resting on the shelf. I backed away cautiously, the image of heavy things dropping on me from overhead flitting through my mind, and went down another row.

Then the heavy steel door slammed against the wall and the whole building trembled.

I'd seen three dockworkers, one forklift driver, Wingtips, and Renee. While it was possible all six had come inside to look for us, I thought it unlikely.

But I wasn't willing to bet my life on it.

I had my gun ready, a pair of knives in easy reach in my pockets. I was the predator, not the prey. The men looking for me just didn't know it.

So I waited, listening for the sound of soft footsteps and breathing to break the silence.

Chapter 16

The first one to die was one of the dockworkers.

His squeaky shoes gave him away. An almost imperceptible *creak* signaling every step he took. He'd probably never noticed it before.

I noticed.

He led with his gun, a Beretta 92, whose matte-black muzzle poked out from the end of the row only inches from my eyes. I stayed still, the Glock in my waistband, a knife in my hand, – I wanted a quiet kill. I stood with my back pressed to the stack of boxes filling the shelf at the end of the row, just shielding me from view. I had my head turned toward him, waiting for him to come into striking range.

One step. Now his wrist was so close that even in the shadows I could read the time on his digital watch: 4:23.

With his arms extended, he could defend against a throat strike. All he would need to do was lower his arms to trap me before my blade ever touched him. But his extended arms left his core open and vulnerable. I turned my wrist slightly.

Another step. *Creak.*

I spun toward him, grabbing the metal shelving frame at the corner for leverage. The knife swung upward, almost of its own accord, the tip plunging into his solar plexus, driving up under his ribcage, seeking his heart.

He was dead before he knew he'd been hit.

His arms sagged and he staggered back, his body folding over the knife, pushing the blade even deeper as I released it. His grip on the Beretta loosened. I caught the gun as it slipped from his hand and dropped it into my pocket, then dragged his body around the end of the row, the sound camouflaged by the rumble of a passing semi. I rolled him into the shadows at the base of the shelving where he would be less visible.

And then I was on the move, looking for a new place to hide.

There were surprisingly few good hiding places. The aisles and rows were wide open, providing clear views from one end to the other, with only limited places to crouch effectively in the shadows. Slipping into open spots in the shelving was an option, but what it offered in terms of concealment the restricted movement effectively negated. Grates at the back of each shelf unit, placed there to prevent the pallets from sliding onto the unit behind, meant I couldn't move through the shelving from one row to another.

I had no interest in hiding in what I considered little more than a cage.

The shelving units themselves were solidly bolted to the floor, and braced at regular intervals, meaning the action hero trick of toppling them onto the bad guys with a good shove was nothing more than movie magic.

That left only one choice.

I looked up at the stacks of boxes on the higher shelves. Though wrapped in plastic, the sprinkler water had obviously gotten inside many of the wrappings, and the boxes sagged, some still dark where the water had pooled. I moved down the row, looking for boxes that had fared better – or at the very least, that didn't look like they were on the verge of collapse.

I went up.

Warehouse shelving is not made for free climbing. The spacing between the shelves means you're clinging to support struts, holding onto horizontal beams, and pulling yourself up with your arms, hoping you can find footing in pallet's fork gap or at the top of a stack of boxes to help you to the next level.

All while trying not to fall. And not to make any noise.

Ian's laughter echoed in my mind as I climbed, remembering the grueling hours he put the gym rats through – myself included – focusing on upper body strength and endurance in preparation for obstacle course races. I wondered how many of the gym rats had scrambled up a shelving unit, and grinned. Every one of them would take it as a personal challenge if they knew I'd done it.

I pulled myself to the top of the fifth rack and lay flat on my back on the boxes, taking deep breaths that I released slowly and quietly. When I rolled over, moving away from the outside edge of the shelving toward the center of the double-stack, the plastic wrapping covering the boxes under me wrinkled with a gentle *shushing* and the thin film of water on the wrapping dripped over the edge of the boxes, landing with a soft *plop* onto the boxes below.

In the cavernous quiet of the warehouse, the sound dissipating in the rafters might as well have been a shout.

I moved cautiously, testing the boxes for stability before putting my weight on them. I slid forward in a belly crawl, leading with one elbow at a time, moving only when the rumble of a passing truck covered the sound of my movement. It was agonizingly slow. The waterproofing on my anorak held up, but my jeans offered no such protection, the front of my legs soaking up any water my movement didn't displace.

There was nothing to do but lay still or keep moving. I chose to move.

The boxes ahead of me, near the end of the row, tilted precariously toward the floor. It would only take a good shove to send the whole soggy pallet down onto the head of one of the unsuspecting hunters. I moved into position. I toyed with the idea of making a noise to lure someone closer, but thought better of it. My view down through the stack was limited, and the odds of two or more of them being in just the right place at the same time were too small to count on.

I would only have one shot at this. So I waited.

The minutes ticked by.

I wondered where Kaitlyn had hidden. The memory of a child in an old science fiction movie hiding from monsters beneath metal floor grates flashed into my mind. Kaitlyn was slight for her age – I'd estimated her at about thirteen – and might well be able to hide in the small gaps behind stacks of boxes that the adults couldn't fit in. If she'd found a good hiding place, all she had to do was stay quiet.

Being quiet didn't do me much good, my inner child reminded me. The memory flashed into my mind of a young girl huddled in the back of a storage closet, barely breathing as the taunting voice came closer…

I shook off the memory.

You're safe now. We're safe. I'll keep her safe.

I repeated the mantra over and over in my mind, pushing the past away and focusing on the present.

I would make sure Kaitlyn was safe if I had to kill every one of the men hunting for us.

♦

Outside, another truck rumbled.

But instead of continuing on by, as several others had, I heard the distinctive *woosh* of its air brakes, followed by the rhythmic beeping as it backed into place.

The 4:30 truck. It had to be.

I didn't know what time it was, and didn't want to move enough to dig my phone from my pocket. I only knew that it had been more than seven minutes since I'd killed the first of the hunters.

The truck was late.

As if in response to my thought, Renee's voice called out from the direction of the door, echoing in the rafters.

"Robby, Hendricks, I need you. Now."

Footsteps echoed in the distance as one of the two men ran toward the door.

I heard a movement near me. Craning my neck, I strained to see where the sound was coming from. And then I spotted him – his shadow, actually – moving slowly down the aisle, heading into my kill zone. I braced myself, resting my hands lightly on the edge of the soggy boxes.

The shadow moved forward, resolving into the shape of a man. Tall, slim, with long, stringy hair and wearing an orange safety vest over a dirty white t-shirt. He was holding something long and dark in his hand – it might have been a pipe wrench or a piece of rebar, I couldn't tell.

One more step...

I gave a hard shove.

The leaning pile of boxes shifted, then collapsed, pulling the pallet they rested on with them as they topped off the shelf. I jerked back, out of the way, but not before the falling pallet scraped past my upper arm, snagging on the sleeve of my coat, then ripping itself free, tearing a long gash down my left arm.

I felt the sting in my forearm, but didn't waste time looking at it. I scrambled backward, onto the stable boxes.

Down below, I caught the briefest glimpse of the man's horrified face as the pallet bore down on him. He tried to dodge, but he'd waited too long, and the leading edge of the wooden pallet caught him on the back of his neck, driving him to the floor. The boxes exploded over and around him, burying him in piles of colorful, soggy fabric.

The feet protruding from the stack didn't even twitch.

I didn't waste time worrying about making noise now. As multiple sets of footsteps pounded in my direction, I fled down the row in a fast, low crawl, moving much the way my iguana did when offered a piece of melon. Some of the boxes I crawled over were soggy, and once I thought the box I was crawling over might give way under my weight, but I kept moving. By the time the footsteps stopped and the swearing started, I had reached the opposite end of the row and was scrambling down the shelving.

Going down was much faster than going up.

It seemed that I'd buried the one named Robby. There were two men trying to dig him out, one of them cursing up a storm at Renee, at me, and at the other person, who he didn't seem to think was being helpful enough.

"Shut up, Hendricks. Go help Renee," the second person said. I'd heard that voice before – it was Wingtips.

"That bitch killed Robby," Hendricks said. "I'm going after her."

"No, you're not," Wingtips said.

"He was just a kid," Hendricks said.

"I'll get her," Wingtips told him. "Go. Renee needs your help with the truck."

Hendricks swore at him, but a moment later, I heard both his muttered curses and his footsteps receding in the distance.

With Renee, Hendricks, and the forklift driver outside, and Robby and the un-named dockworker dead, that only left Wingtips.

And I knew where he was.

That would change in a matter of seconds. I couldn't waste the opportunity. I pulled the Glock, which was still racked and ready, stepped out from the cover of the shelving, and raised my arms, wincing at the pain from the pallet cut. It was only then that I noticed the blood darkening the sleeve of my jacket and running down my left hand.

I fired.

And missed.

The bullet grazed Wingtips' ear, then flew on to hit the shelving strut with a loud, metallic *clang*.

NOTHING PERSONAL • 147

He didn't waste time reaching up to clap a hand over his bleeding ear. In a smooth, fluid motion, he drew, turned, fired, and started running toward me, firing a second time, and a third.

His shots hit the warehouse wall as I dove out of the way, somersaulting when I hit the floor and rolling back to my feet already on the run, the sound of Wingtips' heavy footfalls right behind me.

I skipped the first row and darted down the next one, sprinting for all I was worth. I'd seen one of the seated forklifts parked nearly at the end of this row, and headed for it now. It was the only available cover in the wide, open rows.

I skidded to a stop, sliding in behind the forklift like a baseball player into home plate, just as a bullet whistled overhead.

So much for hiding. Not that I'd thought I'd fooled him, but I'd hoped to at least be out of sight before he came around the end of the row.

A bullet hit the forklift's engine block, the machine jolting slightly at the impact. Two seconds later, another bullet tore through the driver's seat. I crouched lower.

Wingtips' footsteps had slowed, and he was making no attempt at moving quietly. I heard his footfalls slow as he advanced, clearly intending to walk right up and shoot me in the head.

As if he thought I was going let him.

I raised up slightly, peering through the narrow gap between the driver's seat and the tool compartment at the back of the truck section, the dark wig next to the black vinyl seat keeping him from easily spotting the top of my head. Wingtips was taking no precautions, just walking slowly toward my position, watching for me to make a mistake.

He held his body in a slight crouch, arms raised, gun extended, making a critical core shot difficult. He'd left me two targets: legs or head.

We both knew which I would choose.

I slowly raised the Glock, not wanting to draw his eye with any movement, and hoping the shadows behind the driver's seat would help to conceal the gun's barrel.

There wasn't much room to work here. With the gun in position, the only way I could see Wingtips was to pull my head down so my eyes were level with the top of the gun, my nose tucked behind my hands.

I lined up the sights, looked past them at Wingtips' almost expressionless face, felt the same lack of expression settle over my own features, and pulled the trigger.

This time, I didn't miss.

Chapter 17

I relieved Wingtips of his Sig and a spare magazine, and reached inside his coveralls to take the phones from his pants pockets. There were two of them – one live, which I assumed was his, and one powered-down, which was probably Bouchard's burner phone. I stuffed them both as deep into my over-full pockets as they would go.

I then used one of my knives to cut a long strip of fabric about an inch wide from the sleeve of his coveralls. The pallet had torn the sleeve of my coat from just above the elbow nearly to the wrist. When I peeled the blood-soaked fabric open, I was relieved to see the six-inch gash along my forearm had missed my elbow.

I pulled the sleeve closed, overlapping it like a bandage over the wound, then wrapped the coverall fabric around my arm to hold the fabric closed. I bound it snug, but not too tight, the goal being to hold the gash closed without cutting off circulation, then tied it off one-handed – grateful it was my left arm that was injured and not my right. Then I cut a second strip from the coveralls and repeated the process.

It took three long strips of coverall fabric to mummy-wrap my arm from elbow to wrist. It was tedious and awkward, and more of my attention was on listening for anyone who might be coming than on tending to the injury, but when I was finished, my arm felt better.

I crept back toward the door, checking down each row before I moved on to the next. Everything was quiet inside the warehouse.

The door was still open, late afternoon sunshine pouring in through the bright rectangle.

I edged toward the door, staying close to the wall in case anyone outside was looking in. I moved slowly, quietly, letting my eyes adjust to the brighter light after the dimness of the warehouse. Gradually the hazy bands of gray, green, and blue resolved themselves into the pavement, marshy wetland, and river beyond. The warehouse was much closer to the river than I'd realized – a fact that might have been useful if I'd been planning to get rid of the bodies I'd left laying around the warehouse.

I had no intention of cleaning up after myself.

I hesitated when I reached the door, moving just behind the front edge, like a shield, and looking around it.

The gray van was still there, blocking my view toward the left. But I heard no voices, no one walking around outside, no engine sound from either the forklift or the 4:30 truck.

No hum from the reefer's cooling fan.

I stepped around the door and onto the dock. Someone had moved Richardson's body from where he'd fallen, hiding him between the van and the large bay doors. Beyond the van, the lot was empty. Renee had gone, leaving her henchmen to their own fate.

More importantly, the container was gone.

♦

I was so focused on the missing container, that I didn't notice the cigarette smell until I'd run down the short flight of steps and around the gray van – and came face to face with a pock-faced man leaning against the van, taking his last, long drag.

Hendricks.

We jumped apart, both startled by the appearance of the other.

He flicked the butt aside and slid a hand in his coverall pocket. The motion seemed calm, but his facial expression gave him away, as surprise gave way to anger. "You're the bitch who killed Robby," he said, his mouth twisting into a sneer. He stepped toward me, pulling a knife from his pocket, flipping the switchblade open. "You're gonna pay for that."

I took a step back and then another, putting some distance between us.

I'm good with a knife – but better at throwing than knife-fighting. Given the choice, when it came to knife fights, I preferred to run away rather than engage. Blades are just too chaotic – or perhaps it's the blade-wielders. Regardless, there's no real pattern to follow, and no good defense against a knife. You simply had to accept the fact that you were going to get cut. After that, survival is mostly in not taking a critical hit before you could inflict one on your opponent.

I had a small arsenal of guns– Bouchard's Glock in my jacket pocket, Squeaky Shoe's Beretta tucked in the back of my jeans, and Wingtips' Sig in tucked in the front of my jeans – and none of them would be of any use to me if Pock Face closed in on me before I had a chance to draw and fire.

I took a third step back, moving my hand toward my pocket.

"That's right, be afraid," Hendricks said, misinterpreting my movement. He lunged toward me, slashing with the blade. I twisted away, my hand closing on the Glock in my pocket as I ducked around to the back of the gray van.

Still moving backwards, I pulled the gun out of my pocket. I was raising my left hand to rack the slide when Pock Face came around the back of the van, swinging the blade at me again and catching the top of my right arm, just below my shoulder.

As he raised the knife for another strike, his eyes fell on the gun in my hand, and widened in surprise. I caught the slide, racked it, and fired as he dove toward me. The bullet tore through his sternum, throwing him back against the van, his knife dragging across my collar bone as he fell.

I staggered back, knowing I'd been hit, but not sure how badly.

Pressing the torn jacket against the cut in the hopes of slowing the bleeding, I backed away from Hendricks' body. Then I turned and ran up the steps and back into the warehouse.

◆

I had only a passing knowledge of where things were in the warehouse – the rows of shelving, the offices, the bathrooms. It was the bathroom I was heading to, hoping it had been spared in the fire. I needed paper towels, soap, water, a mirror.

I needed to see how deep the cut was.

"Kaitlyn," I shouted. "Kaitlyn, it's Emma. I need your help." I didn't stop, or even slow down to look for her or wait for a response. "I'm going to the women's restroom, by your mother's office. Come quick."

Keeping as much pressure against the wound as I could stand, I speed-walked through the warehouse, trying to maintain something close to an even heartrate. I only paused when I reached the row where the orange-vested dockworker lay buried under a mountain of wet t-shirts. There I stopped and grabbed an armful of the shirts, swaying dizzily as I bent to scoop them up.

The stink of mildew nearly made me gag.

Mildew or not, I didn't have anything I could use as either a towel or a bandage. The t-shirts would just have to do. And the stinking armful of shirts pressed to my shoulder had the additional benefit of acting like smelling salts, keeping me alert and focused as I headed toward the big yellow "X" of police tape that marked the double glass doors leading to the Raeburn offices.

Kaitlyn met me at the doors.

"You're hurt," she said, skidding to a stop and then backing away.

"Knife wound. Nothing serious," I said through gritted teeth. "But I need your help to bandage it up."

I pushed the yellow police tape away and reached for the door.

"We can't go in there," Kaitlyn said, pointing at the tape.

I ignored her and pushed the door open. No one had bothered to lock it, thinking it was secure enough with the entire building shut down. I was glad for the oversight. I wasn't up to picking another lock just at that moment.

I'd grown so accustomed to the smoky, burned-plastic and wiring smell in the warehouse that I'd all but forgotten about it. But as we walked into the burned-out office, the smell practically hit us in the face.

The short hallway was a charred ruin, the wall to Bouchard's office burnt down to the metal studs. The remains of the LED board hung askew from the studs, wires melted together.

"Where did you hide?" I asked, as I steered her away from the wreckage and toward the bathroom. I hoped to distract her before she had a chance to look through the rubble and see the melted remnants of her mother's desk.

This day had been traumatizing enough for her as it was.

"Sometimes the boxes they put on the higher shelves aren't as big," Kaitlyn said, picking her way through the rubble. "If you're small enough, you can squeeze in behind them and no one can see you. I'm almost too big, now."

"No one found you today," I said. "That's all that matters."

The bathroom door was gone, and the room in pretty bad shape, but one of the overhead lights flickered to life, and the sink farthest from the door still worked. We used one of the t-shirts to wipe the soot and grime from the mirror.

"Is it okay if I use the toilet?" Kaitlyn asked.

"Sure," I said, unzipping my jacket and gingerly peeling it away from the knife wound.

Blood was still oozing from the cut, but it wasn't pumping freely, which I decided was a good sign. I hoped that meant it was only a surface wound, and that Hendricks hadn't done any serious damage. I was still upright, so he hadn't hit a vein, and still breathing okay, so he hadn't punctured my lung.

Unlike my arm, though, which I was now barely even aware of, it hurt like hell. I wondered if he'd actually cracked my collar bone, or if my body was just reacting to being cut.

More than that, I couldn't begin to diagnose.

"Emma? The toilet won't flush," Kaitlyn said from inside the stall.

"Leave it," I said. "No one will know it was you."

She came out, a sheepish expression on her young face, and I stepped away from the sink so she could wash her hands.

"That looks bad," she said, looking at the cut in the mirror.

"It could have been worse," I said. "Soon as you're cleaned up, can you help me bandage it?"

Kaitlyn looked at the pile of t-shirts sitting in the second sink. "You're gonna use one of those? They stink. Won't you get an infection or something?"

"It's all I've got," I said. "There's hot water, and soap. We can wash one of the shirts and fold it like a bandage, then use one of the others to pad it. The jacket's a wreck, but it should hold everything in place long enough."

Kaitlyn listened, frowning. "There are bandages in the break room," she said. "But probably not any big enough for that."

"Where there are bandages, there will also be aspirin," I said. "And I bet there's a vending machine, too. A soda would be great."

"I can go get some—"

"After. Help me with this first."

While Kaitlyn washed out one of the t-shirts, I stripped off my blood-soaked gloves and tossed them in the sink with the t-shirts, then tugged off the now useless bandage covering the blister on my hand, wadded it into a ball, and stuffed it into my pocket to dispose of later. Finally, I grabbed one of the dry t-shirts from the other sink and awkwardly folded it into a thick pad about the length and width of my hand.

After she'd squeezed as much water as she could from the t-shirt she'd washed, Kaitlyn folded it up as well.

"This is gonna hurt," she said apologetically, raising the pad to the angry cut.

"I know," I said. "You don't need to press hard; just hold it steady while I get the second one in place."

Once we had the t-shirts positioned, I had Kaitlyn hold them while I pulled the jacket over the top and zipped it up. We ended up having to add a third shirt to the padding, to keep the others from slipping, and by the time we finally managed it, I thought Kaitlyn's face looked almost as pale as my own reflection in the dirty mirror.

"Okay, where's the break room?" I hoped my forced enthusiasm wasn't too obvious.

Kaitlyn pointed at the wall behind the toilet stalls. "On the other side of the wall," she said.

"Go ahead," I told her. "Figure out what you want. I'll be right there."

She looked up at me, puzzled.

"I need to use the toilet."

"Oh, okay," she said, and started toward the door. Then she turned back, her face turning bright pink. "Oh! I'm so sorry—"

"Not your fault," I said. I waved her away. "Pick out a candy bar. I won't be long."

She left the room and I did my business, then washed up, finished rinsing the blood off my gloves, and followed. I hoped she'd been focused on the candy bar, and hadn't lingered near her mother's desk for too long – although I had to admit that I paused on my way by Mindy's, dipping my head in a moment of silence.

Mindy had been in the wrong place at the wrong time. But she'd tried to do the right thing anyway. The container girls might be on their way west, but I knew where they were headed, and thanks to the FBI contact the Researcher had given me, I would make sure they were picked up and received proper care.

The job was almost done. Now I just needed to get Kaitlyn home.

"What did you pick? Are the machines working, or do I need to break one open for you?" I asked, pulling on the second of my still-wet gloves as I walked into the break room.

The room was good-sized, almost square, with plenty of space for two long tables down the middle with a decent aisle between them. A counter, dominated by a trio of industrial-sized coffee makers, ran along the far wall, a row of vending machines filled the wall nearest me. In the center of the wall opposite me, a set of double doors, currently closed, led back into the warehouse.

I noted the layout in a glance, and dismissed it as quickly. The detail that mattered was that the room was empty.

There was no sign of Kaitlyn.

And now that I looked more closely, I realized that the two steps I'd taken from the doorway were the only footprints in the room. Even the many large footprints, presumably from the firefighters and police, had stopped in the door, their owners not bothering to enter once they saw the room was unoccupied.

I turned around and retraced my steps, following my footprints in the soot and ash on the floor back across the cubicle space toward Mindy's desk.

Kaitlyn's small footprints stood out among the firefighter's heavy-tread prints, showing where the girl had stepped into her mother's cubicle, stopped, and turned around. But instead of heading toward the break room, a second set of prints joined hers.

Boot prints.

From cowboy boots.

Dragging the sneaker-prints…

I raced past the few cubicles toward the front of the building, bursting through the front door just in time to see a dark blue Camry – the one I'd seen at the end of the warehouse, I was sure – tearing out of the small parking lot, Renee at the wheel, and a terrified Kaitlyn in the seat beside her.

Chapter 18

I dashed across the lot to my car.

I was backing out when the blue Camry passed right behind me, heading in the opposite direction. I followed her, seeing the reason for her change of direction in my rear-view. A pair of semis – one backing up to a loading dock, the other waiting to leave - blocked the way. It wouldn't take them long to clear the path, but nothing about Renee suggested she was patient woman.

And with a kidnapped teenager in her car, she couldn't afford to wait around.

I sped after her, my black Altima easily keeping pace with the Camry. In point of fact, the cars were almost too well matched, running over the pavement toward the stacks like a pair of horses let out of the barn. Whether or not I caught up with Renee and got Kaitlyn away from her would depend more on my driving than on the car.

I didn't know if I was up to the challenge – but I was damn well going to do my best.

The gash on my left forearm was a dull throb, the strips of cloth I'd wound around it keeping it as well supported as possible. I hadn't seen evidence of any new bleeding, though the wine-red color of the jacket hid most of the blood anyway.

Driving with the slice across my shoulder, though, was agony. I felt every bump like a new cut, and it was all I could do not to scream in pain as I turned the steering wheel this way and that. My right hand was growing weak, and the wheel often slid through my hand whether I wanted it to or not, forcing me to rely on my left hand as I followed Renee into the stacks.

Renee turned down a row bordered on either side with reefers, the stacked white boxes a grim reminder of the container girls she'd sent to their awful fate a short time before.

I followed, twisting the wheel to dodge an oncoming semi, just slipping between the truck and the container stack.

Up ahead, Renee took a sharp right.

I stomped on the gas, skidding as I turned to follow her, catching sight of her just as she skidded into her own next turn, now entering the colorful container canyons, long, wide rows bordered with the multi-color boxes rising in walls on either side.

We wound around through the stacks, dodging semis, who blew their horns at us in annoyance. Once I thought a truck was going to pull into Renee's path, but she was better at playing chicken than he was, and barreled forward. The semi turned aside at the last possible moment, forcing me to swerve as it headed directly at me.

After her last turn, I understood where she was headed.

Instead of the low cement wall at the end of each row we'd been on to this point, a thousand feet ahead of us was a gate. Beyond lay a warehouse, and visible just past the building a street, with traffic running in each direction.

Renee sped up.

I followed suit. Thirty, forty, fifty miles per hour, our speed building as we chewed up the distance of three football fields, racing down the open, empty row toward what I could now see was a closed and locked chain link gate.

She was planning to ram it, break through, and disappear in the traffic.

I closed the distance between us, not crazy about the possible ramifications of an impact, but intending to tap her rear bumper anyway.

I couldn't let her get away with Kaitlyn.

I hoped the kid had buckled her seat belt.

I couldn't have been more than a foot or two behind the Camry when it hit the gate. The heavy chain holding the padlock stretched and snapped, the fence warping and flying off to either side as first Renee and then my own car blew through the opening.

Renee's car went into a wild half-spin carrying her toward the end of the warehouse. I fought my own steering wheel, turning in the opposite direction to avoid her, repeatedly tapping at the brakes to control my own spin.

I came to a stop twenty feet to the left of the gate, my rear bumper kissing the cement wall that separated the lot I was in from the container yard.

Renee's Camry – which probably Richardson's now that I thought about it, commandeered after she discovered the gray van's flat tire – hadn't made it to the building. It had bumped up over a curb onto the grass near the corner of the building, and come to a stop with the driver's side rear door up against a medium-sized tree. As I forced myself out of my own car and half-staggered, half-ran toward them, I could see the puffy white pillows of the airbags.

Inside the car, no one moved.

I grabbed the Glock from my pocket, racking it as I ran, my right hand barely strong enough to hold it.

From down the length of the warehouse, people were shouting, running toward us.

When I got to the car, I yanked Kaitlyn's door open, stooping to catch her as she flipped the latch on her seatbelt and tumbled out into my arms.

When I looked up, Renee was staring me, her pistol low on her lap, the muzzle just visible beneath the airbag.

"Two can play that game," I said, a slight tilt of my head indicating my own gun, which was pointing at her and half-hidden by Kaitlyn's airbag. "I wonder which of us will be faster on the trigger."

At this range, neither of us would miss.

"It would be interesting to find out," Renee said. The footsteps were getting closer. "But perhaps we should save it for another day? When we don't have an audience?"

"The girl comes with me," I said.

Renee shrugged. "So you saved one girl. We do these runs all the time, there are always more girls." She lowered her gun, pushed the airbag out of the way.

Kaitlyn stood. "Go to the car," I told her, gesturing toward my Altima.

She glanced from one gun to the other and her already pale face drained what little color it held, but with a little nod did as she'd been told, taking a few shaky steps before running to the car and practically diving into it.

The first of the warehouse workers had nearly reached us. Renee shifted the car into gear, and I took advantage of her attention being elsewhere to force myself to my feet.

I closed the car door, keeping the Glock low, but ready.

I didn't trust Renee for one minute.

She pulled away from the tree, the scraping of wood on metal doing at least as much damage to the car as it to the tree, and pulled around, forcing the warehouse workers to jump back out of her way.

As she circled around, Renee put down her window.

"I'll be seeing you," she called out. Then, with a little wave, she drove away.

"Not if I see you first," I muttered. I pocketed the Glock and walked over to the Altima, letting the long, dark – and now very messy – hair hang down around my face, and ignoring the looks and questions from the warehouse workers who had gathered.

They all had the good sense to stay back.

"Are you okay?" Kaitlyn asked when I got in the car.

"I've been better," I said. "Let's get out of here."

♦

"How do you know my mom?" Kaitlyn asked as we drove back to her house.

We'd stopped at a drive-thru restaurant, and I'd sent her inside with instructions to get us milkshakes, fries, and a bunch of napkins. I needed a hit of carbs and sugar if I was going to get past the shakes that were rapidly overtaking me, and I'd left the rest of the mildewy t-shirts in the bathroom sink back at Raeburn.

My shoulder was bleeding again.

"I did some work for her boss," I said as I stuffed napkins around the blood-soaked padding. It's easiest to remember a lie when there's some truth in it.

"Mom said he was creepy," Kaitlyn said, munching on a fry. "She didn't like him very much."

"Neither did I," I said. "I didn't work for him long. But that was where I met your mom. She was a good person. She cared about you and your brother."

Kaitlyn was quiet. She sat there, sipping at her milkshake while I finished packing my shoulder, and I was glad to give her the time. This had probably been the worst day of her life, and other than not letting her be sold into the sex trade, there just wasn't much I could do to help her deal with everything she'd seen and heard.

We were on the expressway, crossing the second of the three rivers, before she spoke again.

"You look a little like her."

"Yeah, a few people have said that," I replied.

"Why did she call you?"

"She'd learned some things about her boss that worried her. And when she figured out more – what he was really doing – she was afraid."

"Why didn't she call the police?"

"She was going to – maybe she did, just not soon enough. I don't know."

Kaitlyn fell quiet again, and neither of us spoke until after we crossed the third bridge.

"I know you live in West Ashley," I said. "But I don't know the way. Where am I taking you?"

When she didn't answer, I glanced over. The tears she'd held back all this time had finally welled up, spilling down her cheeks. She scrubbed at her face with the back of her hand.

"Hey, hey," I said, reaching out and patting her on the leg. I was at a loss here, driving nowhere with a distressed teen. I tried to think what Bonnie would do in this situation, but with my bad shoulder, hugging wasn't an option, not that I could hug her while I was driving anyway.

I pulled off the road and into a shopping center parking lot at the first opportunity, and just let her cry, stroking her hair awkwardly. After a few minutes, I looked in the bag of fries and found a couple of napkins that weren't too greasy.

"Here," I said. "These are the last two. They're probably salty, so keep them away from your eyes."

Kaitlyn laughed weakly, and took the napkins. "You don't have kids, do you?" she asked, wiping her face.

"No. Why?"

"I don't know. You just seem like you're more used to talking to other adults than to kids."

"That's true," I said. "You okay now?"

"I suppose," she said. "Can you take me to my dad's house? I can tell you the way."

"I can do that."

She gave me directions toward the eastern part of the peninsula, and we were able to make the trip with only a few missed turns. But when she pointed out the house up ahead of us in the middle of the block, lights blazing even though it was barely after six o'clock, I drove past it, then turned the corner.

"Are you okay to walk from here?" I asked. It was a neighborhood of neat, tidy houses with well-tended yards that stopped just shy of being manicured. I could see her house from where we sat – and the unmarked police car parked in front of it.

Kaitlyn frowned. "Yes, but why? Are you not coming to the house with me?"

I glanced down at my shoulder and then back at her. "Look at me, Kaitlyn. Your family doesn't want someone who looks a little like your mom to show up at their door, covered in blood. They want to see you, home, safe and well."

"Where will you go?" she asked.

"I'll go to a hospital, get put back together." I reached out and squeezed her hand. "I'll wait until I see you get to your house before I leave."

Abruptly, she twisted in her seat and threw her arms around me, careful to avoid my shoulder. "I won't see you again, will I?" she asked, her voice muffled by my coat.

"Probably not," I said, patting her awkwardly on her shoulder with my left hand. "You'll be just fine. You were so brave, Kaitlyn. Your mother would have been very proud of you."

"Thank you," she said, drawing away. "For helping my mom. For saving me."

"It's what I do," I said.

Most of the time that would have been a lie. Today, it was actually the truth.

Chapter 19

I'll admit, when Kaitlyn's father ran out of the house and met his daughter halfway up the sidewalk, wrapping her in a bear hug that lifted her feet off the ground, I got a little teary-eyed.

Or maybe it was just the pain in my shoulder finally getting to me, now that I didn't have anything else to focus on.

Either way, it was time to go. I accelerated slowly, letting the car roll forward slowly until it was beyond view of Kaitlyn's house, then pulled away from the curb and drove away.

I'd told Kaitlyn that I was going to a hospital. And I probably needed to. But with everything that had happened at Raeburn, I knew the police would be watching the hospitals for anyone coming in with unexplained injuries.

So no hospitals.

In my current condition, I couldn't go back to my hotel, either. Or anyplace public. The medical attention I needed wasn't going to come from a conventional source.

That left me with only one option.

I retraced the route out of the neighborhood and pulled off the road at the first large shopping plaza parking lot I came to. Large lots are good, because you can park far enough away from prying eyes that nobody notices the fact that you're sitting in your car, covered in blood.

With a great deal of difficulty, and a near nausea-inducing level of pain, I succeeded in retrieving the plastic bag containing my cell phone from its hiding place under the passenger seat. I sat there with it on my lap for what might have been several minutes before the rumble of a passing motorcycle jolted me back to alertness.

This was not the time to relax. But at least the nausea had passed.

I put the battery in my phone, powered it up, and made the call.

"Hey, you," Ian said, the unmistakable grunts and shouts of the gym rats sparring in the background confirming that he was at the gym. "I thought you were out of town."

His voice was warm, welcome. I hated making him worry, but I didn't have a choice.

"I am. I'm in Charleston."

"What's wrong—"

"I need a medic," I said, not letting him finish the question.

He was instantly the Special Forces soldier turned freelance 'fixer,' gathering information, assessing the situation. "Charleston. Okay. What kind of injury?"

"Knife wound. Shoulder."

"How bad?"

"Bad."

"Hold on." The gym sounds were replaced with the tapping of a keyboard as Ian went into his office, closed the door, and went to work on his computer.

Injuries happen in our line of work. And just as there are sources on the dark web for picking up illicit contracts, there are also people who provide support services for contractors who get hurt.

That included the medics. A dark web variation on *Doctors Without Borders*, the medics specialized in patching up covert operatives in private facilities well out of the public eye. If I'd had access to my own computer, I could have looked for a local medic myself.

"Do you have a burner?" Ian asked.

"Yes." I'd forgotten about the burner phone in my pocket – the phone I should have used for this call. I pulled it out and gave Ian the number.

"Sending you the contact." A moment later, the burner phone buzzed quietly in my hand.

"Thank you," I said.

"Do you need me to come down?" he asked, his voice heavy with concern.

"I'll be okay," I told him. "Kyle will be here tomorrow."

"I see." I could almost feel his jaw clench.

"Ian—" I began.

"Call the medic. Get yourself put back together. We'll talk later."

"Dammit, Ian—"

"This isn't the time, Meg." His voice softened, "Call the medic."

The line went dead.

I called the medic.

♦

The phone rang, five, six, seven times. I was about to hang up when a man answered, "Hello?"

"I need a medic," I said, knowing that if I'd reached the right person, he would recognize the phrase as the request for covert, confidential services that it was.

"Of course," he said. "For yourself or a friend?" His tone was friendly, professional, with a hint of Southern drawl.

"Myself," I said. "Knife wound, right shoulder, heavy bleeding."

"Where are you?"

"I'm not sure. Somewhere in West Ashley. Not far from the bridge to downtown."

"Are you mobile?"

"For the moment."

"What is your blood type?"

"A positive."

"All right. I am going to text you an address. Rush hour's winding down, so it shouldn't take much more than twenty minutes to get there. I'll meet you. What are you driving?"

"Altima. Black."

"When you arrive, come to the back of the building and pull into the garage – I'll leave it open for thirty minutes. If you are delayed by more than ten minutes for any reason, call me and I will come to you."

"Open garage around back. Call if delayed. Okay."

The burner phone had a rudimentary GPS app on it. I entered the address, turned on the speaker, and began driving. I hadn't thought to bring a charging cord, and now hoped that the phone's remaining forty percent battery power wouldn't fail me.

It failed me.

When I left the parking lot, the GPS had indicated that I was twenty-three minutes from my destination. I'd followed the app's instructions like a drunk person, muttering back at it when it revised a route and mocking its mechanical monotone.

Twenty-five minutes and several route recalculations later – mostly due to the mechanical voice informing me of the need to turn as I was passing the indicated street – the phone beeped a low-battery warning.

"No, no, no," I moaned. I had no idea where I was, the GPS said I was still seven minutes from my destination, and I didn't even have enough juice left to call the medic back.

I pulled over, grabbed the phone from the cup-holder, and swiped at the screen, trying to memorize the remaining few turns and street names. I'm normally pretty good at that sort of thing, but the blood loss was taking its toll on my ability to think clearly.

"*My* phone has a *real* battery, you cheap piece of…" I left the sentence hanging as I remembered that my phone – my actual, personal phone – was sitting right there, where it had slid into the crevice at the back of the passenger seat.

I lunged for it, the sharp, sudden pain in my shoulder reminding me just how badly I'd been cut – and of the fact that I'd been driving almost exclusively left-handed. My hand was weak, my arm numb from the elbow to just below my ear.

That was not good.

At least the fingers of my right hand still worked. I entered the medic's address in my phone's GPS app, then shut down everything on the burner phone I didn't need. I left the phone powered on, in case the medic called me back, but I didn't know how much longer the battery would last.

It occurred to me as I pulled back into traffic that the low battery warning might have saved my life. I'd been driving around in a blur for I didn't know how long; how I'd avoided an accident I had no idea. Now I was awake and alert, in much the same way a drowsy driver drifting off the side of the highway is jolted back to consciousness when their tires hit the rumble strip at the edge of the shoulder.

The kinder, friendlier voice of my own GPS directed me to the medic's address with no additional drama.

I thought I'd taken another wrong turn when it directed me into the parking lot of a large, old-fashioned church, but when I pulled around to the more modern addition at the back of the building, I saw an open garage door.

I pulled into the garage, shut off the engine, and leaned my head against the headrest. I was peripherally aware of the groan of the garage door closing behind me, and then someone was tapping on my window.

I touched the window control.

An older man, his curly, brown hair liberally sprinkled with gray, looked down at me from behind dark glasses much like the Mindy glasses I only then remembered I was still wearing. He was dressed in black, with a priest's collar at his throat.

"I'm Father Leonard," he said. "I'm the medic. Come, let's get you sorted out."

He wasn't what I'd expected – then again, I hadn't known what to expect – but I was in no position to argue.

I did as he directed, and put myself into the care of the man of God.

♦

Things got hazy after that.

Father Leonard went through the standard list of questions doctors always asked – allergies, any other medications, was I pregnant. The questions blurred together in my mind. I only knew that they were easy questions that all had the same answer: No.

It was a good thing, too, because I don't think I could have answered anything complicated at that point.

The next thing I knew, he was wrapping a bandage around my left forearm. I didn't remember him unwinding the fabric strips binding my jacket to my arm, and had only a vague recollection of him helping me out of my jacket.

I turned my head – slowly, because even small movements left me dizzy – and saw the clean, white bandages covering my right shoulder, only partially hidden by a light cotton hospital gown. I was laying on a hospital bed, the head elevated slightly, a colorful quilt covering me, intravenous lines snaking over the bed rail and feeding into the back of my right hand.

"Thirsty," I croaked.

Father Leonard glanced up, then leaned over and grabbed a short water bottle fitted with a bent straw from the supply cart beside him. He held it out to me, giving a little shake of his head when he realized I couldn't hold it for myself, then held the straw to my mouth.

I sipped at it gratefully, nodding when I was finished.

He set the bottle on the cart and went back to work wrapping my arm with gauze tape.

"They teach you to do this in priest school?" I asked, my voice coming out in a hoarse whisper.

"Med school, actually."

"Why the career change?"

"I was in Afghanistan…" his voice trailed off.

"I'm sorry. It's none of my business," I said. "I shouldn't have asked."

"Hmm? No. It's okay," he said, reaching for a pair of long, narrow scissors. He cut the tape, and tucked the end under a lower layer of gauze, talking as he moved my arm into a more comfortable position at my side. "I was there as a chaplain, which meant I spent a lot of time in medical facilities, saw a lot of injured soldiers. Assisting with minor medical tasks was another way to serve. When I came home, I enrolled in med school."

"Makes sense."

"I thought so." He moved around to the other side of the bed and adjusted the drip on the half-full bag of mostly-clear liquid near my shoulder. "Are you expected anywhere?"

"Why?"

"So I know when to wake you up, if you don't wake up in time on your own."

That seemed fair. "Airport, ten a.m."

He frowned, shook his head. "I wouldn't recommend flying – or any travel – for at least a few days, if you can avoid it."

"I'll keep that in mind," I said. I nodded toward the bag he was fiddling with. "What's that?" I asked, my eyes suddenly heavy.

"This one's saline solution." He nodded to a second line, connected to another bag I had to twist my head to see. "That one's blood. You lost a fair amount. Wrapping and packing the cuts the way you did probably helped keep you from losing more, but it's a good thing you got here as quickly as you did."

"Would have… come sooner, but…" I began.

I blinked, feeling myself slipping away, and briefly wondered what he'd added to the saline solution.

"…had to take the girl home." I finished.

I was talking to empty air. I looked around, confused. Halfway through my sentence, Father Leonard had turned the lights down low, left the room, leaving the door open. The light in the hallway was only a little brighter, but when I tried to sit up, my body refused to cooperate, and I fell back against the pillows.

I wasn't sure how many times I surfaced then sank back into oblivion through the night. One of the times my eyes fluttered briefly open, I thought I saw Ian at the side of the bed, changing the saline bag.

"You came anyway," I whispered.

Ian turned, his close-cropped hair lengthening and graying, his facial features blurring so that all that I could make out were the dark rectangles of his glasses. A white line ran around his throat, contrasting with his black shirt.

"Why are you wearing a collar?" I murmured.

"Shh," he said, passing his hand over my eyes. "Rest now. Talk later."

Chapter 20

The next thing I knew, the sun was peeking in between strips in the mini-blinds covering a window I hadn't even noticed the room having the night before.

Father Leonard was sitting in an easy chair in the corner near the door, reading a book. A pole lamp glowed in the corner behind the chair, and an end table beside it, with a mug of coffee next to a small stack of books, suggested that this was a place he frequented often.

He sat there so quietly, I wasn't entirely sure if he was actually awake until he reached up and turned the page.

"How long have I been out?" I asked.

He looked up, smiled. "You got here a little before seven last night, it's about eight-thirty a.m. now," he said, marking his page with a slip of paper and setting the book on the table. "You've been asleep most of that time."

I glanced at the intravenous line, then back at him. "That wasn't just saline. You put something in it."

"I did," he said, his tone unapologetic. "A broad-spectrum antibiotic, and something very mild to help you sleep. Your body needed the rest to help it recover."

"You should have asked."

"You weren't in any condition for a consultation," he said. He stood and came over, checked my pulse, temperature, blood pressure. He didn't say anything, but seemed satisfied with the results.

"I used local anesthetics around your injuries for the pain," he said, handing me a new water bottle. "They'll have worn off, I trust?"

"Yes," I said. "I feel like I got run over." I drank some of the water. "You do anything else while I was out?"

"I gave you a tetanus shot."

I shrugged, then winced when my shoulder protested the movement. "I was probably due," I said. "I don't remember the last one."

"Most people don't."

"Not to sound ungrateful, but how long before I can leave?"

"Why is that always the first questions people ask?" he said, the smile accompanying the rhetorical question crinkling his eyes. "Let's try getting you on your feet first, see how far you can walk without falling down. You only made it about six feet last night."

I had a brief recollection of him catching me as I collapsed, easing me into a wheelchair. It had been close. But I was awake and alert now, and decided to focus on that instead.

My left arm, where the pallet had torn past me, was in surprisingly good shape, all things considered. I couldn't brace my full weight on it, but it was strong enough that I was able to lever myself to a sitting position without assistance.

"Are you okay?" Father Leonard asked.

"I've been better."

He shook his head. "You all have such high pain tolerances. You push yourselves too hard as a result."

"It's part of the job," I said, sliding off the high bed.

The pain in my right shoulder was tolerable as long as I didn't move my arm too much – a fact I discovered as I reached out to catch hold of the I.V. stand. I ground my teeth together, breathing my way through the wave of pain that washed over me.

Father Leonard just stood by the window, his arms folded across his chest, an amused expression on his face.

I didn't give him the satisfaction.

"Which way is the coffee?" I asked, taking a step forward.

◆

"You should know that the police are looking for someone matching your description," Father Leonard said.

I'd been up and ambulatory for about a half hour, had gotten cleaned up and dressed in fresh clothes. My own, blood-soaked clothes had been consigned to the furnace, and I was wearing a loose-fitting button-up shirt, faded jeans, and bulky sweater I found on the rack of donations for the homeless made by parishioners. There was nothing fashionable about either, but I could put them on without straining the stitches in either my upper arm or my shoulder, and the long sleeves covered the bandage on my arm. I was still wearing the dark wig and glasses, even though we both knew they were a lame disguise.

I said nothing, just sipped at my coffee.

"I just thought you would want to know," he continued.

I met his eyes over the rim of my cup and nodded slightly. We were sitting in the small kitchen in the older part of the church. The prescription-strength acetaminophen he'd given me was only barely kicking in, and though my stomach was grumbling at me, I wasn't ready for food yet.

I wasn't carrying a weapon, out of respect for being in the church. I'd left the guns in the cabinet where Father Leonard had put them the night before, in a paper bag with my other personal belongs, and donated the pair of cardboard-sheathed knives to the church's kitchen. But I had put my gloves back on and wiped my fingerprints off anything I thought I might have touched.

I looked across the table at him, sitting there so relaxed. "How can you be okay with this," I asked, "helping people who do what we do?"

"We all fill our roles," he said, setting down his mug, "and it's not mine to judge yours. I do what I can, help where I'm needed. And what I earn by helping you and your colleagues helps fund this facility."

"The church?" I frowned.

"No, the parishioners' donations support the church and keep the lights on," he said, smiling. "They're very generous. I'm talking about the clinic. We do good work here, helping people who don't have access to other resources. You only saw part of it."

"I wish I had time to see more," I said.

I genuinely meant it.

He'd sparked my curiosity, this doctor-priest who had found a way to cleanse the money that came to him, covered in blood.

♦

I left the guns behind. I couldn't travel with them, and wouldn't be lifting a gun for several days, much less firing one. So after making sure he'd neither cleaned them nor left his own fingerprints on them, I asked Father Leonard to quietly pass them on to the local authorities, if he could do so without bringing undue attention to himself.

Maybe it would do some good.

While I'd slept, the good Father had detailed my car, removing all traces of blood and fingerprints. He'd also filled the tank, and even charged both my phone and the burner. The man was good at his job.

In return, I'd left him with most of the cash I'd been carrying – a few hundred dollars, from Mindy's stash – and the emergency VISA gift card, which was loaded to its five hundred dollar maximum. I'd send a few more as a donation to his clinic after I got home. I suspected others whose lives he'd saved had done the same.

We may operate in morally gray areas, but we look out for our own as much as is possible for people who operate in the shadows.

The airport was only a short drive from the clinic. I removed the wig and glasses as I drove and stuffed them under my seat, then ran my fingers through my matted hair to get rid of the hat-head look.

I got to the airport's cell phone waiting lot about twenty minutes before Kyle's plane was scheduled to touch down – just enough time for the last thing on my to-do list.

I opened the note-taking app on my phone and found the shipping details for the truck taking the container girls west. Next, I opened the contacts app on my phone, and scrolled down to the entry for L. Brady, the FBI agent whose number the Researcher had given me.

On the list of things I never thought I'd do, deliberately contacting an FBI agent was probably near the top of the list.

First time for everything.

I pulled out the burner phone and dialed the number.

Brady picked up after three rings – during which I imagined him picking up the phone, staring at the unfamiliar number, and moving to a private area. It was Saturday morning. He might have been at home, at the gym, at the grocery store. Didn't matter. When he answered, he was all agent.

"Brady."

"Agent Brady," I said, pressing my free hand to my nose to alter the timbre of my voice. I had to assume that the call was being monitored, probably recorded for later analysis. No sense in making it too easy for them to identify me. "I have information for you about a trafficking operation in progress."

"I'm listening."

I messaged over the photos I'd taken of the reefer and its registration number.

"The refrigerated container in these photographs left the Port of Charleston about five o'clock yesterday afternoon, on a westbound semi headed for Kansas City," I told him. "It holds six Colombian girls, shipped here against their will."

"Where did you get this information?"

"Mindy Collier, of Raeburn Shipping, Charleston. She discovered the operation and reached out to me for assistance."

"Why didn't she take this to the police?"

"I didn't ask." And I didn't want to answer any more questions. "I also have partial details about the truck's destination, which I'll send you immediately following this call."

"What do you expect me to do?"

I stared at the phone for a moment before answering. "Perhaps I've called the wrong agency. I'm sorry for wasting your time. Good bye."

"No," he said. "Wait."

"Why? So you can track my location? I'm not the problem here, Agent Brady. The truck is scheduled to make delivery in a little over an hour, local time. I know it's not much notice, but if your people aren't there to meet it, the girls will be lost to the sex trade, and your chances of shutting down the operation will vanish with them. I'm sure neither of us wants that to happen."

"No, of course not."

"Good. I'll send you the details. If I see on the news that the girls have been recovered, I'll send you any other information that comes my way."

After a brief pause, I added, "If not, I won't bother you again."

I didn't wait for him to respond. I hung up, copied the truck's delivery information into a text message and sent it, then powered down the phone and removed the battery.

"That's all I can do for them, Mindy," I whispered, staring out the window at the cars passing by the waiting lot, on their way toward the airport. They blurred together, people going about their business, oblivious to the darker elements that hovered around the edges of society. People like Bouchard. Renee. Me.

Overhead, the sky was a bright, perfect blue, scattered clouds drifting overhead like shredded puffs of cotton. An airplane coming in for a landing grew from a dark, silent speck to a full-throated roar, and I wondered if it was Kyle's. The Charleston airport wasn't large or particularly busy, and the timing was right.

I triggered the button to pop the trunk, then took the wig and glasses to the back and dropped them into the paper bag containing Bouchard's and Wingtips' phones – powered off, their batteries removed. I added the pieces of my own burner phone to the bag, along with my fake driver's license. Then I folded the bag down tight and stuffed it into the spare tire compartment.

When I closed and locked the trunk, I also locked away most of my concerns about the container girls, and turned my thoughts to a more immediate problem:

How was I going to explain my injuries to Kyle?

Chapter 21

I took the easy way out – I blamed it on a bicycle.

There were enough cyclists cruising the streets that it was a believable enough story. Kyle had commented on them as we drove to the hotel, making them an obvious choice.

I didn't mention it at first – when I first picked him up at the curb, there was only time for a brief kiss in greeting before we had to drive out of the pickup zone. And driving back to the hotel wasn't particularly taxing.

It wasn't like I was chasing anyone at the moment.

So it wasn't until we reached the hotel and Kyle hugged me that I backed off with an involuntary gasp of pain.

"It was my own fault," I said, opening my shirt enough to reveal the wide elastic sports wrap Father Leonard had wound around my upper arm, then looped across my chest and around my back to hold the bandage in place and stabilize my arm and shoulder. "I looked the wrong way down a one-way street, and stepped right out in front of a couple of cyclists. It could have been much worse, really."

That much, at least, was true.

"I'd hate to see what 'much worse' looks like," Kyle said.

"Concussion, broken bones, landing in the street and being hit by a car," I said, ticking off a few possibilities. I didn't mention nearly bleeding to death.

There was no need to get too close to the truth.

"I see you've thought this through," Kyle said. He stepped closer, slipped an arm around my waist, brushed his fingers through my hair. "I'm sorry I wasn't there to help."

If you'd been there, you'd be dead.

"There's nothing to be sorry for," I said, leaning my head against his shoulder.

We stood there together near the open balcony, just enjoying each other's company, dancing to the faint strains of a street performer playing a saxophone, the light, bluesy tune coming from somewhere just out of sight.

Kyle was the perfect complement to the legitimate side of my life. Educated, successful, and not at all pretentious about it. And about as easy on the eye as a man could be.

But I didn't like thinking about him close to the shadows.

It was the shadows – and the secrets I kept hidden there – that kept me from fully relaxing into the relationship.

The song ended, the music changing key and shifting into something more lively as the audience that had gathered around the street performer applauded.

"Look, if you're not feeling up to it—"

"I've got good drugs," I said, laughing. In addition to a full week's supply of pain medication, Father Leonard had given me enough of the prescription-strength acetaminophen to last three or four days – and instructions to not overdo them – as well as a couple of stronger pills in case I needed them to help me sleep. Pain-wise, I was set.

I continued. "There's a little beach town out there somewhere," I said, pointing over the balcony and toward the water. "The concierge says it's only about a half-hour's drive. I thought maybe we'd go find it, get away from the city for the day."

I needed to get away from the city. Needed to not watch the clock, not constantly surf the web like a news junkie, not wait to see if Brady had marshalled the FBI to rescue the container girls.

It wasn't that I didn't trust him to do his job.

I just wasn't sure I trusted him to do mine.

♦

We headed out to Foley Island. We wandered the quaint tourist traps and laughed over beach-town souvenirs and ice cream cones. We bought shirts printed with palm trees and dolphins, flip-flop sandals and shorts, and big floppy hats, then went down to the beach, where we spent the afternoon taking photos of the lighthouse and oddly-shaped driftwood and making small castles in the wet sand.

When we got hungry, we headed back into town and tried to remember which of the many restaurants we'd seen earlier had looked like a good choice at the time. We weren't sure if the one we finally ended up at was the same one, but the fries were perfectly golden and the fish was fresh and prepared Southern-style, rolled in a corn meal breading, then fried quickly in boiling oil – or so the server told us. However they did it, the crust was crispy and the flesh flaky and delicious and hot enough we had to chase it with vast quantities of ice cold sweet tea.

It was after nine when we finally got back to Charleston, tired but happy, cares all but forgotten. My left arm had barely bothered me, and the pain meds had kept my shoulder from ruining the day.

Rather than go straight back to our room, we wandered into town, following the route I'd taken that first morning through the charming alleys in the historic district. Kyle was as fascinated by them as I was – clean, paved with brick or cobbles, small sconces set high on the walls providing just the right amount of soft light. They were nothing like the alleys we were familiar with back in Philadelphia.

We had just passed an alcove in one alleyway, a shadowed passage with a set of dimly lit stairs that we were curious about but decided not to follow, when we heard the voice behind us.

"You got a few bucks?"

We turned. A man stood at the opening to the alcove – he must have just come down the stairs, because we hadn't seen anyone there before. He was wearing jeans and a dark, hooded sweatshirt, and his hair was pulled back into a short, stubby knot at the back of his head.

He held his hand out and asked again. "You got a few bucks? I could really use a few bucks."

"I'm sorry," Kyle said. "I can't help you."

"What about her?" the beggar said, eyeing me. He took a step forward. "Hey, lady, you got something for me, don'cha?"

Kyle took a half-step toward the beggar, putting himself between us – a sweet, but unnecessary gesture that was just going to anger the man.

I reached out, pressed my fingertips to Kyle's arm. "Don't," I said, my voice barely even a whisper. I'd seen a movement in the shadows behind the beggar.

He wasn't alone.

"Come on," I whispered, tugging at Kyle's arm.

Kyle didn't respond, didn't react. He just stood there, staring the beggar down as though he thought that was going to intimidate him into slinking back into the shadows.

I know about things that live in the shadows. We should never have stopped walking.

The beggar leapt toward Kyle, covering the short distance between them more quickly than might have seemed possible. Kyle stepped forward, into the fight, and then the two connected, fists flying as they punched and jabbed and dodged and whirled in the narrow confines of the alley.

If I hadn't caught a glimpse of the second beggar, I might have been caught unawares – which I suspected was part of their plan. But I had seen him, so when he burst out of the alcove toward me, I was prepared.

He likely expected me to jump back, startled and afraid. Instead, I moved forward, my left hand darting at his throat, fingers pressed tightly together in a flat, locked position.

A finger-strike is damaging enough without nails. I keep my nails trimmed, but they do extend slightly beyond my fingertips – just enough for my finger-strike to the base of the second beggar's throat to leave him gasping for breath. He staggered back, choking, almost tripping over the third man who I hadn't seen coming.

"Oh, give me a break," I muttered.

Kyle was still fighting with the first beggar, who was doing a great job of staying just out of reach, and leading him farther away from me.

In the meantime, the third beggar shoved his still-choking companion back into the shadows of the alcove, then turned on me, a knife glittering in his hand.

I was so done with knives.

I stepped back, doing my own bit of leading my attacker. I wanted him focused on me, and nowhere near Kyle with that blade. He followed, waving the knife threateningly an almost maniacal grin spreading across his face as he sensed what he thought was weakness on the part of his prey.

With no gun, an injured arm that ached slightly from the impact of the finger-strike, and nowhere to run, the beggar should have had an easy time overpowering me. But my hands weren't my only weapons. There was a good chance what I was planning wouldn't work, and only a fair chance it would, but I'd been trained to use the weapons at my disposal, and my choices were limited.

I kept my right arm pressed close to my body, minimizing my shoulder's movement while I danced back, out of range of the blade. Then, when we were far enough from Kyle and the first beggar, I decided it was safe to go on the offensive.

The knife-wielder's attack had a clear pattern. Each time he stepped forward, he swept the blade toward me in a large arc that crossed his body from right to left. He drew his arm back to the right when he stepped back.

He was at his most vulnerable at the top of the arc, the point when he was still leaning slightly forward, with the blade close to his left shoulder.

He stepped forward.

This time I didn't move back. Instead, I stepped forward, too, leading with my left foot, then raised my right foot, swinging it in a roundhouse kick to his face.

The impact spun him around, his body following his face as he crashed into the alley wall.

At that same moment, Kyle landed a solid punch to the first beggar's chin, sending him onto his butt on the alley's brick paving.

It had all happened in little more than two minutes. Less than the time it would take to listen to a song on the radio. I wondered which of the crazy metal songs the gym rats favored they would have chosen as the soundtrack.

Kyle turned to me, satisfaction turning to shock as he took in the scene that had played out behind his back. The second beggar was still choking in the alcove, while the third beggar had slid to the ground, and was laying there, face pressed to the bricks.

He looked at the beggars, then back at me.

"You?" he said.

I glanced around. "You see anyone else?"

"Wow." Kyle looked at me, his face running through several expressions, from amazement to curiosity to admiration. "I know you go to the gym all the time, but I never thought..." his voice trailed off. Then he grinned. "Okay, I've gotta say it. That's totally hot."

I rolled my eyes.

He reached into his pocket for his cell phone.

"No," I said, stepping forward and covering the phone with my hand. "Leave them. Let's just get out of here."

"We've got to report them, Meg."

"Do you really want to spend the night with the police? That doesn't sound like my idea of a fun way to end the day."

He looked at the three beggars, then back at me. "They'll just do this again," he said.

"Not tonight, they won't," I said. I took a step away from him, then held out my hand. "Are you coming?"

Chapter 22

We walked back to the hotel in silence, the lighthearted mood of the day shattered. We didn't argue – Kyle wasn't the arguing sort – but frustration and annoyance rolled off him in almost palpable waves, like an unseen fog that filled the air.

There was nothing I could do, nothing I could say. Even if I'd truly only been a visiting tourist, reporting the attempted mugging to the police was not an option. There was too much I couldn't explain. Like how I'd defended myself, when I was clearly sporting injuries that should have made me an easy target. How I'd come by those injuries in the first place and who had treated them.

And if the investigating officer was even the least bit on the ball, there would be other questions. Harder questions.

Where I'd been over the past few days, when an unknown woman – with different hair color and style, true, but we all know that's easy enough to change – took down several people in a local warehouse. Possibly set the warehouse on fire, killing someone else in the blaze. Might have had something to do with the accidental death of a warehouse employee a few days before, and the recovery of that same employee's teenage daughter who had been abducted by one of the men who had later been found dead in the aforementioned warehouse.

Had been seen driving the same make, model, and color car as the one I'd rented.

Just like in a knife fight, the best way not to get cut was not to engage, to put as much distance between yourself and your attacker as possible. I'd already been cut this week. It wasn't happening again.

As much as Kyle meant to me, I couldn't explain to him why talking to the police for any reason was not something I could do. Not now. Not ever.

Instead, I walked alongside him, pulling my sweater tighter around me like a shroud of secrets and shadows, insulating myself from his disapproval.

♦

Sleep did not come easily. I'd avoided taking the stronger pill Father Leonard had given me to help me sleep, preferring the acetaminophen tablets to the opioid. I'd thought the long day would have worn me out, but while I was emotionally tired, I wasn't physically sleepy.

I cleaned and awkwardly re-bandaged my wounds, trying to figure out what I could say to Kyle to possibly salvage the evening. But by the time I came out of the bathroom, he had already gone to bed.

So I lay there, listening to him breathe. We were on opposite sides of the big bed, our backs to each other, the lighthearted closeness of the day having fallen victim to the mugging.

I hadn't realized I'd drifted off until I was already in the dream.

"She saved me," Kaitlyn said. "You can trust her."

She was sitting on a filthy blanket on the floor of the reefer, surrounded by the six container girls. She reached out to them, the blood from my shoulder crusted under her fingernails and leaving streaks of red on their greasy hair as she pushed it from their eyes, revealing their tear-stained faces.

Maggie walked into the scene, then, carrying a plastic grocery bag, and began distributing packets of snacks and water bottles – packets I'd left with Father Leonard. But she gave out far more than the handful of packets

I'd put together, moving through the ever-deepening container, putting packets into hands that reached out to her from the dark.

"She saved me," Maggie said, echoing Kaitlyn's words. "You can trust her."

But when she turned and looked back at me across the sea of container girls, her hands now empty, her expression was one of rebuke.

I woke with a gasp.

I'd turned in my sleep, and was laying on my back. Kyle hadn't moved, and I focused on his slow, rhythmic breathing to help settle my racing heart.

I slid out of the bed, found my robe, and slipped quietly from the bedroom, closing the door separating it from the sitting room, then went to the desk and powered up my laptop.

I scanned every reputable news source I could think of and searched the internet using multiple variations on Kansas City, shipping container, and trafficking, but found no recent news, no suggestion that any girls had been recovered or arrests had been made.

"Damn you, Brady," I muttered.

While there was a small chance the news had been kept quiet pending further investigation – something I knew the authorities liked to do – I didn't know Brady and didn't trust him enough to give him the benefit of the doubt.

As far as I was concerned, I'd handed off the assignment, and he'd either botched the job or ignored it.

I closed the browser and paced around the sitting room, holding my robe closed against the light chill that emanated from the glass of the balcony doors when I paused to stare out across the harbor. At two a.m., fewer lights twinkled in the distance than had earlier in the evening, the shine of streetlights along the shores of the neighboring peninsulas outlining the harbor.

Other lights moved slowly across the darkness, ships either coming to port or heading out to sea. There were dolphins in those waters.

Sharks swam there, too.

I thought again of the container girls. How many groups had Bouchard smuggled into the country, selling them with no more thought than he would give to the sale of an imported car – or less, like for a car stereo?

Bouchard was gone. I didn't consider his death a suitable punishment, but if an afterlife existed, he answered to a higher power now.

On the other hand, there were others who were just as much at fault.

I returned to my laptop, all thoughts of sleep banished from my system. For the next two hours, I poured over Bouchard's spreadsheets and the information from Mindy's flash drive, correlating data, summarizing findings into a list of targets.

When I was satisfied with my work, I went to the dark web.

For the most part, those of us who frequent the illicit job listings site work alone, as solitary, anonymous contractors. It's just not the kind of job that lends itself to water-cooler chats and team bonding activities.

But when we need help, we have ways to reach out.

Just as Ian had located the medic through the dark web, contractors like me also had access to a private bulletin board, where we periodically posted calls for assistance jobs that were either too big or too geographically dispersed for a single contractor to complete on their own.

I went to this section of the board now. I listed the names of nine buyers, located in major cities across the eastern half of the country, and watched as the feeding frenzy of contractors raced to claim their prey.

The tenth name on my list – Renee, taking over for Haskell – I kept for myself.

♦

Share the load.

The following individuals, listed below, have engaged in child sex trafficking.

Double-tap execution within the next seventy-two hours is preferred; however, as long as the target is eliminated within this timeframe, you may use your own discretion and preference regarding the method of their death.

The account each used to purchase underage girls is provided. If you accept the contract, disposition of the funds from the associated account is up to you. As I have no control over these accounts, and do not know their current balances, I recommend you withdraw your fee immediately, using any method that safeguards your identity.

If it is within your power to locate any of the trafficked girls, and report their locations to the appropriate authorities, that would be greatly appreciated, but is not required as part of this contract.

Chapter 23

"That's going to leave a scar," Kyle said, running his finger near the row of neat stitches on my left forearm.

He'd awakened in a better mood than he'd been in the night before – but whether it was real or one that developed when he found me sleeping in the easy chair next to the fireplace in the suite's sitting room, wrapped in one of the spare blankets – I didn't know.

Nor did I care.

We hadn't talked about the mugging.

I had no regrets over not reporting it. If Kyle couldn't accept that, couldn't walk that close to my shadows, we weren't going to last anyway.

I did care about that.

I squeezed antibacterial ointment onto the cut, grimacing as I spread it over the stitches. It was healing well, and showing none of the signs of potential infection Father Leonard had warned me to watch out for, but it was still much more tender than I had patience for.

I wanted it to heal faster.

"Maybe I'll get a tattoo to cover it up," I said.

"A bit of bicycle chain?" Kyle teased, referring to the cover story I'd told him about the accident.

I shook my head, scrunching up my nose at the idea. "I don't want to commemorate it," I said as he unfolded a fresh gauze pad and spread it out over the cut. "Maybe a lizard."

"That would make Glau happy. And you could do a beach scene on your shoulder. A lighthouse, palm trees…"

"A shark in the water."

He laughed, but I couldn't tell if it was forced, or if the perceived strain was just my imagination.

It was all idle chatter anyway. The scars would fade, or I could cover them with makeup if I needed to. While I had nothing against well-drawn tattoos, in a profession that required me to be as invisible as possible, a tattoo would be noticeable. Recognizable. An identifying mark.

Anything but invisible.

I would never get a tattoo.

Dressing the wound on my shoulder was more complicated. The stitches had oozed and then dried during the night, and we had to soak the gauze pad to soften it enough to peel it away without pulling at the stitches.

"You fall on the derailleur?" Kyle asked, frowning as he studied the line of the cut, his logical mind trying to recreate the accident.

"I have no idea," I said. "Whatever I landed on, it was sharp, and the doctor said I was lucky it didn't go any deeper."

"Yeah," he was silent for a minute as he applied a thick line of ointment. I flinched when he pressed the gauze to it, and he apologized.

"Not your fault," I said forcing a smile. "It's not my favorite way to 'play doctor,' but it needs to be done."

"Meg—"

His warm breath on my neck sent a shiver down my back and goosebumps raced across skin. I was standing there in nothing but jeans and a bra, and suddenly felt unreasonably exposed.

"Let's finish this, okay?" I said.

I handed him the wide athletic bandage he'd unwound from around my torso a few minutes before. I'd rolled it up while he'd soaked the gauze from my shoulder, and now he reversed the process, running the elasticized fabric around the cut on my upper arm, then up over my shoulder and angling down over my chest to cover the diagonal cut that had nicked my collar bone.

Rather than moving around me to loop the bandage across my back and up under my arm on the other side, Kyle stepped closer, reaching around my body, and transferring the bandage from one hand to the other.

"I'm sorry about last night," he said, his voice so low I wouldn't have heard it if I hadn't been standing in his arms.

"It's okay," I said.

"I mean it. I was afraid that guy was going to hurt you," he said. He continued winding the bandage around me as he spoke, standing so close that I couldn't see his face. "And then you fought the other two on your own – and with your shoulder like this…" he trailed off.

"Kyle—"

"Let me finish," he said. He pulled the bandage snug and anchored it with a row of little clips that hooked into the fabric. Then he stepped back, leaned against the edge of the bathroom sink so we were closer in height, and took my hands in his.

"I was as impressed as hell with what you did – and equally confused about why you just wanted to walk away afterward." He met my eyes, his expression serious. "You've been attacked before, haven't you? And the police didn't do anything about it? That's why you didn't want to report it, isn't it?"

There was enough of the truth in what he'd guessed that I could answer honestly. "Yes," I said.

He nodded. "That's why you go to the gym. Why you teach the self-defense class."

He wasn't asking now, just putting pieces of the puzzle together. Trying to make sense of behaviors he'd observed over the past six months, but not understood.

"I get it," he said. "Or at least I think I get some of it, anyway. I'm not going to push you, but if you ever need to, *want* to talk about it, I'm here. I'll always be here for you."

"I'm pretty much past the 'talking about it' stage," I said with a shrug. "But thanks."

"You're a complicated woman," he said. "And utterly fascinating. Maybe you'll tell me how you managed to take out two thugs in the time it took me to bring down one?"

"Maybe," I said. I stepped closer to him and kissed him. "Or maybe I should keep that a secret – just in case I ever need to use the same techniques on you."

♦

By the time we packed our things, had brunch, and checked out of the hotel, there were only a couple of hours until we had to head to the airport. We'd both gotten seats on the same afternoon flight back to Philadelphia, and wanted to get to the airport early enough to see if we could change our seating assignments so we could sit together on the two-hour flight.

Not that it really mattered – after being up half the night, I was probably going to spend most of the flight sleeping anyway. But it would be a nice way to end the trip.

We were in luck – the businessman assigned to the seat next to mine agreed to swap places with Ian's place two rows forward, commenting on how he'd gotten the worse end of the deal. With that arranged, we settled into the hard plastic seats to wait for the attendant to call the flight.

Above us, a television monitor alternated between displaying on-screen announcements and the news, the volume just loud enough to hear, but low enough that you had to concentrate on it if you wanted to know what the announcer was saying.

Kyle was saying something about his meetings in Charlotte when the words "Kansas City" caught my ear. I held up a hand to Kyle, and looked up at the television.

The image displayed a white reefer, the door hanging open, indistinct shapes barely visible in the dark interior. In the foreground, a news reporter was talking to a man in a dark jacket. I'd missed most of the story, but the closed caption text at the bottom of the image told me everything I needed to know:

> *"...the six Colombian girls have been taken to a nearby medical facility. We have a number of people in custody in connection with the trafficking operation, and are pursuing all leads..."*

Brady had come through after all.

In the back of my mind, my younger self finally relaxed. For the time being, at least.

♦

I took the only empty parking space on the street, about six doors down from the rowhouse, and sat there for a few minutes chewing myself out for being such a chicken.

When I couldn't justify sitting there any more, I got out of the car and walked up to the rowhouse. And then I stood on the porch, dithering like a schoolgirl for several seconds before I finally got up the courage to knock.

The door opened almost instantly.

"I wondered how long you were going to stand there," Ian said.

He'd known I was there.

Of course he had. He'd probably spotted my car when I first turned onto the block. It wasn't that he was paranoid – I'd never known anyone less fearful, actually – but Ian was extremely security conscious and his situational awareness was dialed up even when he was otherwise totally relaxed.

Even after all the years I'd known him, all the times I'd visited his rowhouse, I still didn't know the full details of his security system.

"I just got back," I said.

"I can see that," he said. He leaned against the doorframe, a tall, muscular man in a snug white t-shirt, pale khakis, and bare feet, seemingly at ease on a warm, Sunday evening. But his arms, folded across his broad chest, expressed all the tension his Zen training usually helped him conceal.

He jutted his chin toward my shoulder. "Looks like you survived," he said. "How's the other guy?"

"Regretting his poor life choices," I said with a mild shrug. "And Kyle?"

There it was, the challenge I'd been waiting for, said so casually that someone who didn't know Ian wouldn't have even noticed the slight tightening of his jaw.

"Probably still fighting his way through traffic," I said. "I don't know."

We stood there for a long moment, neither of us sure what to expect from the other, and to be completely honest, probably not sure what we even wanted.

From inside the house, a timer began to beep.

"Up for a pizza?" Ian asked, straightening. "It's just coming out of the oven."

"You make it from scratch?"

"Only way."

I stepped closer. "I wouldn't miss it for the world."

Ian smiled, put his arm around my waist, and together we went into the house.

Chapter 24

The next morning, I sat at my desk, staring at a spreadsheet, my thoughts wandering far from the financial benefits of the possible merger I was reviewing.

Jessica had gone out to pick up some necessary office supplies, so the office was quiet, leaving me alone with my thoughts.

Two of the nine targets had already been marked as eliminated when I'd checked the dark web listing that morning. That left seven who would be dealt with over the next two days.

Not counting the names I'd reserved for myself.

I pulled open my lower desk drawer, and from a hanging file at the back retrieved a new burner phone – I usually keep two or three on-hand, just in case. I activated the phone, then dialed a familiar number.

"The soup was just right," I said when the gruff voice answered.

There was barely a pause before the Researcher replied. "Well, well, if it isn't Goldilocks. Glad to know it wasn't too hot."

"Exactly what I ordered," I said. Changing the subject, I continued. "I'm looking for a couple of friends."

"These friends have names?"

"Possibly. First is Haskell, from… I'm not sure, actually. I think there's a Chicago connection. May or may not still be active."

"And the second?"

"Renee. Might also be Chicago-based., but I doubt it. There's a tie of some sort to Haskell. May also have ties to St. Louis or Kansas City."

"You don't ask for much, do you?"

"Just let me know when you find them. Whatever it costs."

◆

The gash on my left arm from the falling pallet hadn't been deep, just messy, and was almost entirely healed by the middle of the following week. I picked out the ragged line of stitches while I was watching television, with Glau lounging on the floor, his head resting on one of my feet like a lumpy pillow.

My upper arm and shoulder took longer to heal.

I'd avoided any heavy lifting or extreme training that I thought might pull at either the visible stitches or the dissolving stitches Father Leonard had used deeper inside the wound to pull the severed flesh together. But as the days passed and my mobility increased – as the medic had said it would – I'd gradually begun mild strength and flexibility training.

Three weeks after Hendricks sank his knife into my upper arm and dragged it across my shoulder blade – conveniently dying before his blade reached my throat – I stood in front of my bathroom mirror, armed with cuticle scissors and a pair of tweezers.

My options were limited. I couldn't go to a doctor – they'd ask too many questions. I'd said nothing about the injury to either Jessica or Bonnie for the same reason, choosing lightweight clothing appropriate for the early summer weather, and that also hid my bandages.

Asking Kyle for help would have re-opened the argument about the muggers, as well as had him questioning why I didn't just go to a doctor.

In all honesty, the only person I thought seriously about calling was my friend, Deb, who actually was a nurse and could have had the stitches out before I'd finished making the request. But once again, I held off, holding her in reserve in case the wound got infected.

My priority was to keep my friends as far from my alternate life as possible.

And while Ian was fully aware of my injuries, he'd already reminded me about how dangerous our work was. I wasn't in the mood to have him to go into over-protective mode, like he sometimes did.

Which brought me back to my bathroom-turned-clinic.

I have no formal medical training, only what I've learned online and in an EMT prep class I took as part of my self-assigned continuing education curriculum. So, I try to err on the side of caution when it comes to anything even vaguely medical. I wiped down my hands, my tools, and my stitches with peroxide, and then got started.

Angling the scissors to clip the threads near the knots with my left hand was awkward, even more so with the need to locate the knots in the mirror image. Grasping the clipped threads with the tweezers and gently tugging them out was also backward, but much easier. I only missed one knot that I had to go back and pull from the opposite direction.

I followed up with more peroxide, then studied the injury in the mirror as I tested my shoulder. I had full, free range of motion, with no pain and no visible difference between the movement of my right shoulder and my left.

I'd been lucky. Luckier than I deserved, considering it had been my own carelessness that had gotten me cut in the first place.

I covered the tiny stitch-marks with a liberal slathering of antibiotic ointment, and a couple of wide gauze bandages to keep it all clean. I wasn't taking any chances. The Researcher had finally sent over full dossiers on both Haskell and Renee, and I needed to be in fighting form before I went hunting again.

♦

Ryan Haskell was dead.

Apparently, he'd led a moderately successful operation – working at the small-business level – and had been tolerated by the larger organized crime kingpins in the Chicago area. As his ambition grew, he moved south to St. Louis and established his own small empire there, extending from the banks of the Mississippi River across Missouri and Kansas and northward into Iowa. His recent death, and the upheaval that had caused, had made him easy enough for the Researcher to find. Since he was already out of the picture, I read his dossier with less interest than I might otherwise have.

Haskell's role in the trafficking ring had primarily been as an idea man and a distributor. Bouchard had credited him with the idea of using the reefers rather than transporting the girls in regular containers. Shipments had increased almost exponentially after that, with Bouchard handling the import side and Haskell's midwestern operation initially taking the lead on distribution – and a cut of the profits on the sale of the girls.

With a reliable supply, the other distributors had popped up like mushrooms.

But now that I'd had the other distributors in Bouchard's network eliminated, and the supply chain had been broken, former customers were looking for other suppliers.

Many had turned to the person who had inadvertently brought me into the picture in the first place – the person who killed Haskell, took over his operation, and been the other party on the phone call Mindy had overheard.

His not so devoted daughter, Renee Sullivan.

When Haskell went to St. Louis, Renee and her mother had moved to the opposite side of the state and settled in Kansas City. Raised by her mother – and using her mother's last name – Renee had followed in Haskell's footsteps with the all-too-obvious intention of one-upping her father. I had to give her credit, she'd been successful at it. Despite the tendency toward impatience and quick temper I'd seen, she apparently had a good head for business.

Renee now controlled the heartland's drugs, gambling, and prostitution trade. She'd established Kansas City – on both sides of the Kansas-Missouri border – as her base, and ruled her operation with an iron hand.

It seemed "the Madam of Kansas City" was a much more powerful individual than I'd initially assumed.

I leaned back in my chair and looked at the montage of color photographs filling the dual monitors in my secret office. Renee was a few years older than me, in her mid-forties. She had sharp features not helped by her choice of heavy makeup and a figure that bordered on anorexic.

Her wardrobe consisted of fashions that pushed stylish to the edge of tacky – garish colors in clashing patterns, worn skin-tight, but cut just a little too low or with hems just a little too high. I'd seen New York fashion designers pull off look on the runway, but outside of Midtown, it always seemed overdressed, or like the wearer was trying too hard.

She wore her thick, red hair long, often cascading around her shoulders, making me wonder if it her hair real or an affectation chosen to distract her male subordinates. I suspected Renee's hair was probably as fake as the rest of her look.

But none of that mattered. What did matter was that I now knew where to find her. And as soon as I could look myself in the mirror and honestly declare myself fit, I was going after her.

I owed it to Mindy.

♦

Fitting physical training around a busy day job is a challenge. I told Jessica, Bonnie, Kyle, and anyone else who wondered about my intensive workout regimen that I was getting ready for a marathon, and adapted my routine to suit my schedule.

I started my day with an early morning yoga or Pilates session, followed by a sprint around the block. I did planks while the coffee brewed, ignoring Glau's quizzical gaze as I rebuilt my core strength.

I biked to work to build up my stamina, and even convinced Kyle to go biking with me on the weekends. I ran up and down stairs on breaks, and spent my lunch hours at a nearby downtown fitness center. Once or twice a week, Bonnie joined me at the gym, chatting up the miles as we climbed invisible mountains on the elliptical.

Jessica stocked the office kitchen with water bottles, and brought me a new bottle every two hours, whether I'd finished the previous one or not. When I went looking for an afternoon snack, I also discovered that she'd replaced the chips and chocolate with fresh and dried fruit, nuts, and protein bars. It was overkill, but she meant well. As long as she didn't hide the coffee or try to replace it with a green smoothie, I wasn't going to argue with her. I grabbed a banana and a handful of unsalted almonds and rolled my eyes at her when I went back to my desk.

After work, I hit the gym. Every day. I wasn't up to sparring with the gym rats, but took it easy, starting at beginner levels with the weights and time at the punching bag, gradually increasing time and intensity to bring my arm and shoulder back into form for actual hand-to-hand fighting.

I also needed to make sure my arm and shoulder were fit enough to hold and fire a gun.

"You're prepping for something," Ian said one evening at the gym. It was a statement, not a question.

"What makes you say that?" I asked, not pausing in my routine – a combination of squats and kettle-bell flips that neither arm had been up to only a couple of months before.

"You've just been... I don't know... *driven* since you got back from Charleston," he said. He stood near the end of the mat, feet spread slightly apart to support his weight, arms folded across his chest. This wasn't my friend, my lover talking. He was in trainer-mode, head tilted at a slight angle as he watched me, evaluating my combat readiness. "It's been a while since I saw you take your training this seriously."

"I let myself get out of shape," I said, setting the kettle-bell down and grabbing a towel to wipe the perspiration from my forehead. "I got hurt. Not letting that be a factor again."

"Sleeping better?"

The question made me pause. I *had* been sleeping better since coming back from Charleston. My inner child still watched from the shadows of my mind with the ghosts of the container girls in the background, but they no longer tormented me. It was as if they knew the only way I could avenge them was to first get strong. So they were patient, and let me sleep – for now, at least.

"Yeah," I said.

He nodded. "Good. Sounds like you're getting your feet back under you," he said. "I'm glad to see it. Ready to start sparring again?"

I grinned and tossed the towel back onto the bench. "Looking forward to it," I said, shifting into a low crouch.

Sparring at Ian's gym is as close to real fighting as you're going to get without wandering down a dark alley on the bad side of town. There are only a few rules: Anyone can challenge another gym member at any time – except on Tuesdays, which are excluded because that's self-defense class day. No one is under any obligation to fight. Don't damage the gym equipment unless you're prepared to replace it. Don't deliberately break bones or cause lasting injury. And if your opponent taps out, the challenge is over.

Gym rats often jump each other without warning, and for the most part, the rest of us just continue with our workouts. But some challenges will draw an audience, and plenty of money has been passed back and forth in friendly wagers on the outcome of a challenge.

Any time Ian was part of a challenge, a crowd was sure to gather, and today was no exception. We'd barely begun to circle each other before someone noticed, and moments after he'd taken his first swipe at me – which I'd dodged – we were surrounded by a small crowd of sweaty, men and women, elbowing each other for a better view.

"Stay out of his reach," one voice shouted from somewhere off to my left.

"He gets hold of you and you're done," called another. This voice seemed like it was behind me, but I was moving around quite a bit and couldn't pinpoint the speaker and watch Ian at the same time.

"You've never watched them fight, have ya?" said a deep voice from the opposite side of the circle. Most of the rest of the group laughed at the newcomers.

I couldn't blame them for their assumption. Ian is seven inches taller than me, all speed and muscle and with a longer reach. I'm faster than he is, and half his bulk, but I'd learned to use that seeming weakness to my advantage, as many of the men now surrounding us had learned from first-hand experience.

Ian's real advantage was that he'd been the one to teach me the majority of what I knew about fighting. It was almost impossible to use a move on him he hadn't anticipated, and he knew how to counter most of my defenses.

Ian swiped at me again.

I grabbed his hand at it flew past, twisting the wrist and shoving his arm toward his opposite shoulder to block his free hand, landed a couple of quick kicks to his exposed ribs, then released his hand jumping back out of the way as he reached for me.

"First hit to Meg!" someone shouted. I hadn't heard them placing bets, but money was already changing hands.

It was no time to rest on my laurels, though. Ian closed in fast, catching my foot in the crook of his arm when I went to kick him again and pinning it against his back. I knew better – the move left me exposed, hopping on one foot as he landed a solid punch to my stomach. I twisted as I fell, pulling my foot free, and somersaulted away, feeling the air rush past my ear from the follow-up strike I'd only barely avoided.

I was rising to my feet just in time for him to reach for my throat.

I blocked his arm, using my momentum to throw my full weight against Ian's shoulder. We rolled, our audience jumping back out of our way as we tumbled sideways to the floor.

He was flat on his back for half a moment, just long enough for me to get a couple of good punches to his chin and jaw before he grabbed me and flipped me over his shoulder. I'd been expecting something like that, and landed in a crouch. Ian rolled toward me, and I supported myself on my hands, using my foot to swipe his arm out from under him when he started to rise.

I jumped on his back, bracing one knee on his buttocks, catching his arms by the elbows and pulling them backwards, forcing him to arch his body up toward me.

A shout went up from the assembled gym rats, but the fight wasn't over yet.

Ian managed to slip one arm free, pressed it to the floor, and pushed himself up. I couldn't keep my balance, and slid off him, rolling away – but not fast enough. He caught my foot and dragged me back toward him.

I rolled so I was facing him, kicking at his knees and ankles with my other foot, not wanting to get close enough to his hands for him to catch it as well. He bent down to catch it anyway, and I punched him in the nose.

He let go of my foot, wrapping an arm around my waist and dragging me to my feet as he stood, then threw me over his shoulder and onto the mat.

I rolled away, the wind knocked out of me, but there was no time to catch my breath. I was no sooner looking up again than he was there, his foot raised to stomp down on me.

I caught his foot, twisted his ankle and shoved it aside, barely succeeding in redirecting the force of his blow to the floor while I twisted away.

We faced off again, him with arms raised, ready to strike, me back in the low crouch that gave him few easy targets. To all appearances, his best choice would have been to have kicked at my face – in fact, a few of the gym rats were shouting out that suggestion – but I'd tricked him with that lure before, catching his foot before he connected. He didn't take the bait this time.

Instead, I lunged forward, drawing my body up and swinging my foot up toward his face as I spun. He jerked back, as my foot sailed harmlessly past his nose, but he hadn't anticipated me following through the spin to throw a second kick. This one connected solidly with his jaw.

As he staggered back, I ran forward and jumped up onto his hips, wrapping my legs around his waist. Holding myself up with one arm around the back of his neck, I got three good hits in – slaps, instead of closed-fist punches – before he was able to shove me of him.

I bounced down and back, dancing on the balls of my feet. The gym rats were hooting and hollering, and I was breathing hard, but I was having a great time. Ian's face had settled into his single-minded combat expression, and barely changed during the course of the fight. When I'd been clinging to him, he'd barely seemed to be exerting himself. It was part of what made him such a dangerous opponent – and such a good trainer. I knew he wouldn't pull his punches with me; he expected my best.

I dove at him, sliding in under his guard and taking his legs out from under him. He returned fire, slamming the flat of his hand against my recently-injured shoulder, sending me spinning across the mat.

I couldn't decide if the fire I felt radiating across my shoulder was from some as-yet unhealed portion of the knife-wound or the handprint I would surely see if I looked down. But discretion is the better part of valor, or so they say.

I tapped out.

Ian's combat persona dropped away instantly. He'd been only a half-step from me when I tapped out; now he extended his hand to help me to my feet.

"Well done," he said as the gym rats drifted away.

"Thanks," I said, rotating my shoulder experimentally. No damage done, as far as I could tell. I looked up at him. "Yes, I'm prepping for something."

He didn't say anything, just waited for me to finish.

"I have unfinished business from Charleston. The target has moved, but I know where to find them," I said. "It's time to finish the job."

Chapter 25

Two weeks later, I was in a neighborhood sports bar in Kansas City.

I found a seat in a corner near the front, that offered a clear view of most of the interior, most importantly of the front door. I and ordered a veggie burger – in Mindy's memory – and a Guinness, then settled back to study the crowd.

Happy hour had ended, but the no-frills, homestyle bar was still lively, filled with an eclectic mix of patrons that ranged from older retirees to university students. The predominant demographic was in their thirties and forties, ordinary men and women who'd stopped in for a pint on their way home from work and decided to stick around for a few laughs.

I'd chosen a mousey-brown wig, cut in a shoulder length flip, and was once again wearing the dark-framed Mindy-style reading glasses. Combined with a relaxed, business-casual outfit of a navy blue, tunic-style t-shirt, and dark leggings, I blended in with the thirty-something crowd, becoming just another forgettable face.

I could see why my contact had suggested we meet here. It felt like a comfortable gathering place, and not somewhere an assassin might meet with a weapons supplier.

I specialize in quiet kills, the kind that are often mistaken as accidental deaths, even by law enforcement and the members of the victim's family. It's easier not to get caught when no one's actively looking for you.

But this was to be an execution, just as I'd requested of the other contractors who'd gone after the rest of the traffickers. And for an execution, I needed a gun.

I don't bother trying to carry a gun when I travel. It's just not worth the effort required to get one through TSA, when I could just obtain one through a black-market dealer after I reached my destination.

For this job, I'd reached out through the dark web to a Kansas City dealer, who had suggested this location for our meeting. I'd arrived a half-hour early, using the time to eat and get a feeling for the usual clientele. Look for anyone who stood out. Any reason to cancel the meet.

There are reasons I work alone. I'm not a particularly trusting person. And the fewer people who see my face, know who I am and what I do, the fewer people who can point to me on those occasions when someone does decide to go looking.

So I ate my burger, drank my beer, and people-watched.

By five minutes after the scheduled appointment time, I'd identified three people who might have been my contact: a man in an ill-fitting suit, who sat at the bar with his briefcase at his feet and kept looking around the room and fidgeting with his napkin, one of the waiters, who seemed particularly attentive to detail in his dealings with the customers, and a woman in an outfit similar to my own, who had arrived just after the man in the suit, but taken a seat deeper in the bar.

I wouldn't do business with the man in the suit. His nervous energy made me uncomfortable. And I doubted the woman was my contact, as she'd arrived with nothing more than a clutch purse that was far too small to conceal the gun I'd come here to purchase. She'd settled down with a drink and was almost entirely absorbed with whatever she was doing on her phone.

That left the waiter. He might simply have been good at his job, but I got the sense that there was more to him than that. He looked to be in his late twenties or early thirties, but had the air of quiet confidence about him that said he was a man who had bigger aspirations than working in a neighborhood bar.

He also seemed to be looking for someone, and after the second time he'd passed by the woman's table and been sent on his way, I decided to take pity on him.

I'd seen no one who exhibited any of the markers of law enforcement, so when he next came my way, I flagged him down.

"I was wondering," I said, pulling a bright red wallet from my pocket and setting it on the table, "If my take-out order is ready."

There was a subtle shift in his demeanor as he recognized the signal we'd agreed – the red wallet on the table. A hint of a flush, barely visible in the poor lighting of the bar, rose above his collar as he glanced across the room at the other woman, who was still busily engaged with her phone.

"Of course," he said, recovering himself almost immediately. "Let me get that for you."

He disappeared into the kitchen, returning quickly with a folded-over take-out bag, which he placed very carefully on the table. He set a folio with the bill for my meal alongside it.

"As requested," he said. "Steak, medium-rare, and sides, fully loaded."

"Salad?" I asked.

"Yes. And dessert." He seemed pleased with himself.

While I knew there was no food in the bag, I secretly hoped he'd actually added a real dessert. I'd seen some tasty items listed on the menu. But it was too late to modify the order now. Anyone nearby would have overheard and ignored a routine restaurant transaction – one the kitchen would have had no record of. Asking for something else would have risked calling attention to the bag now sitting on the table in front of me.

Not worth it for a piece of cake.

I opened the wallet and removed enough cash to pay for my beer and burger plus a generous tip, then slid a hundred dollar bill under the stack as I set them on the open folio. "Keep the change," I said.

He picked up the folio, palming the hundred as he closed the folder. "Thanks," he said.

"My compliments to the chef," I said.

The waiter nodded and disappeared with the folio. I took a last swallow of my beer and used my napkin to wipe my fingerprints from the glass. Then I picked up the take-out bag, and headed out of the bar and into the muggy twilight of a Kansas City summer evening.

◆

The first thing I saw when I opened the bag was a small, clear plastic container with a large slice of chocolate cake. Now that was what I called good customer service.

I set the cake and accompanying utensils and napkins aside with a chuckle.

Under the cake, were two large, square, take-out containers. In the first was a disassembled Glock 19, with a threaded barrel and loaded magazine, wrapped in a piece of microfiber cloth. I took the pieces out of the package one by one, inspected them, and assembled the pistol.

The second take-out container contained a pair of loaded magazines and a long, dark metal tube. A silencer.

I twisted it onto the Glock and tested the feel of the weapon in my hand. The silencer interfered with the front sight, but that wasn't an issue. While I'd initially learned to shoot by lining up the sights, when I started shooting moving targets, I'd had to learn to teach my eyes and hands to work together. There's no time to line up the sights when either you or your target is on the run.

Even with the silencer, I wasn't going to fire off any test rounds in my hotel room. I released the magazine, verified that the chamber was empty, then removed the silencer. I wiped everything down with the microfiber cloth, and after a bit of fuss, managed to pack everything back into one of the take-out containers, which just fit in the room's tiny safe.

Then I plumped up a couple of pillows, grabbed my tablet, and settled down on the bed to eat my cake and review my notes about Renee's operation.

The Researcher hadn't indicated the source of his information – he never did – but they'd been thorough. In addition to addresses for both her home and primary office, he'd provided photographs not only of Renee, but of the bodyguards who accompanied her virtually everywhere. One of the bodyguards – identified as Martin – might have been Wingtips' twin. He was of similar height and build as the man I'd shot almost two months before: a little over six feet with a broad, muscular chest that seemed to strain the buttons of his shirt. He wore his blond hair close-cropped, in a military-style flat top, that suited his square jaw and hard expression. And there wasn't a single photo of him that didn't show the bulge of his gun that was just visible under his suit jacket, if you knew what to look for.

Of course, that description varied only slightly for the second bodyguard – Walker – who was of similar height and build, but whose skin was as dark as Martin's was fair. Both men looked like linebackers turned mercenary. Just the type Renee seemed to prefer.

In addition to the Researcher's data, I'd gone back to the dark web and hired a couple of contractors. I'd specifically asked for a contractor from the Midwest, who was willing to relocate for up to a month. I'd deliberately avoided any mention of Kansas City.

In addition to minimizing the chances of word getting back to Renee that she was being watched, I knew from my own experience that it was easier to blend in if you're from the same general region. Accents and cultural norms vary across the country – and significant cultural differences and rivalries often occur within a region. But unless you're an extremely good chameleon, it's generally easier to blend in when you're from an area that has something even marginally in common with the target location. Similar weather and clothing styles, similar foods, even similar industries – they all provided a bit of common ground that was helpful for an operative attempting to blend in with the locals.

I received a half-dozen responses to my listing, and after brief, online conversations with the applicants ended up hiring two of them: Williams, who claimed St. Louis as his home base, and Vern, who said he'd travelled quite a bit and currently lived in Omaha.

I assumed neither was using his real name. I never did.

For this job, I was going by "Emma," the same name I'd used with Kaitlyn. I negotiated with the candidates individually, not telling either about the other – again, trust issues – and asked them to provide an ongoing photo record of Renee's activities. I wanted to know where she went, who she saw, when she was alone.

They'd been uploading their photos to a cloud storage account for a little over two weeks, enabling me to build a decent profile on Renee. Williams' photos came in more consistently, a new photo every time Renee left a building, got into a car, and got out of the car at her destination, each labeled with the address, date, and time they were taken. The photos were usually distance-shots, with only occasional interior shots of her in restaurants, nightclubs, and casinos, but the thoroughness of the record had me wondering if he had a crew of his own following her. It was entirely possible.

Vern wasn't as good at tailing Renee as Williams was, and turned in fewer photos overall, but he was better at getting the close-ups. It was his photos – sometimes several for a single meeting, and always with either Martin or Walker visible in the background – that gave me a glimpse into how Renee ran her operation.

It was all in the body language.

With most men, she was flirty, using her over-the-top sexuality to get her way, but men she'd had to intimidate into cooperation saw a different side of her. These men dealt with the cold, hard businesswoman, and their reactions were always subservient, often annoyed or resigned. She was generally dismissive toward women, treating them as useful but not measuring up to her standards.

Interestingly, after studying hundreds of photos, I never saw a single one where Renee looked genuinely relaxed, comfortable, or with her guard down. She never leaned over and whispered in a confidant's ear, none of her smiles reached her eyes. If she trusted anyone with that level of intimacy, it was behind closed doors.

In an unsettling way, it was like watching a version of myself, as seen through a funhouse mirror.

I shoved that thought aside, and focused on the immediate problem: how to get close enough to Renee to kill her without getting caught or killed in the process.

Unfortunately, taking her out from a distance wasn't an option. I know how to shoot a rifle, but it's not my preferred choice for a number of reasons – not least of all being how difficult they are to conceal. Also, the strategies for setting up a distance shot are entirely different, and I'd not seen anything in the photographs or the research I'd done based on the patterns of Renee's activities, that suggested good vantage points for basing a good distance shot.

However, there had been a few times when she didn't have a bodyguard glued to her side.

The bodyguard waited outside when Renee went to the salon for her weekly appointment. I would need to see if the building had a back door.

The bodyguard checked her condo before she went inside for the night, but did not stay. I would need to check the condo for best entry points, and places to hide.

And there were enough photos showing Renee, one of the guards, and one or two other people in one frame and the bodyguard standing outside the door in the next to confirm that she regularly took meetings in private. She'd done the same thing in Charleston when she met with Bouchard and left Wingtips in the hall. I assumed she went to these meetings armed, as she had that night.

I knew Renee was more than willing to shoot someone out of frustration or annoyance; what I didn't know was how capable she was when it came to defending herself. It's a different skill, and not everyone who knows how to use a gun is automatically good at the defensive draw. But I had to assume she was adept, and wouldn't freeze like a deer in the headlights when confronted on her own turf.

I would have to hit her quickly, before she had a chance to fight back.

Chapter 26

I didn't tell Williams or Vern that I'd arrived in Kansas City. They didn't need to know, and it kept a layer of anonymity between us. That said, the next morning I followed Renee's usual route, watching for her, while keeping an eye out for my own contractors.

I made Vern easily. I'd seen the wiry, middle-aged man with thinning hair in several of Williams' photographs, and suspected his identity. Now watching him in action, I was certain.

Vern wasn't following Renee in any obvious way, but as his pictures had shown, he had a reporter's boldness, and often got much closer to her than seemed prudent. But her bodyguards paid no attention to him, or the odd angles he held his cell phone camera when capturing photos of Renee and her entourage, which led me to believe he was a regular feature of her route.

It was probably the reporter persona he'd adopted. Unless they were actively shoving a microphone in a celebrity's face, after a while they got used to seeing them, dismissing them as part of the background noise. I'd seen the pattern before. A lucky reporter might become so invisible to the celebrity they're pursuing that they're able to catch an off-hand quote or snap a saleable photo.

It was a clever ploy. Not without risk, but it appeared to be working, and that was all that mattered to me.

Williams, however, was trickier to identify.

Over the course of the day, I spotted five individuals I thought were part of his crew – three men and two women. Which of the men was him, I wasn't sure. The crew worked in pairs, two watching each location, never interacting with each other.

I might not have tagged them if I hadn't been actively looking. But when I spotted one of the two men from the condo surveillance team with an Asian woman I'd seen at the coffee shop at Renee's gym later in the day, I made a note of the second appearance.

Then a Black man who had also been the coffee shop showed up across the street from Renee's office, his lightweight blazer from that morning discarded as the day had warmed up. He "accidentally" dropped something about the size of a matchbook as he passed the fifth person, a young woman who was sitting on a bus bench reading a tablet. When the tablet reader casually put her foot on the matchbook and slid it toward her, that confirmed it.

I turned away before either operative caught me watching.

Williams had a skilled team, one that had been working together long enough to have developed a level of trust in each other.

There were few people I trusted enough to work with that closely.

When I checked the image uploads that evening, over a room-service dinner in a blissfully air-conditioned suite, I wasn't surprised to find my Emma persona as a background character in some of the day's photos.

I studied the images, and formulated my plan.

Vern uploaded his images after Renee had returned to her condo each night, which was sometimes quite late. Williams-and-team uploaded theirs at random intervals throughout the day. I'd hired two contractors so there would always be someone covering her, so one would fill in any gaps in time the other might miss. And while the coverage was thorough, the timing of the uploads meant I didn't have a complete chronology until the following day. That had been fine for the "discovery" phase of this operation; now that I was in town, I needed reports that were closer to real-time.

I messaged both contractors and asked them to upload hourly, Williams on the hour, and Vern on the half-hour.

Not surprisingly, Williams acknowledged the request with a simple "Will do," while Vern balked. His reply was almost petulant.

V: Not sure if I can do that.
Me: You having upload issues?
V: No. Why do you need the photos so often? Who is she to you?
Me: My business. Not yours.
V: Would be helpful to know.
Me: If you can't do the job, I'll find someone else.
V: Didn't say that. I'll upload hourly.

I stared at the phone in my hand.

I hoped to deal with Renee quickly; I also knew that there was no telling when the opportunity I was waiting for would present itself. I could be on my way home tomorrow night, or I could be here all week.

Either way, I didn't need Vern any more.

Me: I only need you to watch her for another twenty-four hours. Through tomorrow night. So the hourly reporting won't last long.
V: Whatever.

I powered down the phone. Williams' team was doing an exceptional job. A professional job. Cutting Vern loose was the right decision.

♦

The heavy, muggy thunderstorm-prone mid-July weather persisted through the night, and the next morning dawned gray and oppressive, with heavy clouds looming and the news predicting thunderstorms for later in the day.

So, of course, the photos began arriving at seven thirty, when Vern uploaded his first pictures of the morning. Renee was on the move early, dressed in jeans, a bright plaid shirt, and her unmistakable alligator cowboy boots. She'd pulled her hair back into a French braid, a good choice for a hot, windy day, and got into a big, black SUV with Walker.

Renee wasn't usually out and about this early. I didn't know what it meant, but took the next half hour to get showered and ready for the day.

Like Renee, I wore jeans, but instead of cowboy boots, I wore a pair of lightweight chukka boots with good ankle support and great tread. And instead of her bright plaid, I kept it simple, with a soft, dark t-shirt that cushioned the double holster I slid on over it, and kept the straps from chafing against my skin. I put the Glock in the holster along my left ribs, for fast and easy drawing, then secured the magazines and silencer in the loops along my right ribs, where they'd be easy to retrieve as needed. It may sound cumbersome, but it's surprisingly comfortable, especially when worn with a jacket that keeps it from rubbing against the inside of your arms.

Williams' eight o'clock upload hit the cloud right on time. I studied the images while towel-drying my hair.

Renee hadn't slipped past Williams' team. The photos also showed her early departure, as well as shots of Renee and Walker heading into the Lucky Linda twenty minutes later.

The bar had shown up in the photos a couple of times before. It was just close enough to the Power and Light District to see the lights and hear the echo of bands playing on the outdoor stage, but far enough away to miss out on most of the action – and the customers – of the trendy nightlife district.

According to my research, Renee had bought the Lucky Linda a few months ago, and it was currently closed for renovations.

Along with a photographic record of the stormfront heading into town, the next few uploads from both Vern and Williams showed Renee, Walker, and several people in coveralls and paint-splattered caps coming and going from the Lucky Linda. Vern's photos were centered on the bar, while Williams' showed Renee and Walker picking up coffee, coming out of a hardware store with bags of supplies, and running a variety of other errands.

It looked like renovations were well underway.

Then again...

I don't know if I'm naturally suspicious, or if it's a byproduct of years of covert dealings. But as I flipped through the photos – Vern's focusing exclusively on the front doors, while Williams' team had expanded their coverage to include the alley entrance as well – I couldn't help feeling like Renee was playing an elaborate shell game.

Had she spotted the surveillance?

If she had, it would have been Vern. His paparazzi persona would have set her teeth on edge. And if she didn't want to attract unwanted attention by killing him, I had no doubt she'd have gone to great lengths to shake him – especially if she had plans for the day that she didn't want caught on camera.

I set the towel aside and went back to the first photos of the day. Working through the images one by one, and assigning identifiers to each person who appeared even once, I built a timeline, recording their comings and goings in a spreadsheet.

Two people in, two people out. Renee and Walker.

Two people in. Renee and Walker.

Three more people in. Renovation crew.

One person out, then three people in. All renovation crew.

Three people out. Renee, Walker, one painter.

Five people in. Renee, Walker, three renovators.

On and on, over the course of the morning and into the early afternoon, I added and removed players from the list until only five remained.

Vern's two-thirty upload showed a total of four people leaving the bar, the last three members of the construction crew heading out just a few minutes after two. They all walked close together, heads down, hands half-obscuring their faces as they held onto their hats against the wind. Then Walker left, only moments before Vern uploaded the photos at two-thirty.

There was no sign of Renee.

I flipped back through the photos, scanning them for any sign of bright red hair tied up in a French braid, either at the front door or the back, but saw nothing. I zoomed in on the images of the last four construction crewmembers, but couldn't see their faces clearly enough to tell if they were men or women, much less spot Renee in their mad rush to get out of the storm and into their truck.

If the photos were to be believed, she hadn't left the building since the last time she'd arrived, a little over an hour before.

I pushed back from my computer. With Walker gone, that meant she was alone.

I messaged Vern.

Me: Did Renee leave the bar after you uploaded your photos?

V: No. Unless I've lost count, she's the last one there.

Me: Stay in place. Message me if the bodyguard returns before your next upload time.

The Lucky Linda was only a few blocks from my hotel. If luck was with me, I could get there before Walker returned.

I quickly wound the wig-grip band around my head and settled the shoulder-length, mousey-brown wig firmly into place. I pulled on a short, lightweight leather jacket, then put on the Mindy glasses and left my room.

I was heading toward the parking garage, pulling my gloves on as I walked, when my phone buzzed again.

V: I think I see her through the window. I'm going to get closer.
Me: Too dangerous. Stay in place.
V: I'm going in.

The idiot was going to get himself killed, and spoil my chance to catch Renee in the process. I shoved my phone in my pocket and ran.

◆

The alley entrance was closer and less obvious.

I was driving a dark gray Acura rental, with plates I'd stolen the day before, and parked near the mouth of the alley, then walked cautiously up the narrow passage. A garbage dumpster sat at the far end of the alley. If a truck backed in here to collect the trash, the driver had to be very skilled to not scrape his side mirrors against the brick walls on either side or roll over the back steps of the several businesses that opened onto either side.

But there was no trash truck today, no other vehicles, and no people. A small cat – or large rat – disappeared into the shadows at the far end of the alley, but beyond that, the rain pelting down and flowing in rivulets past my feet was the only other movement.

I shivered, pulling the collar of my jacket closer. When I reached the door with *"_ucky Lind_"* written across the hazy glass in the upper window, the letters at either end smudged and faded beyond recognition, I paused under the slight overhang. Pressing myself flat against the wall, I listened for any sound – voices, music, the clatter of dishes – anything that might tell me if someone was inside.

The door didn't seem particularly thick, but I couldn't hear a thing through it over the storm. I tried the knob.

It was unlocked.

An oversight? Or an invitation?

I drew the Glock and chambered a round, then twisted the silencer into place.

I turned it cautiously, then eased the door open with my foot, standing to one side while it drifted open on surprisingly quiet hinges. The door opened into a short, dark hallway, a slight glint of light on the wall identifying a small window in a nearby door, possibly leading into the kitchen. At the end of the hall a pair of saloon-style swinging doors were outlined by the dim light from the main part of the bar.

I slipped into the building, closing the alley door quietly – and locking it – behind me.

Opposite the kitchen, were two, single-person bathrooms. I quickly checked each, then closed and locked the doors. I didn't want anyone taking advantage of them as possible hiding places, now that I'd checked them.

And if I needed a hiding place later, I would find another option – preferably one that had a second exit. I didn't like the idea of being trapped like a fish in a barrel.

I backed away from the swinging doors and back toward the kitchen.

The door with the small window swung open easily, opening onto a dim room lit only by what little light filtered in through the long, narrow windows set high in the wall overlooking the alley.

Other than the random cockroach, which I didn't see but thought I heard scuttle across the floor, the kitchen was empty.

It was a small room, with a large worktable in the center, and smelled faintly of old grease, stale beer, and harsh detergent. It was an odd combination, and suggested that the bar probably served a limited selection of fried appetizers, but left little room for doubt that the kitchen's primary function was for washing the various glasses used for serving the beer and harder drinks that were the bar's primary trade. There were several glasses in the sink now, the remains of the drinks they'd held still sharp and fragrant.

I crossed to the swinging door near the opposite corner of the room, the Glock raised to my shoulder, ready to swing down and fire.

The window was hazy with grime. I couldn't make out anything through it, and didn't want to make myself a target for anyone watching from the other side. Instead, I pressed up against the leading edge of the door and rolled out, keeping my back against the wood as I pushed it open. When I came around to the front of the door, I stepped backward, still keeping my back to the door as it swung into the kitchen, to prevent it from swinging freely.

I took one last glance in the kitchen to ensure it remained empty, then slowly took a single step forward, moving away from the now-stable swinging door.

I had not come in sight of the bar yet, but was still concealed by the end of the heavy wooden cabinet that held the liquor, when a man's voice said.

"All that sneaking around must be thirsty work. Would you like a drink?"

I stepped around the end of the cabinet, lowering my gun toward the voice as I turned, and found myself facing Vern. He was standing behind the bar, a drink in one hand, looking at the collection of liquor bottles on the shelves on the wall.

He looked over at me. "Renee's not here. She must have gone out the back before I came in." He shrugged, then gestured with his glass toward the whiskey bottle on the counter and asked a second time, "Want a drink?"

"No," I said, taking a few steps to the side and coming deeper into the room. I didn't lower the Glock, though I pulled my arms in a little closer to my body as I alternated between studying Vern and glancing around the bar.

Vern had turned on a light behind the bar, which bathed the otherwise darkened interior in a faint golden glow that faded the farther it got from the counter. The chairs and tables had been moved away from the center of the room and stacked in the booths along the far wall. Most of the barstools were lined up behind the bar.

"I think they're getting ready to refinish the floor," Vern said, in answer to my unspoken question.

"Why are you still here?" I asked. The wind howled outside, but our voices still seemed to echo in the empty space.

"I was waiting for you."

"How did you know I'd come?"

"I didn't," he said with a shrug, then took a drink of his whiskey. "Wasn't even sure you were in town. Hoped you'd show up, though, prove me right."

"What are you talking about?"

A clap of thunder shook the building, the dim light flickering in accompaniment.

"You shouldn't have fired me," Vern said as the thunder faded. His eyes flicked just past me, and I started to turn, extending the Glock, but it was too late.

A large, powerful fist connected with my jaw, the impact sending me spinning, the Mindy glasses flying off my face.

I briefly recognized Martin's close-cropped blond hair, then my head connected with the end of the bar, and I slid to the floor, the bodyguard towering over me while Vern laughed in the background.

Chapter 27

I came to sitting on a wooden chair in the middle of the empty room, my jaw aching, my hands zip-tied on my lap. Martin had at least done me the kindness of crossing one wrist over the other before looping the zip tie around them, and hadn't removed either my gloves or my wristband-style bracelet, which doubled as a concealed wallet holding a fake ID, a VISA gift card, and a bit of spare cash. Presumably, the band just looked like a bit of frippery to be ignored.

But that was pretty much the only good things about my present situation.

They'd taken my gun and from the lack of weight along my right ribcage, I'd been relieved of the spare magazines as well. I pressed my elbows gently against my pants pockets and couldn't feel either my phone or the multi-tool I usually carry, so had to assume that they, along with my lock picks, had also been taken.

Vern and Martin were over at the bar, talking. I stayed quiet, my head bowed as though I was still out, and listened.

"...I caught her, I should at least get to watch," Vern was saying.

"Renee wanted to be notified as soon as we had her," Martin growled.

"So call her. I don't want to go out in that."

"She's out of cell service."

There was a pause, as though one or both of them might have looked my way. I kept my breathing easy and didn't move.

Martin continued, his voice lower, "You know where to find her."

"That's halfway across town," Vern said. He wasn't exactly whining, but at this point, even I was losing patience with him.

"Then you'd better get going," Martin said, his tone neutral. Almost clinical. As though it didn't matter to him one way or another. "She won't be happy if she finds out you kept her waiting."

"The thanks I get," Vern muttered.

There was some rustling around, that I used as an excuse to stir slightly, and then Vern stomped out.

Martin came over.

I looked up at him, noting the bulge of the gun in the shoulder holster he wore under his jacket. He hadn't drawn it, clearly not seeing me as any sort of threat.

He stared down at me, his expression utterly neutral.

"I figured Vern was lying when he told Renee about you," he said. He reached into his pocket, pulled out the Mindy glasses, and slipped them on my face, apparently assuming I needed them. "Never would have guessed the little weasel would have come up with some useful intel."

"I should have shot him."

"I wouldn't have blamed you if you had," he said. "I've been tempted to a few times myself. But he's in Renee's good graces for now." He shrugged. "You know how it goes."

He crossed over to one of the booths and disentangled another chair off the puzzle of furniture at the top of the stack. I took advantage of the ten second distraction to flatten my hand against my lap and begin wiggling it ever so slightly in an effort to slide my thumb past the loop of the zip tie.

Not counting simply cutting it, there are three ways out of a zip tie. The easiest is pressing the catch and sliding the loop open. With my gloves on, covering my fingernails, and no other flat tool within reach, that option was a no-go.

The second, which I was currently attempting, was to work your flattened hand backwards, taking advantage of any wiggle room afforded by poor placement of the tie. I was making progress, and had gotten my lower, not-visible-to-Martin hand backed out of the loop just to the knuckle at the top of my thumb, when the other side of the tie caught on the bracelet.

I was trying to work it free, the fingers of my upper hand twisting awkwardly in the attempt, when Martin turned back toward me. He saw what I was doing, and the first hint of an expression crossed his face. He looked disappointed.

"Don't try anything stupid," he said. "The only reason you're still alive is because Renee wants answers. She won't be happy if I kill you, but I will if I have to."

He placed the chair in front of me and took a seat, facing me, his blond hair glowing in the dim light.

"Shall we begin?"

♦

Martin began asking questions – who I was, why I was here, who sent me. That sort of thing.

When I didn't answer, he hit me.

He started with simple slaps – not gentle, but not damaging. After about four slaps that neither earned him answers nor a reaction from me, he backhanded me, his knuckles bruising my face.

I tasted blood and turned my face to the side to spit it out. Then I faced Martin, staring at him as I licked the blood from my lips.

He grinned.

"You're tough, I'll give you that," Martin said then. "Play nice and Renee might even offer you a spot on her crew. She'll pay you more than your current employer will, that's for sure. She's fair with her people."

Until she gets tired of them and shoots them in the head.

I didn't say anything. I just sat there, staring at him.

"Who sent you?" he asked again, backhanding me again after a three-second count.

I didn't like being hit, but there was a method to my madness. As long as I had Martin's attention focused on my face, and away from my hands, I could continue trying to slip out of the zip tie. Doing it without his noticing was slow-going, but I'd managed to untangle the tie from my bracelet, and almost had my thumb free.

After that, my hand would be able to slide right out.

I ignored Martin's next question as well, my thumb slipping out of the zip tie loop the next time he hit me. My hand would slide free now, but I held off, instead shaking my head as though to recover from his backhand and giving him a nasty glare.

Martin was armed. He was taller than me, stronger than me. I would have one chance – and barely even that – to take him by surprise. This wasn't like sparring with Ian or the random challenges from the gym rats.

Nobody was going to tap out in this one.

But like Wingtips before him, Martin was too trusting of his size, strength, and apparent invulnerability. It had never occurred to Wingtips that I would shoot him as he bore down on me. And by not tying me to the chair, not securing my feet to the chair legs, binding my hands together in my lap instead of behind my back, Martin had demonstrated the same lack of concern. He didn't think of me as a threat.

And that was going to cost him.

The third time Martin backhanded me, I shifted my feet, sliding them closer together and back by a couple of inches. I also closed my upper hand over the side of my lower hand, tightening my grip around my glove as I slid my hand out of it so it wouldn't move.

The blood was in my mouth again, but this time I didn't shake it off or spit it out. As Martin leaned back from delivering the blow, I lunged at him, teeth bared in an almost feral snarl.

My left hand, closed into a knuckle-punch, struck him in the trachea with all the strength I could deliver. He jerked back, choking, one hand flying toward his throat, his other arm windmilling to keep him from tipping backwards.

I didn't wait to see if I'd crushed his windpipe, if he would fall over, if he would choke himself to death, or rebound after me. Even as I'd delivered the blow with my left hand, my right hand had reached inside his jacket, closing around the butt of his pistol. As I pulled away from him and stepped back, I raised the gun, chambered a round.

And fired.

He'd been in the middle of rising to come after me, and his forward momentum continued to carry him toward me. He was choking, one hand on his throat, his eyes wide with a mixture of fury and fear as he struggled for breath.

The wind howled and thunder crashed outside as I fired again, two, three rounds into his chest, continuing to back away as he came at me.

He moved like a zombie, each shot pushing him back a step before he shook them off and continued staggering forward, arm outstretched, the fingers on that hand curled into a hook that would tear me to pieces if he caught me.

Dammit. He was wearing a bulletproof vest under his shirt. He had to be.

My back hit the wall. I raised the gun higher and fired again. The first round tore through the hand at his throat, ripping the flesh open. The second round went through his eye.

Blood exploded from his throat, accompanied by a harsh gurgling sound as he fell, first to his knees and then onto his face. Blood pooled around him, just one more stain to be sanded out of the floors before the bar could reopen.

I pocketed Martin's gun – a Beretta 92 – and stepped away, retrieving my other glove from where it had fallen on the floor near my chair. Only then did I notice the blood that had splattered onto my hands, sleeves, and the front of my jacket and jeans.

With a sigh, I went behind the bar, found a cloth, and used the small sink to wash off, wiping the blood from my face, clothes, and boots. I then went back and made sure I'd not left any bloody boot-prints on the floor. Why leave any extra clues if I could avoid it?

The storm might have covered some of the gunshots, but I couldn't count on it. Someone was sure to have called the authorities. I needed to get out of there before the police showed up.

I stuffed the bloody rag into my empty coat pocket, then retrieved my Glock, phone, and other belongings from where Martin had left them on the bar.

Vern had left the open bottle of whiskey on the counter, along with an empty glass. I poured a single finger and tossed it back, then wiped the rim to smear any lip-prints.

That had been too close.

I was about to pocket my phone when I noticed the time: it was nearly three-thirty.

Vern wouldn't be uploading any more photos to the cloud, but unless Williams had also turned traitor, there should be another set. I quickly browsed to the site. A dozen images had been posted, right on schedule. I scanned the most recent uploads.

Vern, entering the bar from the front door.

A black SUV stopping in the alley outside the back door. Martin exiting, handing the keys to Walker. Renee and Walker driving away in the truck as Martin entered through the back door. The timestamps on these images were within a minute of Vern's coming in at the front. There hadn't been any time for him to negotiate a deal with Renee in that minute – he'd clearly turned on me and contacted her earlier, probably even the night before, setting up this whole charade.

Which would explain the "workers" coming in and out all day, the glasses in the kitchen sink. They'd set the room up, then lazed around having a drink or two between their randomly-timed comings and goings.

I'd been played.

I flipped through the rest of the photos.

Me, entering through the back door.

Vern, leaving about ten minutes later. Which gave me an idea for how long I'd been out after Martin hit me the first time.

The last image was of a black SUV, heading into a tunnel. I looked at it, frowning. There were trees all around and the street sign in the near corner of the photo was blurred, and zooming in on it only blurred it further – the first such error I'd seen from Williams' team. Other than a set of numbers painted in a vertical column along the side of the tunnel entrance, I couldn't make out anything about the location to tell me where it was or where it led.

I tapped my fingers on the bar. The clock was ticking. I needed to go... but go where?

I'd never been fully comfortable with Vern – and he'd sold me out. But Williams had delivered. And after watching his team in action, I was still of the opinion that they were professionals.

Sometimes you've just got to trust your gut.

I dialed Williams' number. He answered on the second ring.

"I need to know where Renee is, right now," I said, not bothering to introduce myself.

"She's in a cave near Lenexa," Williams said.

"Excuse me?"

"There are several businesses operating out of former limestone mines all over the Kansas City region," Williams explained. "Renee appears to have found one that isn't part of a business development. She may be using it as a warehouse or a base of operations – I can't tell without going inside, and I haven't done that. She and one of her bodyguards drove into the cave about an hour ago. They haven't come out."

So the photo had been of a cave entrance, and not a tunnel. Interesting.

"Has anyone else gone in?"

"No."

"Is there another way out?"

"I don't know. It's not one of the commercially mapped mines."

I considered this for a moment. I didn't know the caves, didn't know Renee's strength. She could be in there with only Walker – and soon, Vern – with her, or she could have her whole crew with her.

"Do you still have someone watching the Lucky Linda?"

"Yes. With as much activity as there's been there today, it seemed prudent." He didn't seem at all surprised that I knew he wasn't working alone.

"Is your team as good in a fight as they are at surveillance? And are they currently armed?"

"Yes, and yes," he said, without hesitation.

"Would you be interested in expanding the terms of our arrangement?" I asked.

Out of courtesy, I added, "It's probably going to be dangerous."

"Didn't want to intrude," Williams said, "But I was hoping you'd ask." I could almost hear him smiling.

Chapter 28

It didn't take long for Williams and me to come to a mutually acceptable agreement and for me to leave the bar by the back entrance and head toward my car.

A slim figure, of medium height, stood in the alcove of the building across the alley. She wore a long, dark, hooded coat that brushed the tops of calf-high, heavy-soled boots with leather straps and wide buckles. Her raised hood protected her from the pouring rain, as well as obscured her features. A half-remembered image from a video game crossed my mind, and I wouldn't have been surprised if she'd had a pair of swords crossed over her back. But of course, she didn't.

She did have a gun at her hip.

"Stevie?" I asked as I neared the alcove.

"Yeah."

"Emma. You're with me."

Stevie fell into step beside me. She was young, maybe in her early twenties. The top of her head barely reached my ear, but she easily matched my stride.

We were in my car, and had just pulled away from the alley, when Stevie spoke. "We've got company," she murmured, her eyes on the passenger-side rear view mirror.

"I see them."

I'd seen the police cruiser half a moment before in my own mirror, as it turned the corner half a block behind us.

It's easy to panic when the police show up, especially if you've done something they'd be all to happy to lock you up for, like shooting someone five times and leaving them lying in a pool of their own blood. I'd wiped myself down enough for it not to be messy or too obvious, but a cop looking closely would surely notice the bloodstains on my clothes.

So yes, there were plenty of reasons to panic. There were more reasons not to. All panicking would do was attract their attention, like a swimmer flailing about in the water attracts a shark.

I didn't panic.

I drove away like a normal, innocent bystander just going about my business – and watched the cruiser in my rearview. When it reached the center of the block and turned into the alley, I accelerated, but only a little.

The police didn't seem to have been interested in the car or what we were doing in the area.

Yet.

The Acura's actual license plates and rental agency paperwork in the spare tire compartment in the trunk, so even if they'd caught the plate number on their car, they wouldn't be able to connect the car directly to me. They'd find records for another dark gray Acura – the one whose plates I'd stolen, and pay the unsuspecting owner a visit.

I stifled a growl. I wanted to go after Renee, get this job over with. But first I needed to swap the current plates for another set.

We drove in silence for a couple of blocks before I spoke.

"Williams gave me an address in Lenexa," I said, handing Stevie my phone. "Can you tell me how to get there, or do I need to plug it into the GPS?"

Stevie looked at the address, frowned. "I'll map it."

The mapping app directed us to follow Highway 35 about twenty minutes to the southwest. On our way to the highway, I pulled through a packed movie theater parking lot and then an apartment complex lot, scanning for another dark gray Acura. Stevie spotted one parked in the shadows of the apartment complex's carport-style covered parking.

We swapped plates with it, working quickly. It was raining hard by then, which meant almost no one was out, but by the time we got back into the car we were both soaked.

I turned up the heater and headed to the highway.

"You take a lot of precautions," Stevie said, shaking off her wet hood. Her hair was short and blonde, cut in a rough, choppy style and highlighted with rust-colored tips. She ran her hands through her hair fluffing out the wet ends around her face.

"I don't want to get caught," I said.

"Fair enough."

I couldn't tell if she was naturally quiet or just suspicious. Other than providing the occasional navigational update, she said very little, instead spending most of the ride in a flurry of text-based conversation. Her long, slim fingers flew over the phone's tiny keypad, as line after line of type scrolled along the screen.

"Who are you talking to?"

"The crew. They're asking a lot of questions about you."

"What did you tell them?"

Stevie looked over at me. "That you seem to know what you're doing." She grinned. "That you'll probably kill us all when the job is finished."

"Only if you try to double-cross me." I was completely serious, and spoke without a trace of humor.

Stevie's grin faded. "Is that what Renee did?"

"No."

She grew quiet again, leaning back in her seat and staring out the window at the rain. We'd left the dark, heavy clouds mostly behind, drenching downtown Kansas City, but we hadn't escaped the rain and probably wouldn't until we reached Lenexa.

I'm too used to working alone.

It occurred to me that part of Stevie's silence was probably my fault. She'd stopped texting, which I saw as a sign of her heightened stress. If we were going to survive this – and I was sure it was going to be at least a little bit messy – she was going to have to relax and trust me enough that we could work together.

I tried to think of something, anything to talk about besides the weather.

"Are you from around here?" I asked. I knew it was lame, but it was all I could come up with. I'm not even forty yet, but the realization that I had no idea what to talk about with a twenty-something made me feel suddenly old.

"I've visited a few times" Stevie said, not looking at me.

I tried again. "What do you know about the caves?"

"There's not much to tell," she said. "There used to be a lot of limestone mining around here, way back. Somebody got the bright idea that they could store stuff in the caves, and somebody else figured out how to make money off them."

"Someone always does. Have you ever been in them?"

"Only once," she said. She shifted, turning sideways to face me. "One of the mines has a paintball range in it. A bunch of us went one time. I thought it was gonna be all dark and creepy, ya' know? Like with spiders and bats and shit? But it wasn't like that at all." She'd livened up, talking about the memory.

"In what way?"

"Well, it's rock, right? And sure, there's dirt, but not like you'd expect. It was almost... clean, I guess. And kinda dim, but not that dark."

"So there were a lot of ventilation shafts?" I was trying to imagine being in an old mine, and all I could come up with were images from stories and movies of Old West silver mines.

"No, they ran some of those long tube lights along the ceiling."

"I suppose they'd need to, if people were going to be working down there. How far down do you have to go?"

"You can walk right in – or drive in, depending on the cave," Stevie said. "It's like you're going into a tunnel under this big hill, right? Only instead of going in one side and out the other, you're in this crazy place that's just a maze of roads and big fat piles of rock holding up the ceiling."

I looked over at her. "You're kidding, right?"

"Swear to God," she said, shaking her head. "You'll see."

The mapping app buzzed an alert. Stevie looked down at her phone. "We're almost there."

♦

Williams was in an extended cab pickup truck within sight of the cave entrance, but not so close as to be obviously waiting. He hopped out of the truck when we pulled up behind him.

He was about my height, with dark hair and darker skin, a neat goatee, and a wrestler's stocky build. His long, leather duster was open, the straps of a pair of shoulder holsters visible where they crossed his broad chest. I got out of my car and we exchanged greetings while Stevie came around to the front of the Acura, leaned casually against the hood, and pulled out an e-cig. A sweet-spicy scent wafted our direction as Williams brought me up-to-date.

"Another car drove into the cave, about ten minutes after you called," Williams said. "Skinny, weasely-looking guy—"

"Losing his hair?"

"That's the one. He's been around a lot. I think he's a reporter."

"He's the other spotter I hired to follow Renee." I watched Williams for a reaction; was pleased to see nothing more than a raised eyebrow. "I didn't know you had a crew."

"I don't advertise them."

"No reason to," I said. I gestured toward his double holsters. "You look like you're loaded for bear."

His serious expression gave way to a grin. "You said it could be dangerous. I loaded up." He looked past me to Stevie. "You set, kid?"

"I got my piece," she said, pulling her coat back to display the gun at her hip.

Williams looked at me, then jerked his thumb toward the truck. "You'll need more than that. Take what you need from the cargo box in the back seat."

Stevie tried to act casual as she tucked the e-cig in an inside pocket, but she was practically radiating excitement, and almost skipped toward the truck.

"She's green," I said.

"A bit," Williams agreed. "But she's got a good head for the game. Switches her personality off when she's working."

I looked toward the truck, where Stevie was rummaging through the contents of the back seat. The ability to go clinical, to not let your emotions run away with you during a fight, was key to surviving in this business. Even after all these years, I still had to wrestle my inner demons into submission too often in order to work efficiently – and suffered whenever they got the better of me during a job.

"If you say she's ready…" I said, leaving the sentence unfinished.

Williams understood. "She'll surprise you."

"If she lives, *that* will surprise me."

I turned away. Another car had approached while we talked – a late-model Chevy Malibu – and parked behind my Acura.

"Gang's all here," Williams said. "Let me introduce you around."

We walked over to the car, and Williams identified the remaining three members of his crew as they got out of the car. First was Mai, a Thai woman of about Stevie's height, dressed simply in black jeans and a black t-shirt. She nodded in greeting, while adjusting the straps on an armored vest.

Next was Hatch, who looked more like an accountant than an operative, with his neat haircut, button-down shirt, dark tie, and wire-rimmed glasses. It was the hardened look in his eyes that said he was used to doing more than working with numbers.

The last member of Williams' crew was Dalton. I did a double-take as I studied his dark, patient face, the athletic posture. Then my memory replaced his jeans and dark hooded sweatshirt with a baseball jersey.

"You were a ball player," I said. "Hit a home run—"

"And destroyed my knee on a bad slide into home," he said with a grimace. He lifted his foot, swung it back and forth. "Replaced the knee, but the game was over for me after that." He stepped forward, extended his hand. "Joe Dalton."

"Emma Peel," I said, fully claiming the BBC character's name. "I was at that game. Had seats along the third base line."

"Nice view," he said.

Williams cleared his throat, and we looked over. He was leaning against the side of my car, his hands folded across his chest, head tilted to one side. Stevie had come back to join him, an HK SP5 semiautomatic with a heavy-duty suppressor slung over her shoulder. All four of the other operatives were giving me and Dalton some curious looks.

"Right," I said. I stepped away from Dalton, turning so I could see Williams and his entire crew.

Williams clapped his hands together. "Okay. You've all met Emma. I told you what I know, and you decided to show up, so I assume that means you're good with the risk." No one disagreed, and he continued. "Emma's the boss on this one, so you'll take your lead from her."

"Thanks," I said. "The woman I've had you following is Renee Sullivan. She and her crew smuggle high-tech electronics and run illegal gambling operations across Iowa, Kansas, and Missouri – frankly, I could care less about that. But she is also involved with kidnapping and importing underage illegals and selling them into the sex trade. That I do care about."

There was some uncomfortable throat-clearing, and one of the guys growled, low in his throat, but no one said anything.

I continued.

"We know that Renee, her bodyguard, Walker, and the weasel, Vern, all went into this cave in the last half hour or so. Unless they've left by some other route, they're in there still. I'm going in after them, and would greatly appreciate having a crew at my back."

"How big is her operation?" Mai asked.

"Big enough. Her father controlled the region from his base in St. Louis. Renee killed him while he was on a business trip to Chicago a couple of months ago and took over."

"Cold," said Dalton.

"She takes what she wants, and has no patience with anyone who gets in her way. The members of her father's crew who opposed her are dead or disappeared."

"And the rest are working for her, because it's better than being shot by her," Mai said. "I've heard of her."

"You knew—" Hatch began.

Williams shut him down. "Not the time." He gestured to me to continue.

"I've been hired to bring her down – with primary focus on the sex trafficking enterprise," I said. "As far as how many people she has in the cave with her… I don't know. It could be only the three of them, and this is just a good place for a secret meeting. It could house a major branch of her operation and several dozen armed guards. Realistically, it's somewhere in between."

"So we'll be in for a fight," said Hatch.

"Possibly a big one, yes," I said. "One last thing. If you spot any of the underage illegals I mentioned, don't shot them – unless they're shooting at you. In a perfect world, if she's holding any in there, I want to get them out unharmed."

I looked around. "Any questions?"

There was a low round of "no's" and head-shakes. We moved out, heading across the street in two groups, staying under the treeline along the edges of the short drive leading to the cave entrance.

I led my group, Williams behind me, Stevie bringing up the rear. We moved in almost complete silence. Just before we reached the cave entrance, Stevie murmured, "We're not usually the good guys."

We raised our weapons and stepped into the darkness.

Chapter 29

It was noticeably cooler inside the cave, and dry, too, after the first few steps. We crept forward cautiously, keeping close to the wall while our eyes adjusted to the lower light, not sure what lay ahead.

Despite what Stevie had told me, it still felt more like I'd walked into a tunnel than a cave. The floor here was smooth, the exterior pavement giving way to hard-packed ground that barely showed the tracks of the cars that had entered ahead of us. The walls were artificially straight, clearly manmade, and I could see no discernible variation in width or ceiling height that I would have expected from a naturally occurring cave.

About ten feet in, the tunnel made a hard turn to the right.

I looked across at the other group. Mai was in the lead, with Hatch and Dalton following. Without hesitation, they continued forward, crossing to the far wall, then moving up to remain opposite our group.

I was about to make the turn when Mai held up her fist, then pointed first at her eyes and then ahead and upwards, toward the ceiling, and again at her eyes.

There was a camera.

We flattened ourselves against the wall and watched as Hatch moved forward, passing Mai. A moment later I heard the soft hissing sound of a can of spray paint.

I had no idea how high up the camera was, or if Hatch had been able to disable it, but Mai seemed satisfied, and gestured Dalton to follow as she moved forward. I followed her lead, taking the corner, Williams and Stevie at my back.

Stevie had insisted the caves leftover from the former limestone mining operation would be nothing like I'd imagined. But I think I still half-expected to see low ceilings with bats fluttering overhead around low-hanging stalactites. Or maybe a cobweb-covered ore carts on rusted rails, the skeleton of a miner with a pick-axe propped up against a pile of rubble.

I didn't expect to find myself in a cool, dim, but otherwise perfectly serviceable warehouse easily the size of a football field. Air moved through the cave, not so much to call it a breeze, but more than enough to keep the air from being stale or stagnant.

A dotted line of fluorescent tubes ran along the ceiling, disappearing into the distance. Only a fraction of the lights were in use, the cave comfortably dim, but pools of light shone at irregular intervals from side passages up ahead.

Shadows moved in the distance. A generator whirred, creating a low, background hum, like an idling lawn mower. And there was music – classical rock performed in dubstep style, heavy with drums, bass, electronics, and strings. From the way sound echoed off the stone walls, it was difficult to tell where anyone was, but it was clear that we were not alone.

I gestured my team forward. Mai did the same, both teams keeping close to the walls, in the shadows, Hatch serving as our camera-disabler. We hadn't seen any sign of Renee's or Vern's cars yet, other than the dusty tire tracks, but eventually someone was going to notice the cameras going down and decide to investigate. We kept moving, evaluating the terrain as we went, ready to meet them when they appeared.

As we moved deeper into the cave, it became clear that the walls and passages had been formed by a huge gridwork of massive stone pillars, rough limestone squares easily twenty feet or more across on each side, held up the ceiling. There was about forty feet between pillars, the spacing forming large "rooms" of sorts. Even the central aisle where we were walking was nothing more than an arbitrary path between the pillars, where a series of connecting rooms had been left open.

Like a peg-board, the space could be configured as needed. It was the ultimate in flexible space.

Renee appeared to use several of the rooms to organize contraband. These spaces were well lit, and after Hatch disabled the cameras, we darted past the lit spaces, regrouping in the shadows. In the first one I passed, wrapped pallets of flat-screen televisions were lined up in neat rows; in another, cases of video game cartridges were sorted on metal shelving units. A third room had tables stacked with laptop computers and assorted peripherals.

The rooms on the opposite side of the central aisle appeared to have been similarly utilized – creating a combination warehouse and sorting facility.

It made sense, after a fashion. Renee had an almost unlimited amount of space here. Distributing their ill-gotten gains over a larger physical space would make it harder for a rival to sneak in and easily relieve them of their entire ill-gotten product line.

I briefly wondered if the music, which had increased in volume as we'd gotten closer to the source – and which now rumbled through the cave like thunder at slightly below concert volume – was playing on stolen speakers. I brushed the thought aside. The music would have covered any noises we might have made in our approach, but every time Hatch painted over a camera, it was one more announcement of our presence.

It couldn't be helped. I'd watched for any alarms, but seen none. But if they were paying any attention at all to their cameras, they would know we were here. Painting over them would only slow them down a little.

The fourth room I came to held a twenty-foot, white refrigerator container. It wasn't the same one I'd seen in

Charleston – I didn't remember all of the markings on that one, but I did remember a brand logo on it that this one didn't have.

Still, I was curious.

I signaled for Williams and Stevie to wait, then went to investigate. The door in the reefer's side hung open. There was no hum of the refrigeration unit – not that it needed it here, in the naturally cool, dry climate of the cave.

I moved forward cautiously and looked inside. The dark interior of the container reeked of vomit, sweat, and urine, but I saw no one huddled in the blankets piled against the walls.

I was just turning to rejoin Williams and Stevie, when from across the central aisle Mai raised a closed fist.

I froze.

She flattened her hand, resting it across her brow as though looking ahead, then lowered it, palm facing forward, thumb and first two fingers extended.

Enemy ahead, three people.

Mai looked to me. I nodded, raising my hand in a thumbs-up gesture to indicate that I understood, then circled my hand above my head and pointed past her, to the room where she and her team hugged the wall.

Acknowledged. Take cover and defend your position.

She nodded, then turned to Hatch and Dalton. I couldn't see her gestures to them, but a moment later, all three had scattered, finding places to hide amid the shrink-wrapped pallets and assorted boxes.

I moved toward the opposite end of the reefer, then between it and the forklift parked alongside it, coming around to the back of the container. Williams and Stevie were back there as well, at the opposite end. I pointed to Stevie and signaled for her to climb up and take a sniper position. I left Williams at the end of the reefer, and returned to the other end, where I crouched down, hidden by the forklift.

Then we waited for Renee's people.

♦

Stevie took the first shot.

The SP5's suppressor did a good job of muffling the sound – I barely heard the soft *pop* over the heavy electric violin reverberating through the cave, and never heard the *thud* of a body falling to the ground. Even the three or four shots of return fire sounded like little more than mis-timed drumbeats, the sound echoing off the stone pillars. The heavy bass beat of the piece that was currently playing did as much to cover our attacker's movements now as our own.

I crept to the edge of the reefer, peered around it, and saw no one. I ran, in a half-crouch, to the nearest stack of boxes, moved to the far side, and looked again. But though I heard the *pop* of Stevie's SP5 as she brought down another target, I again saw no one. Near the center of the room as I was, I could hear the shots being fired and returned, but couldn't see past the limestone pillar from my current position.

I crouched behind the boxes for only a moment, my ears already ringing from the gunfire, which was increasing in frequency as Williams' team engaged with Renee's men.

I had a bad feeling – one that had nothing to do with the firefight taking place only a few feet ahead of me.

I've learned to trust my instincts. Rather than dart forward, I moved in the opposite direction. The pillar that blocked my view of the fight offered Renee's men the opportunity to circle around behind us, equally unobserved.

I went to the pillar and moved to its far end, both my Glock and the Beretta I'd taken from Martin raised and ready. I felt – or perhaps simply imagined – the pulsating rhythm of the music through the stone, my own heart matching it. Taking a deep breath, I rounded the pillar, keeping my back to the rough stone.

Ten feet away, four men were creeping forward, two-and-two, barely more than shadows in the unlit passage.

Their guns were lowered – shielded from view by the pillar, they clearly hadn't expected to encounter anyone. I fired before they realized I was there.

The first dropped, nearly tripping the man behind him. The second fell toward the wall, crashing against it and sliding into a heap.

The third raised his gun, but fell before he got his finger to the trigger. The fourth, who was still recovering from stumbling over the first, died with his head down, my bullet slamming into the top of his skull.

I went to them and knelt, grabbing the guns from the four fallen men – two handguns, which I dropped into my jacket pockets, an SP5 like the one Stevie was using, and an old Uzi that I slung across my back on its wide strap. I tucked Martin's Beretta in my waistband, holstered my Glock, and moved forward, the SP5 pressed against my shoulder, safety off.

I could mount a sneak assault on their base as easily as they'd attempted it on mine – and hopefully, be more successful in the attempt.

The limestone pillars supporting the roof were about twenty-five feet on a side, which meant I had about fifteen feet of darkness to cross before reaching the next corner. Light pooled into the darkness from the room just ahead, much the same as the dim, single fluorescent tubes that had lit the previous rooms.

While it was entirely possible that the next room was just another storage space, like the ones before had been, I suspected otherwise. The music was too loud, for one thing, for the speakers to be much farther away, although here the sound competed with the thrum of the generator for dominance.

And the two men who came around the corner, talking to each other as though there wasn't a gunfight taking place on the other side of the pillar, the two men I shot before they even saw me in the shadows a few feet away, only confirmed my suspicion.

Renee was close.

I was almost at the end of the pillar – too close to safely take the time to relieve these bodies of their weapons. I stepped over them and continued forward, my back to the wall, the SP5 facing the room at the end of the pillar.

Ready for just about anything at this point, I turned the corner.

A dozen cars – including Renee's black SUV – were parked in two rows in front of me, their noses aligned roughly down the middle of the room. Along the far side of the room, just beyond the SUV, sat a twenty-foot mobile office trailer, the rumbling generator at the near end.

The trailer door was at the center of the unit, up a short flight of steps, a lighted window to either side.

That was where I would find Renee.

I moved forward through the middle of the row, staying low and using the parked cars as cover. I fired a shot into the front tires as I passed each vehicle, barely able to hear my own gunshots over the roaring of the generator and the music that blasted from speakers somewhere near the far end of the office trailer.

There would be no quick escape for anyone who survived the gunfight.

I had reached the SUV, but had not yet shot out its tires, when the trailer door opened. Three men carrying guns burst out, pounding down the stairs and running off down the central aisle.

I wasted no time on them – Williams' team were clearly putting up a respectable fight if Renee felt the need to send reinforcements. I darted around the SUV, up the steps, and jerked open the door.

The trailer was divided into three rooms – a main one in the center, and smaller rooms at either end. The main room was empty, a table along the wall opposite the door scattered with water bottles, beer and soda cans, and coffee mugs, and a few odd chairs around the perimeter of the room.

I pulled the trailer door closed behind me and locked it.

Renee would not have chosen the room close to the generator for her office, so I checked and cleared it first. It was empty, a desk scattered with papers and an unattended computer, the desk chair tipped as though hastily pushed back from the desk.

I crossed the main room to Renee's office.

But when I threw open the door, it wasn't Renee who dove for the gun laying on the desk, wasn't Renee who I shot three times, wasn't Renee who fell back against the chair pushing it into the wall.

It was Vern.

And while I took a certain satisfaction in the flash of recognition that crossed his face in the instant before he died, he wasn't who I was looking for.

Renee and Walker were still out there.

I bolted from the trailer, looking in every direction at once as I wrenched open the door and flew down the steps.

And dropped like a stone when a bullet whizzed past my ear, ripping through the trailer wall behind me like paper.

Chapter 30

I practically threw myself toward the SUV in a frog-like leap, the bullets flying past me, those that didn't tear into the trailer pinging off the stair railing.

I crouched by the rear tire for only half a breath, then turned, glancing under the back of the truck, and firing at a shadow that was moving toward me. It fell, but I didn't dare wait to see if whoever it had been was alone.

I backed up, moving to the truck's front tire, and easing up to look over the hood. The truck's tinted windows blocked my view of anyone who might have been in the shadows beyond. Unfortunately, the overhead light let the shooters spot my movement, and I ducked down again as a series of bullets shattered the windows, sending fragments of safety glass showering over my head.

I raised the SP5 sent a burst of shots in their general direction, shattering car windows and the fluorescent tube above, and hoped taking out the light – which had been my goal – looked like an accident. The room fell into a deep twilight, the only light coming from the room across the central aisle.

If they moved past the opposite room, they would be silhouetted – unless they blasted that light, too. I expected they'd figure that out before too long,

I scooted around past the front of the SUV and moved along the row the same way I had come, looking over the hoods of the cars and through the vehicle windows for any sign of my pursuers, and checking between each pair of cars before crossing the space to the next one.

At the third set, the last of the SP5 bullets caught one of Renee's men by surprise but didn't kill him. I used the empty gun like a hammer, smashing at his face, then caught the pistol he was raising and twisted his wrist, turning the pistol toward his own chin before forcing him to fire.

I left the SP5 and kept his pistol – another Glock – and grabbed the spare magazine sticking out of the pocket of his hooded sweatshirt. Then I stepped over his body, edging toward the central aisle, pulling my own Glock as I moved forward. When I reached the end of the sedan, I crouched beside it, scanning in all directions, a loaded Glock in each hand.

I saw no movement back toward the trailer, and no one in the lit room across the central aisle.

But there was a movement near the pillar, someone tall. I fired at the shape, and missed, the shot hitting the stone and sending chips flying.

The person turned and shot back, his three quick shots missing me and hitting one of the vehicles beyond me. I fired again, the muzzle of my gun almost resting on the back of the sedan. The Glock's suppressor minimized the muzzle flash, but his eyes must have been better adjusted to the dark than mine, because his next shots were much closer.

I moved back, watching for other shooters as I circled around to the opposite side of the car, so that I was between the shorter sedan and a jacked up pickup truck. Then I once again headed toward the central aisle.

The shadow was gone when I looked around the end of the truck, but the shot that shook the vehicle when it hit the opposite side of the pickup bed, forcing me to duck behind the jacked-up tires, told me that he'd either crossed the central aisle or wasn't alone.

Stepping around from behind the truck would be suicide.

The truck hadn't been lifted so high that I could see through to the other side across the top of the tires, so I crouched down and began firing around the side of the rear tire, under the pickup's lifted bed.

We exchanged several shots, his blasting through the truck, mine taking bites out of the pillar he was hiding behind, no more than twenty feet from me.

When my gun clicked dry, I released the empty magazine, pocketed it, and popped a new one in without even a thought.

The shooter must have mistaken my reloading for having been hit, because when I next looked under the truck bed, I saw him coming toward me, inching stealthily forward in a half-crouch, his body pressed tight against the end of one of the cars further down the row.

It was Walker, the second of Renee's bodyguards. I recognized him from the momentary glimpse of oddly familiar features – features I'd seen in dozens of grainy, surveillance photos.

The adrenaline of a fight changes how you think, how you move. Your aim gets worse, your fine motor coordination drops off. Trying to aim at any specific spot on Walker's body – a dark shape against a larger dark shape – would be an exercise in futility.

So I didn't try for precision. I just shot at the parts of the shadow that wouldn't be protected by the body armor I assumed he was wearing.

I fell to my side and fired from the ground, shooting with both my suppressed Glock and the second Glock I'd taken from the dead man. I shot where I thought he would be most vulnerable: his legs, the slight bulge at the top of the shadow that seemed like it might be his head, the edges of the shadow that should be his arms.

A bullet caught his knee, and he almost lost his balance, then used the back of the car to support his weight and kept firing. I thought a couple of my bullets caught him center-mass, but other than rocking him slightly, they did no damage. No surprise.

But he was firing high now, the distortion of the darkness leading him to believe I was up in the truck bed and shooting down at him, the impact of the bullets muffled by the tarp-covered objects in the back of the truck bed – a pair of kegs, from the sharp smell of beer that now filled the air.

The dead guy's Glock ran dry. I had his spare magazine, but didn't want to take the time to swap out the empty one. I dropped it into one of my jacket pockets, trading for the other gun I'd stashed there earlier, and kept shooting.

I hit Walker's gun arm, then hit it again. His gun lowered before he fired again, and this time his bullet hit the ground dangerously close to my shoulder, sending shrapnel into my face and chipping one lens of the Mindy glasses I still wore.

I needed to end this.

I sat up, moved back behind the monster truck tire, then looked around it, focusing on the shape that I knew was Walker. Breathing deeply to calm my heartbeat, I took aim and fired.

The shadow crumpled, like a balloon with a slow leak.

Walker was dead. Now I just had to find Renee.

♦

As it turned out, I didn't even have to go looking. Renee came to me, a shadow coming out of the dark, crossing the central aisle.

I didn't know it was her at first, only that someone was firing, one shot after another, the brief muzzle flashes moving steadily toward me, the bullets pounding their way through the side and back of the truck, finishing the job Walker had started on the tarp-covered kegs in the truck bed.

One of her bullets caught me – slicing across the outside of my left arm. The nerves in my arm screamed out, but I ignored them and kept shooting.

I moved back, shooting in the general direction of her muzzle flash while mostly concentrating on putting the bulk of the truck between us. Her bullets might rip the truck to shreds, but the engine block would give me some protection.

The first gun from my pocket ran dry. I dropped it and grabbed the second one, the thought briefly flashing through my mind that I was no longer acquiring either weapons or ammo and might want to be more judicious with both.

I gave the thought all the consideration it was due, noting at the same time that the electric violin had been joined by a full orchestra – or maybe it was just the booming of the guns that I was mistaking for drums – and that the rhythm had moved into the crescendo.

The truck's windshield exploded at my face. I jerked back, instinctively, but did not duck. The truck was tall, but I could just see over the hood.

With no glass in the windows to distort my view, I could see Renee clearly, at the rear of the truck, head and shoulders silhouetted by the light across the central aisle.

I raised my pistols and fired, hitting her left shoulder and right almost simultaneously. Renee staggered, turning slightly from the impact. I fired again, but while I hit her again with my own Glock, the borrowed gun in my left hand clicked dry.

We stared at each other across the shredded interior of the pickup. The shooting around us had subsided, and for an instant, it seemed as though time had slowed.

Renee leaned forward, bracing herself against the tailgate.

I dropped the empty pistol.

Renee raised her gun, her hand unsteady.

I took hold of my Glock with both hands.

We fired.

Renee's single shot grazed the top of my shoulder and kept going.

My shot opened a hole at the bridge of her nose, perfectly centered between the drawn-on tips of her eyebrows.

Renee fell, her chin hitting the edge of the tailgate as she went down.

I walked to the end of the truck and knelt down, pushing the guns away from her hands and turning what was left of her face this way and that. After all the effort it had taken to find and kill her, I needed to verify that it was, in fact, Renee.

Pale eyes stared vacantly up at me from a too-thin face – a face that wore a death mask of rage and surprise. Deep red hair pooled around her head in a sticky cloud of blood.

I stared down at her, feeling the cold expression that had settled on my own face, and pressed the tip of my Glock to her chest, where her heart would have been if she'd possessed one, and pulled the trigger.

Click

I shook my head at the cosmic irony of our two lives being decided by a single bullet. I swapped out the empty magazine for a new one, fired a "make sure" shot into her heart, then walked away, leaving Renee's body where she lay.

The only sound in the cave the grumble of the generator and the sad notes of the violin – a requiem echoing off the pillars in the dark.

Somehow, it seemed fitting.

Chapter 31

I managed to rejoin Williams and his team without getting shot, but only by throwing the Beretta I'd taken from Martin down the middle of the central aisle ahead of me, shouting repeatedly that I was coming, and walking toward them with my hands raised, signaling surrender.

I shouted and slowly waved my hands high above my head as I picked my way forward through the bodies. Thankfully, both Mai and Williams recognized me before anyone shot me.

We were all mostly deaf, and I wasn't the only one who'd taken a bit of damage, though no one had received any major injuries. When Stevie climbed down off the container, her face streaked with sweat and dirt and a few flecks of blood from shards of metal that had nicked the side of her face, she was shaking so badly she could barely stand and finally slid to the floor and sat there puffing on her e-cig.

Dalton had taken up a position at the end of the pillar on their side of the aisle, just as I'd gone around the one on my side, and taken a bullet to the knee – the same one that he'd already had replacement surgery done on once before. Hatch had jogged off to bring back his car while Mai wrapped Dalton's knee with a torn shirt she'd pulled off one of the dead guys. When she was finished, she calmly began picking shrapnel out of her long hair.

We'd counted nineteen bodies in the central aisle – idiots, if you ask me, who had never learned anything about guerilla warfare and had put their trust in a frontal assault and safety in numbers. Stevie had brought down at least half of them from her sniper position on top of the container. Adding the ten I'd killed and another dozen Dalton had stopped, brought us up to forty-one.

I'd taken one of the sleeves from the shirt Mai had used on Dalton, and was wrapping it around the slice on my arm while Williams and I talked.

"Where'd you get the Uzi?" Williams asked, gesturing at the old rifle still strapped to my back. I'd almost forgotten about it in the fighting.

"One of the dead guys behind the pillar," I said.

"You planning on keeping it?"

"I have a friend who's into vintage weaponry," I said, thinking of Ian. "Thought I'd give it to him. Christmas in July and all."

Williams nodded, then glanced around at the shredded boxes and shattered glass and plastic remains of pricey electronics. "It's a pity."

"There's plenty left that wasn't damaged," I said. "I have no use for it."

"Really?"

"My job here is done. This is yours, if you want it."

"It's outside our usual line of work," Williams said, his tone thoughtful. Then a grin spread across his face. "But we might be interested in a few souvenirs."

"As you like," I said. "Be out of here in twenty-four hours – twelve would be better. Don't touch the reefer. Use gloves, don't wipe anything down or take too many of the guns; don't leave any trace that you were here. You know the drill. We want this to look like Renee had... personnel issues."

"Deal," Williams said.

While we'd been talking, a movement in the shadows beyond the container where we stood caught my eye. Since all our people were accounted for, I reached into my jacket and slid out my Glock, raised it, and fired.

From her spot near my feet, Stevie squeaked.

"Forty-two," I said as the body crumpled to the floor. "And who knows how many more rats are still crawling around in the dark."

"Point taken," Williams said, as unruffled as ever. He tilted his head. "So, what happens in twenty-four hours?"

"I call in an anonymous tip."

Hatch pulled up, and together he and Williams helped Dalton into the car. I walked over, watching while he got settled.

"You kick puppies or something, Dalton?" I asked, looking down at him.

His head jerked up, the grimace temporarily replaced with a look of utter confusion. "No! Why would you even say that?"

I shrugged. "Just wondering why God keeps knocking that leg out from under you." I said, gesturing at the knee.

Hatch practically howled with laughter. Even Mai was chuckling as she got into the car.

Dalton just rolled his eyes at me. "Very funny," he said. The grimace had returned. I wished I had something I could give him for the pain. Most of the bullet's actual damage had been to the artificial knee joint, but it had torn through flesh, too, before connecting with the metal and plastic.

I crouched down, resting my hand on the ankle of his uninjured leg. "You did good," I said, my voice low, all joking aside. "Probably saved your team. Let me know how much the new knee costs. I'll cover it."

"You don't—" he started, but I cut him off.

"Maybe not. But I'm doing it anyway."

♦

We left the generator running, but turned off the music – and I made a note of the artist. I also grabbed a couple of Bluetooth speakers like the ones that had filled the cave with sound. They were only about the size of large pillar candles, and would easily fit in my luggage.

Before I left, I also took a more thorough look at the contents of the trailer – and at the laptop Vern had been working at when I so rudely interrupted him. While I didn't know if he'd been part of Renee's crew all along, or if she'd taken him on after he turned on me, the files open on his screen suggested that he'd accessed her inventory.

I took the laptop.

A second laptop sat on a table at the side of the room. An image grid of the security system was displayed on the screen, several squares in the upper portion of the screen dark, representing the cameras Hatch had painted.

Nobody needed the visual record of what had happened here today. I found a canvas shopping bag and put both laptops in it, along with the speakers, and slung it over my shoulder, wincing when the strap crossed the already forgotten shallow cut Renee's bullet had drawn across the top of my shoulder. I growled, adjusting the bag, then Williams and Stevie and I walked out of the cave.

The rain had stopped while we were inside. Williams and I stopped just outside the cave entrance and looked at the sky. The clouds were breaking up, revealing tiny patches of blue.

"It's been good working with you," Williams said, extending his hand.

I raised my own, noticing only then, in the better light, that my gloves were covered with dust and spattered with blood. I pulled my glove off, then shook his hand.

"Likewise," I said.

Stevie had gone on across the street, and was waiting near Williams' truck. She'd gotten some of the spring back in her step as we'd walked away from the underground combat zone, but was still pale and a bit shaky.

"Look after her," I said.

"She'll be okay."

"Yeah," I said. "That's what I'm afraid of."

Williams laughed, then pulled out his phone. "I'm sending you an address," he said, quickly tapping out a message. "Best BBQ in Kansas City, in my opinion." He pressed send and pocketed his phone. "We'd be pleased to have you join us."

I reached for my own phone – which I'd kept set to silent – to make sure I'd received the message. "I just might take you up on that," I said, capturing and saving the cave's GPS coordinates using my phone's mapping app while I had my phone out.

We walked back to the road, then separated to go to our own vehicles. I waited until Williams had driven away before making a U-turn and heading back to Kansas City.

I needed to make travel arrangements for the next day.

I needed to take a long, hot shower.

And then I needed to unwind – and a few friends, a pint, and a plate of barbecue ribs sounded just about perfect.

Epilogue

I stepped off the plane in Charleston, the combination of heat and humidity hitting me in the face like a hot washcloth, reminding me why I make my home a little farther inland.

I'd dressed conservatively, in dark slacks, blouse, and lightweight blazer, and was once again wearing the long, dark wig. I'd also picked up a new pair of dark-rimmed reading glasses at an airport newsstand before leaving Kansas City. The wardrobe had been perfect for the artificial environment of the airplane, but left me sweltering in the late afternoon heat.

I collected my rental car, tossed the jacket on the seat, and turned up the AC. Then I swapped the reading glasses for dark sunglasses and followed the GPS directions to a tidy cemetery across the river in West Ashley.

I found the grave with little difficulty.

Mindy Collier

We miss you, Mom

"This all started with you," I said, looking down at the stone and the mound of bright yellow flowers leaning against it. "I thought you might want to be here for the end."

I pulled out a burner phone and dialed the number I had for Agent Brady.

"Brady."

"Hello, Agent Brady," I said, altering my voice as I had the first time I'd spoken to him.

"I wondered if you'd contact me again," he said, after the slightest hesitation. I smiled as I imagined him scrambling to trace the call and quickly turning on an app that would allow him to capture and record the conversation for later forensic analysis.

"I have some information for you," I said, not wanting to get sucked into a chatty conversation with the FBI agent. "In a moment, I will send you a set of GPS coordinates."

"Another shipment of girls being trafficked?" he asked.

"No. However, I have reason to believe the person responsible for the previous shipment can be found at those coordinates." I saw no reason to tell him Renee was dead. He'd discover that on his own.

"And where can I find you?"

"Nice try," I said. "Have a good afternoon, Agent Brady."

"Wait."

"Yes?"

"Why did you reach out to me?"

"You have resources I don't."

"Will I hear from you again?"

"Perhaps. It all depends on what information happens to cross my desk." I paused slightly, then continued before he had a chance to ask another question. "About the coordinates – according to my sources, the situation on the ground is volatile. If you delay too long, the information may grow stale."

"I'll check it out," he said.

I hung up, then entered the coordinates into a text message and sent it to him.

When I was finished, instead of disabling the phone, I wiped it thoroughly for prints, then bent down and tucked it into the flowers leaning against the headstone. I'd told him before that my information had come from Mindy – I actually hoped I'd given Brady's people long enough to trace the call and that they were on their way.

Mindy deserved all the credit, and none of the blame.

"It's done now," I said to her as I stood. I took a step back and nodded in salute. "Rest peacefully, Mindy."

I left the cemetery and drove back to the airport. I'd been briefly tempted to stay in town a little longer, maybe drive by Kaitlyn's house, but dismissed the idea as quickly as it occurred.

Never go back to the scene of the crime.

Visiting Mindy's grave had been risky enough.

The only other reason I considered booking a later flight was to stop by Father Leonard's church, maybe have a cup of coffee with the warrior-turned-medic. But though he'd saved my life, for which I was grateful, that didn't make us friends. I wasn't part of his flock, and didn't feel I had the right to go to his church unannounced.

You don't make many friends in this line of work.

Even sharing a meal with Williams and his crew the previous night had been something of a novelty.

So I checked in for my flight home, and settled down with a drink to wait in the airport's VIP lounge.

While I waited, I pulled out my phone and dialed a familiar number.

"Hey," Ian said.

I smiled. "Hey, you."

"So you survived another trip," he said.

"So far," I said. "Pick me up at the airport?"

"Sure. What time?"

"About eight-thirty."

"I'll be there."

We chatted briefly about nothing in particular. Then Ian asked what my plans were for the rest of the summer.

"Well," I said. "I needed some sort of excuse for why I've been training so hard the last few weeks. Since I haven't managed to get myself killed yet, I guess I'm going to have to run a marathon."

Acknowledgements

While this book was conceived, written, and released during the COVID-19 lockdown, it contains no reference to either the pandemic or the political turmoil that has been part of 2020. This was a deliberate choice on my part.

Instead of focusing on the lockdown, I turned to writing as a way of maintaining my own sanity during this very strange time. I hope reading this book takes you away from the current craziness for a few hours as well.

The lockdown did impact this book in one unexpected way. Because I couldn't travel to the story locations myself, and didn't want to rely solely on Google's "street view" for my location research, I reached out via social media and asked my friends – both local and those scattered across the country – to share their favorite vacation memories and insider secrets about Charleston, South Carolina, and Kansas City (Missouri and Kansas). I wish I could have incorporated more of their generous suggestions.

I guess I'll just have to write more books…

best,

– *Lauryn*

About the Author

As a mystery reader, Lauryn Christopher likes figuring out "whodunit" as much as anyone – but as a mystery writer with a background in psychology, she's much more likely to write from the culprit's point of view, exploring the hidden secrets driving their choices. You can see this in her *Hit Lady for Hire* series, as well as in her short crime fiction and cozy capers, which have appeared in a variety of short fiction anthologies.

Read Lauryn's musings on storytelling, find links to more of her work, and sign up for her occasional newsletter at her website: www.laurynchristopher.com

If you enjoyed this book, please tell a friend or post a review!

Also by Lauryn Christopher

Pro Bono
a Hit Lady for Hire novel

Some jobs just need to be done – even if nobody's paying…

When a friend is accused of murdering her deadbeat ex-husband – a man Meg had on her hit-list for reasons of her own – Meg Harrison sets aside her usual paid assassin's role and takes it on herself to discover what really happened.

But what begins as a routine inquiry dredges up long-buried memories, forcing Meg to deal with her own demons while simultaneously hunt for a man her instincts tell her might not actually be dead.

Can Meg reverse-engineer the murderer's scheme and bring down the real killer before her friend becomes their next victim?

"… turns the hit-man formula on its head, and in doing so gives us a surprising and entertaining read."

– "Big Al" (Books and Pals)

Available at your favorite retailer
https://books2read.com/ProBono

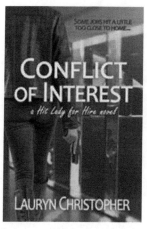

Conflict of Interest
a Hit Lady for Hire novel

When a professional assassin has work-related issues, someone usually ends up dead...

It's a bad idea to piss off a professional assassin, and Meg Harrison – corporate spy and sometimes assassin – is definitely pissed off. Not only has a new, and very irritating, client hired her to kill her own sister, but to top it all off, Meg didn't even know she *had* a sister.

For Meg, this is a contract that hits a little too close to home.

"...Suspend your disbelief and get ready for a ride..."

– Patricia K. Batta

Available at your favorite retailer
https://books2read.com/ConflictOfInterest

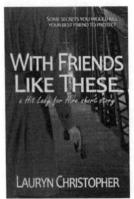

With Friends Like These

a Hit Lady for Hire short story

How well do we really know our friends? Their secret lives? Their hidden pain?

Liz, Deb, Mikki, Anna, and Meg believe they know everything about each other.

But one of them carries too many secrets – secrets that tear at her heart and eat at her friendships.

Secrets she will kill to protect.

"… a powerful piece about friendship, loss, death, and secrets."
— Kristine Kathryn Rusch

Available at your favorite retailer
https://books2read.com/WithFriendsLikeThese

Made in the USA
Middletown, DE
27 October 2023

41376235R00161